Anthony Gilbert and The Murder Room

>>> This title is part of The Murder Room, our series dedicated to making available out-of-print or hard-to-find titles by classic crime writers.

Crime fiction has always held up a mirror to society. The Victorians were fascinated by sensational murder and the emerging science of detection; now we are obsessed with the forensic detail of violent death. And no other genre has so captivated and enthralled readers.

Vast troves of classic crime writing have for a long time been unavailable to all but the most dedicated frequenters of second-hand bookshops. The advent of digital publishing means that we are now able to bring you the backlists of a huge range of titles by classic and contemporary crime writers, some of which have been out of print for decades.

From the genteel amateur private eyes of the Golden Age and the femmes fatales of pulp fiction, to the morally ambiguous hard-boiled detectives of mid twentieth-century America and their descendants who walk our twenty-first century streets, The Murder Room has it all. **>>>**

The Murder Room
Where Criminal Minds

themurderroom.com

Anthony Gilbert (1899–1973)

Anthony Gilbert was the pen name of Lucy Beatrice Malleson. Born in London, she spent all her life there, and her affection for the city is clear from the strong sense of character and place in evidence in her work. She published 69 crime novels, 51 of which featured her best known character, Arthur Crook, a vulgar London lawyer totally (and deliberately) unlike the aristocratic detectives, such as Lord Peter Wimsey, who dominated the mystery field at the time. She also wrote more than 25 radio plays, which were broadcast in Great Britain and overseas. Her thriller *The Woman in Red* (1941) was broadcast in the United States by CBS and made into a film in 1945 under the title *My Name is Julia Ross*. She was an early member of the British Detection Club, which, along with Dorothy L. Sayers, she prevented from disintegrating during World War II. Malleson published her autobiography, *Three-a-Penny*, in 1940, and wrote numerous short stories, which were published in several anthologies and in such periodicals as *Ellery Queen's Mystery Magazine* and *The Saint*. The short story 'You Can't Hang Twice' received a Queens award in 1946. She never married, and evidence of her feminism is elegantly expressed in much of her work.

By Anthony Gilbert

Scott Egerton series

Tragedy at Freyne (1927)

The Murder of Mrs
  Davenport (1928)

Death at Four Corners (1929)

The Mystery of the Open
  Window (1929)

The Night of the Fog (1930)

The Body on the Beam (1932)

The Long Shadow (1932)

The Musical Comedy
  Crime (1933)

An Old Lady Dies (1934)

The Man Who Was Too
  Clever (1935)

**Mr Crook Murder
  Mystery series**

Murder by Experts (1936)

The Man Who Wasn't
  There (1937)

Murder Has No Tongue (1937)

Treason in My Breast (1938)

The Bell of Death (1939)

Dear Dead Woman (1940)
  aka *Death Takes a Redhead*

The Vanishing Corpse (1941)
  aka *She Vanished in the Dawn*

The Woman in Red (1941)
  aka *The Mystery of the
  Woman in Red*

Death in the Blackout (1942)
  aka *The Case of the Tea-
  Cosy's Aunt*

Something Nasty in the
  Woodshed (1942)
  aka *Mystery in the Woodshed*

The Mouse Who Wouldn't
  Play Ball (1943)
  aka *30 Days to Live*

He Came by Night (1944)
  aka *Death at the Door*

The Scarlet Button (1944)
  aka *Murder Is Cheap*

A Spy for Mr Crook (1944)

The Black Stage (1945)
  aka *Murder Cheats the Bride*

Don't Open the Door (1945)
  aka *Death Lifts the Latch*

Lift Up the Lid (1945)
  aka *The Innocent Bottle*

The Spinster's Secret (1946)
  aka *By Hook or by Crook*

Death in the Wrong Room
  (1947)

Die in the Dark (1947)
  aka *The Missing Widow*

Death Knocks Three Times
  (1949)

Murder Comes Home (1950)

A Nice Cup of Tea (1950)
  aka *The Wrong Body*

Lady-Killer (1951)

Miss Pinnegar Disappears (1952)
  aka *A Case for Mr Crook*

Footsteps Behind Me (1953)
  aka *Black Death*

Snake in the Grass (1954)
  aka *Death Won't Wait*

Is She Dead Too? (1955)
  aka *A Question of Murder*

And Death Came Too (1956)

Riddle of a Lady (1956)

Give Death a Name (1957)

Death Against the Clock (1958)

Death Takes a Wife (1959)
  aka *Death Casts a Long Shadow*

Third Crime Lucky (1959)
  aka *Prelude to Murder*

Out for the Kill (1960)

She Shall Die (1961)
  aka *After the Verdict*

Uncertain Death (1961)

No Dust in the Attic (1962)

Ring for a Noose (1963)

The Fingerprint (1964)

The Voice (1964)
  aka *Knock, Knock! Who's There?*

Passenger to Nowhere (1965)

The Looking Glass Murder (1966)

The Visitor (1967)

Night Encounter (1968)
  aka *Murder Anonymous*

Missing from Her Home (1969)

Death Wears a Mask (1970)
  aka *Mr Crook Lifts the Mask*

Murder is a Waiting Game (1972)

Tenant for the Tomb (1971)

A Nice Little Killing (1974)

Standalone Novels

The Case Against Andrew Fane (1931)

Death in Fancy Dress (1933)

The Man in the Button Boots (1934)

Courtier to Death (1936)
  aka *The Dover Train Mystery*

The Clock in the Hatbox (1939)

Lady Killer

Anthony Gilbert

To Irene, with love.

CONTENTS

I

GRETA

IN THE SUMMER of 1948 a young woman called Greta Mannheim, who was employed as a housekeeper by a Mrs. Derry, of London, S.W.7, went for a fortnight's holiday, ostensibly to Torquay, and did not return. She was due back on the Saturday evening and when she did not arrive Mrs. Derry became disturbed.

" The Bannisters are coming to lunch to-morrow," she reminded her husband, " and I don't know how we shall manage without Greta."

" Oh, she probably didn't understand you expected her before Monday," replied easy-going Tom Derry. " Anyway, it's a good excuse for putting the Bannisters off."

" But she must be back to-night," his wife insisted. " She went with the Fillsons, a sort of holiday *au pair*. Gwen Fillson offered to pay her hotel expenses for the fortnight if she would lend a hand with the children, do a bit of baby-sitting and so on, and Greta's so close with her money she jumped at the idea."

" Rather a busman's holiday for her," objected kind-hearted Tom. But May Derry said, " Oh well, she doesn't know anyone, and she doesn't seem to have any relations. As a matter of fact, I believe they were all wiped out by a bomb, one of ours, I'm afraid, in 1944. And then she hates parting with money, never spends a penny if a halfpenny will do. I should think she's saved practically everything she's earned since she's been with us. She does knitting for one of the big shops, too, in her spare time. She must have quite a comfortable little nest-egg laid away."

" Perhaps," said Tom lightly, " she has Someone to Keep." But his wife returned in serious tones that in that case she would hardly have gone to Torquay.

1

And in point of fact, she hadn't.

But that only leaked out later.

"I dare say the Fillsons have changed their plans at the eleventh hour," went on Tom sensibly. "Decided not to come back till to-morrow. I wouldn't worry, old girl. We can take the Bannisters to a restaurant, if you must have them."

There was no sign of Greta the next day, and the Derrys did have to take the Bannisters to a restaurant. It was during the meal that Mrs. Bannister happened to mention that she had seen Gwen Fillson at church that morning.

"So they are back?" exclaimed Mrs. Derry.

"They came back last night. I thought you knew."

"Then what on earth has happened to Greta?"

As soon as they got back to the house May rang up Gwen Fillson.

"Greta?" said Gwen. "But she didn't come with us. You knew that."

"What do you mean—I knew that? I thought——"

"My dear, Greta came to us a day or two before we were to leave, when all our plans were cut and dried, to say that you'd asked her if she could postpone her holiday because your sister was coming to stay."

"My sister's in America," retorted Mrs. Derry grimly. "What a little liar! All I can tell you is that she departed with a suitcase on the Saturday, as arranged, and I understood she was meeting you at Paddington. Well, where on earth can she be?"

Gwen Fillson giggled. "Gone off with a boy-friend, I expect. Had she any?"

Mrs. Derry drew a deep breath. "Now you come to speak of it, I remember that when Tom took me to dinner at the Palace on my birthday, the first person I saw in the dining-room was Greta with a man. She was wearing my dark-red dress that had got too small for me, and she'd altered it very cleverly and added a very striking belt. I must say she looked very distinguished."

Gwen was interested at once. "What was *he* like?"

" One of those dark slightly sinister-looking men who are irresistible to women. They were drinking wine, too, the sort that comes in a wicker cradle. Tom and I drank lager."

" Well," said Gwen, with conviction, " there's your answer. She's gone off with him. I always thought she was almost too good to be true."

" She's very respectable," May began to protest feebly, but Gwen said boisterously, " Oh, I know the Lady-Killer type. Sweep the nicest girls off their feet. And clearly she's not getting married to the creature, or she'd have stayed on a bit longer to get a wedding-present. Listen, May, have you looked in her room ? "

" N-no. I never dreamed——"

" You go and see how many of her things she's left there. Of course, if she hasn't taken them she is coming back, unless, of course, she's been murdered. But my bet would be . . ."

May didn't stay to listen to that. She dashed down the receiver and hurried up the stairs. The missing Greta's room was as empty as a cage with the door wide open. In the wardrobe dangled a few austerity coat-hangers ; the chest of drawers held not so much as a pin. In the waste-paper basket was a crumpled buff envelope marring the complete anonymity of the room. Mrs. Derry automatically picked it up. It was addressed to Greta in the girl's own hand-writing.

" My dear ! " exclaimed Mrs. Bannister, thrilled by this development. " Hadn't you better take a look round and make sure nothing of yours has flitted with her ? "

But there was nothing missing that hadn't belonged to the absent girl.

" I did think it queer there wasn't even a postcard from Torquay," May Derry acknowledged. " Then I remembered how careful Greta was with her money, and, anyway, she'd expect Gwen to be writing, and probably she'd mention Greta."

" And didn't Gwen write ? "

" Not a line. Well, she thought I'd played her a poor sort of trick. I quite understand now."

She laid the crumpled envelope on the table. Paul Bannister, who practically lived on detective stories, leaned over and picked it up.

" The Solitary Clue," he gloated. " Hallo, I say, do you know what this is ? "

" An envelope," said Tom, who didn't like the Bannisters, and on the whole, disliked Paul more than his wife.

" Ah, but what kind of an envelope ? I'll tell you. This once held a Post Office Savings book. Therefore, Superintendent Bannister deduces that the missing girl drew her all before embarking on her mysterious journey."

" Not necessarily her all," objected Tom. " More than three pounds."

" She certainly wouldn't have needed any extra money to go away with Gwen," said May decidedly. " She had a month's pay that was due to her, and I gave her her holiday money, too. She asked for it, now I come to think of it. I thought at the time it was a bit queer."

" Oh, she's gone for the duration, you can depend on that," trumpeted Paul. " You won't see her smiling face again."

And that was true.

" I never want to hear her name again," said Mrs. Derry violently.

And she didn't, not for a long time, and then only as one of a list of credulous females whose hearts had proved considerably stronger than their heads.

Paul wanted Mrs. Derry to go to the police, but Tom wouldn't hear of it.

" What's the sense ? You can't charge her with anything except breach of contract, and you know what the great mutton-headed British Public's like. Poor refugee, both her parents killed by our bombers, runs away from employer. I don't care if you treated her like a princess, before you know where you are, people will be nudging each other and saying there's no smoke without fire, and girls don't leave good homes—oh, everybody will know you starved her and overworked her and probably put her to sleep in a dungeon. And you wouldn't get your money back, and you wouldn't get the girl. No, no. Cut your losses and go round to that fiddle-de-dee agency in the morning and see what they can offer you."

" We shall never get another Greta," mourned his wife. " The house always looked like Buckingham Palace. She could make a kitchen spoon look as if it were made of sterling silver. One thing, she needn't think she can come creeping back to me with a hard-luck story."

But there was no likelihood of Greta Mannheim doing any such thing.

On the very day after this conversation the coroner of Parkmoor Bay held an inquest on the body of a young woman who had signed her landlady's visitors' book as Greta Jones and who had been drowned in a regrettable boating fatality on the previous Friday. The body had been carried down by the action of the tide and had not been recovered until Sunday afternoon, by which time it bore little resemblance to the smart girl who had been the envy of all Mrs. Derry's neighbours.

The inquest was sparsely attended—the dead girl appeared to have no relations, and there was no actual proof—in the absence of documents, all of which had gone down with her—that her real name was Jones. She had handed the landlady an emergency card, and carried all her papers about with her, so the most curious could learn nothing of her past history. The chief witness was a man who gave his name as Henry Grant, a tall, dark personage with the slightly sinister good looks so few women can resist. He said that he had met the deceased on a coach the previous week ; she told him she had come north for a holiday and had just arrived. He did not know her home address or anything about her past life.

" You know how it is," said the witness with a kind of confident distress. " You're on holiday, you meet an attractive girl, she's ready to come half-way and you decide to go about together just while the holiday lasts. There's nothing permanent on either side ; for all I knew she was a married woman though she didn't wear a ring. When we got back from the ride I suggested she might like to meet me that evening, so we had a drink together and then we took a bus into the town and went to the pictures. After that we were together most of the time."

" And she told you nothing about herself ? "

" It wasn't that sort of relationship. The past and the future didn't enter into it. It was one of thousands of similar relationships that start up on boats or trains every year ; each of you is alone, you like the look of the other, you think—Well, why not do things in pairs instead of just on our own ? All Greta told me about herself was that she had a job somewhere, mother's help or something I think it was, but she didn't want to talk about it. I didn't talk about myself either ; we just went about together for a few days."

At the end of the first week Grant suggested that they might take a boat and go for a sail one afternoon, and Greta welcomed the idea. When the day they had fixed came there was a heavy swell on, and he had suggested postponing the excursion until it subsided. But Greta would not listen. " I warned her I couldn't swim," said Henry Grant, " but she simply laughed. She said if there was an accident she was quite capable of life-saving me. She laughed as she said it. We were all joking, you must understand. There were various people standing by and some of them joined in. Well, we went to the café for a cup of coffee, and then I went down to see about the boat. The boatman warned me about the swell, but he didn't refuse to let his boat go out—I wish to heaven now he had—and we set forth. Everything went perfectly well for a time till we were struck by a particularly heavy wave. The boat tilted, Greta screamed, and I shouted to her to keep her head. If there hadn't been another heavy wave almost at once everything would have been all right, but before the girl could pull herself together the second wave struck us and she went over the side. I leaned over and pushed an oar in her direction, shouting to her to catch hold. But she seemed stupefied. I think she must have hit her head on the side of the boat as she went over, because she went down like a stone. I leaned over the side and tried to grab her, and that did it—the boat went over and we were both in the water. I caught at the upturned keel and managed to keep afloat till someone rescued me. We were lucky to be seen from the shore."

There was inevitable criticism of the man's behaviour, the romantics, female for the most part, considering that he should have made greater efforts to save his companion.

" There was nothing more I could do," insisted Henry in a steady voice. " If I had let go the boat I couldn't have saved her, and I should have been drowned myself."

Some of the critics thought this would have been a more suitable development, and certainly it would have saved a lot of subsequent trouble, but the men said it was the girl's own fault, she had insisted on going, and it wasn't fair to blame the fellow. And some of the other women insinuated that any girl who picked up an acquaintance in this casual manner deserved whatever came to her.

The police made the routine inquiries, which got them precisely nowhere. The girl had taken her room on the day of her arrival, and the address in the visitor's book simply said London. She had had no letters and made no confidences.

The landlady said one thing that struck the suspicious —men like Arthur Crook, for instance—as a little odd. She said that once she saw the girl's bag open and it seemed stuffed with notes.

" She carried them everywhere," added Mrs. Mercer, tossing her stiffly-permed head. " Didn't trust me, I suppose. And what's more, I don't believe her name was Jones. She didn't talk English not like you and me."

Medical evidence was to the effect that death was due to drowning, following a blow on the skull, consonant with having struck her head against the side of the boat when it overturned. Verdict—Death by Accidental Drowning.

On the following day Henry Grant left Parkmoor Bay.

" And quite right, too," observed one Mrs. Mopp to another, over their morning cup of char. " I wouldn't let a kitten drown the way he let her. And saying he can't swim ! Believe it or not, dear, I saw him on the beach one morning early, swimming away like a seal."

" You never ! Grace, you ought to tell them that."

" And a nice fool I'd look," said Grace scornfully, " when he said it wasn't him at all. All the same, he done it, you mark my words."

" But why should 'e ? You 'ave to 'ave some reason."

" Not if you're a man, you don't," said Grace darkly. " You needn't tell me. I've 'ad two 'usbands and both of 'em as unreasonable as you could wish. Besides, what about all that money she carried about ? "

" It went down with 'er, in 'er bag."

" That's what 'e says, dear, that's what 'e says. But 'oo's to know if My Lord's telling the truth ? "

Crook said much the same thing. He saw the report of the inquest, if Mrs. Derry didn't. She didn't as it happened, for that was the week when someone tried to assassinate a Cabinet Minister in the name of patriotism, and very nearly succeeded, so that the death by drowning of a foreign national was too small beer to make the London press. Crook loved murder. He paid a press agency a handsome annual fee to send him cuttings of all the so-called accidents, no matter how obscure, and when he didn't agree with the coroner, which occurred quite often, he stuck the report into an enormous book called *Tombstone Serenade*, observing, like another character in a similar lady-killing case, " We shall hear of him again."

IN OCTOBER of the same year the small market town of Marchester was pleasantly stirred by the arrival of a tall dark man of unquestioned charm, calling himself Henry Gardiner. He first attracted the attention of a number of ladies who were in the habit of stopping at Alicia's Tea-Rooms for elevenses five mornings out of six. Alicia was run very capably and profitably by a Miss Beryl Benyon, a spinster in early middle-age, who had bought the derelict tea-rooms known as The Haunt of the Leprechaum immediately after the war, and named them for the aunt whose death at the hands of a Jerry bomber had provided her with the wherewithal to enter the field of private enterprise. Everything comes to him who waits, and sometimes more than he bargains for.

Henry Gardiner was certainly more than Beryl had ever dared to anticipate. Years of patient employment had at last brought her to the haven where she would be —and the trouble about dames, said Arthur Crook, is that they never know where to stop. If Beryl had stopped in Alicia's Tea-Rooms her subsequent history would have been less romantic but a good deal longer. Rumour said she made a packet out of the place, and Mrs. Carstairs, the vicar's wife, thrilled everyone by quoting the case of a woman who made four thousand a year out of a similar establishment. "Not in Marchester," said the Rev. John Carstairs. "Anyone with an income of four thousand pounds here would be as conspicuous as an angel." All the same, she did well. She was a good organiser, the place was clean and pleasant, there were flowers on the tables, the cakes were new and there was no charge for use of cloakroom. This last had more to do with the popularity of Alicia than any man would have believed.

Anyway, at eleven in the morning you could always count on the place being full ; quite often two or three ladies could be seen sitting on the chairs thoughtfully provided beside the counter watching with lynx eyes for the sign of someone preparing to don gloves and pick up her shopping-bag and depart.

" People are so selfish," they would confide to one another in perfectly audible tones. " This is a teashop, not a club. Look at that woman over there, just lighting a fresh cigarette. She finished her coffee quite five minutes ago. Miss Benyon's too good-natured and that's a fact."

For the most part it was ladies who patronised the café. Of course out of term-time mothers brought their sons and aunts brought nephews, but you didn't often see men there. And so the appearance of a tall dark gentleman with an air of distinction—" Possibly a foreigner," said Mrs. Tite to Miss Jenkins—sitting alone at a table with the morning paper, aroused a thrill of interest. So courageous of him, they thought, venturing into this female kingdom.

" A lion among ladies," tittered Miss Bennett, who was the secretary of the local Shakespearian association.

The same thought animated all their minds. Was he a new resident or merely passing through, in which case they couldn't be expected to take any great interest in him. If he was a resident—had he any encumberances ? Bachelors in Marchester as elsewhere, were few and much run after, not only by those seeking a wedding-ring, but because an extra man or two was invaluable at bridge and cocktail parties. And then there were local activities. Could he, for instance, be roped into the Amateur Dramatic Club ? reflected Miss Jenkins, its indefatigable secretary. How about the church choir ? wondered sternly practical Mrs. Carstairs. Would he be good for a lecture to the Writers of To-morrow Association ? Mrs. Tite would like to know. It wasn't easy to get established writers to come to Marchester, and the amateurs could hear each other talk any day of the week. A stranger, even if he didn't prove to be an author, would be a draw. And then he was such a fine figure of a man, so male, if you knew what they meant, as, of course, they all did. The men of the community all wore labels—so-and-so's husband—brother—father. Very few of them were allowed to exist in their own right. And then how debonair, how unconcerned the stranger seemed, so unlike the average unattended male who looked as though he would sooner plunge into a hive of bees than Alicia at eleven o'clock in the morning.

" And so most of them would," said Lady Turner grimly. " Ronald's the greatest coward I know, if he did win the V.C. in 1916."

It was noted that Miss Benyon herself brought the stranger his coffee, and paused for a moment to talk to him before disappearing again into the kitchen premises. The ladies were waited on by " the girls," all of whom had a good stare at the gentleman as they passed. The gentleman apparently unaware of any of them ,finished his coffee, folded his paper, paid his bill and marched out.

Mrs. Tite and Miss Jenkins made a combined rush for his table. They told one another he might be an author—that fine intellectual forehead, the brown lively eyes, the air of concentration. And then what a fine figure, tall and handsome. They wondered if he were married. Mrs. Tite said no. A husband wouldn't have come to Alicia alone.

The next morning rather more residents than usual came to take their morning coffee at the teashop, but if they had hoped to catch another glimpse of the stranger they were disappointed. Then Mrs. Carstairs saw him coming out of the Lamb, and made one of the excuses that come so readily to a vicar's wife to see the wife of the landlord.

" I do hope we can count on you for our jumble sale," she said, and from the jumble sale, though to the uninitiated this may sound improbable, she made an easy passage to the newcomer.

" Late in the year for visitors ? " she offered.

" Dr. Gardiner's come over from South Africa. He's

been in England nearly a year, mostly in London, though he's travelled round a lot."

" I wonder what brought him to Marchester. Is he a medical man ? "

"Well, he's a doctor. Came over here to do some research and he's writing a book about it. Yes, he was telling us about life in South Africa. Makes you wish you could go there yourself."

" Is he staying long ? "

" He's due back home next month, I understand. Would you believe it, he says he'll be sorry to go."

" Don't bother about that man I was telling you about," Mrs. Carstairs told her husband at lunch.

· " What man, dear ? " asked her husband.

" His name's Gardiner and he's a doctor, and he's going back to South Africa."

" Lucky chap," said Mr. Carstairs.

" Why, John, you don't mean——"

" I suppose you couldn't persuade him to take Miss Jenkins with him ? One of these days Marchester will be in the news. A clerical error."

" What nonsense you talk, John. Anyone can see you're not a murderer."

" Don't you be too sure. When I was chaplain at B—— Prison I used to be amazed at the sort of fellows who committed murder. You have an idea they'll carry the brand of Cain in their foreheads, be somehow different from other men, but if you saw a dozen fellows in this room and were told one was a murderer you wouldn't know which was which."

" Why are you telling me this ? " asked Mrs. Carstairs in perplexed tones.

" Because I'm beginning to understand what drives perfectly normal decent men to murder. Good heavens, Georgie, I didn't take orders to fuss about the choir-boys' surplices or embroidered hassocks."

The next day the vicar was driving past the Lamb when Dr. Gardiner came out. Mr. Carstairs stood looking after him. The visitor crossed the street and walked along to Alicia, but he didn't go in by the shop door. Miss Benyon lived on her own premises, with a private entrance round the corner, and it was to this that Dr. Gardiner went. He seemed to have been expected for the door flashed open almost before the bell had stopped ringing. Mr. Carstairs glanced at his watch. It was six-thirty. Alicia did morning coffee, luncheons and teas, but not dinner. There would have been no custom for that meal at Marchester.

" Beryl's got a beau," he told his wife on his return, but though he was smiling there was a puzzled look on his face.

" Where the heck," he was wondering, " have I seen that chap before ? "

That was October.

In November Marchester was staggered to see an advertisement both in the local paper and in the *London Post* to the effect that a thriving teashop in a popular market town was being offered for sale, lock, stock, barrel and goodwill. The annual turnover was put at two thousand pounds. And when inquiries started it was found that the business in question was Alicia. Miss Benyon was bombarded with questions. " You can't be giving up the shop," her customers (many of whom were her friends in the sense that they met at the pictures and other people's modest dinner-tables, and of course in church on Sunday) protested. " Why, it's so successful."

" I'm leaving Marchester," said Beryl. She was smartly dressed, well coiffured, very well turned out generally. She owned to forty-six but didn't look it ; people some-times wondered why she hadn't married, and then it appeared that that was just what she was going to do.

But who ? wondered the neighbourhood. All the bachelors were known by heart, and there wasn't one who seemed to fit the bill. But it seemed that Miss Benyon was going to marry Dr. Gardiner, and go back to South Africa with him. That's why she was selling the business at a great sacrifice, she said frankly. She wanted ready cash. Mortgages were no use if you were going to be the other side of the world and it might be years before Henry could take another long holiday. She thought she had a good prospective buyer and she begged all her clients to give the newcomer a square deal. She flashed a beautiful engagement ring, an emerald set in a rose of diamonds.

Two very nice spinsters were taking Alicia over, such an amusing couple, one tall and fair and very attractive —well, not quite young but very decorative and a definite asset to Marchester—and the other short and dark and very business-like. They were simply devoted to each other, Miss Benyon reported, and the dark one had such a sense of humour.

" We call ourselves Beauty and the Beast," she told Miss Benyon. " We had an arts and crafts shop once called that, but we had to give it up when the slump came. Food's much the most sensible thing to go in for, really, because people never get tired of that."

" Will you be married in the parish church ? " asked Mrs. Tite, disposing of the two spinsters in a breath. Time enough to worry about them when they came. Miss Benyon surprised them all by saying No. It appeared that Dr. Gardiner had got a small cottage in the country, the West Country, and they were going to spend their honeymoon there. He had about a month of his leave left, and then they would go back to South Africa together.

" He's been doing research, but he has the cottage for his writing," Miss Benyon told them. " He comes back to it every week-end. It sounds absolutely ideal for a honeymoon, like a cottage out of Hans Andersen."

" With fairies at the bottom of the garden," suggested someone flippantly. They were very glad about Miss Benyon finding her romance even if she had left it a bit late, but they did think she needn't look quite so delighted to be leaving them. " And why not the parish church ? " asked Mrs. Carstairs.

Then the truth had to be revealed. Dear Henry was a free-thinker. He didn't believe in church marriages and was insisting on a registrar's office. " I don't feel I ought to try to make him go against his conscience," said Miss Benyon seriously.

At the end of November, Beauty and the Beast (really very aptly named, Marchester agreed) took over Alicia, and Beryl departed to love in a cottage, she declared.

" Have you heard from Mrs. Gardiner as I suppose we ought to call her now ? " Miss Jenkins asked Mrs. Lott about a fortnight later.

" Not a line."

" I call it rather ungrateful. After all, we did give her a clock for a wedding-present."

" Oh, being married's a full-time job," smiled Mrs. Lott. " You wouldn't know."

" Did she give anyone the address ? " asked Mrs. Carstairs.

It seemed as though she hadn't. Then came January, the month in which she was due to go to her new country. " Perhaps she'll find time to write on board ship," said her erstwhile friends. But not a card came, not a message, not a hint.

" She might be dead and buried," said Lady Turner sourly.

Well, so she might.

The New Year had come and gone, and now it was February, and still there was no news of the erstwhile Miss Benyon.

" You'd think she'd send us a line," grumbled her friends. " Or a photograph of her house."

" Perhaps she's ill."

" Why should she be ? "

" Marriage takes some women that way."

" Perhaps he's Bluebeard in disguise." That was romantic Miss Jenkins.

Mrs. Carstairs repeated it to her husband. " No, no,

nothing of the kind," said he sharply. " As a matter of fact, I don't mind admitting now I did have qualms. You know I said his face seemed familiar, but I couldn't place it, and then I suddenly remembered a chap called Miller at B—— Prison. Of course it was several years ago, and one's memory of faces grows thin, but the likeness was there."

Even common-sense Mrs. Carstairs held her breath. " What was he in for, John ? "

" Assaulting a woman with intent to robbery."

" John ! But this is terrible. Do you think there's any possibility this is the same man ? "

" My dear, I beg of you to keep calm. No, I can assure you it is not. I was sufficiently troubled to get in touch with the governor, explaining my doubts, of course, and he was good enough to look up the records, and he assures me that Miller died early in the war. Bad company, I'm afraid." The Rector sighed. " Found dead at the foot of a quarry with a broken neck. Fell over when he was intoxicated, one fears. Only identifiable by his documents. Of course, during the war no one had much time to speculate about one rascal the less, for I'm afraid there was no doubt about it, he was a thoroughly bad hat."

" You mean he fell over ? "

" Presumably."

" He might have been pushed."

" There was no evidence to that effect."

" If he wasn't found for ages how could there be any evidence ? "

" And no motive so far as we know."

" We don't know. Still, so long as he's dead he can't be the man who married Beryl. I suppose it's a case of out of sight out of mind, but somehow one wouldn't have expected it of her. Well, it's a relief you made sure."

" Yes. Oh, yes. I'm perfectly easy in my mind that Miller has been dead for several years."

He might have been less easy if he had chanced upon a paragraph in a local paper to the effect that a Mrs. Beryl

Gardiner had had a fatal accident on a hill in a remote West Country district, when her car overturned. She was the sole occupant at the time, her husband, whom she had only recently married, having gone to town on business for the day. He had warned his wife to be careful driving, for he thought her inclined to take risks. The hill on which the accident took place was plainly marked " Dangerous to Motorists," but she had, nevertheless, attempted to take a pre-war car down the steep incline and at a critical moment the brake had refused work. A mechanic said that an essential nut had somehow worked itself loose. The coroner remarked, " If people would realise the duty they owe the community as well as to themselves they would never take these old cars out without thoroughly overhauling them. If she had discovered the nut was loose this tragic accident need never have happened." The mechanic said it was very unusual for this particular part to work itself loose ; it rendered the brake perfectly useless. The husband, a tall dark man, seemed quite dazed. He agreed that they had not been married long, they had been going to return to London as soon as he could find suitable quarters. He had originally hoped to take his bride to South Africa but certain difficulties had presented themselves, and he now proposed to remain in England.

The coroner tendered him the sympathy of the Court and confirmed a verdict of death by misadventure.

Again Henry's luck held.

The news did not make the London papers, for it synchronised with a really terrible rail disaster in the North of England in which fifteen people lost their lives and twice that number sustained serious injury. The widower packed his possessions (and presumably those of the deceased) and left the cottage he had rented for a month some days before the expiry of the lease. During their stay the Gardiners had had little contact with their neighbours, though a few shopkeepers said they had appeared to be a devoted couple.

17

" It does make you wonder what Providence is up to," remarked one woman to another. Arthur Crook, who read the report of the inquest, put it rather differently. It made him wonder what the bereaved husband was up to. It was perhaps the merest coincidence, but this was the second inquest in which the chief witness had been a tall dark man with the initials H. G. In the first case a handbag containing a large sum of money (*vide* the landlady, Mrs. Mercer) had disappeared, gone to the bottom, said Mr. Grant. " Bottom my foot," said the vulgar Mr. Crook. In the second a very little inquiry established the fact that the husband was the sole legatee and that the lady had not been precisely penniless. Mr. Crook's morbid temperament revelled in coincidences of this kind ; he was always on the look out for them, saying you never knew when that sort of information might come in useful. This collection of details about such fatalities might be called Arthur Crook's hobby. Every accident, he held, may conceal a murder, though admittedly the majority do not. Still, like the unfortunate Beryl, he was a natural gambler. " Me, I back a nice little mare name of Murder," he would announce in expansive moments. His was a suspicious nature, and when rich old women or tiresome husbands or obstructive wives passed on at moments exceedingly convenient to their heirs or married partners he always pasted the cutting into *Tombstone Serenade*.

When he read Mr. Gardiner's admission that he couldn't drive he remembered another man, answering to much the same description, who stated at an inquest that he couldn't swim. In each case the man had been seen in the company of the subject of the inquest ; in one case he had been involved but had not lost his life ; in the other he had most fortunately chanced to be out of the car on the sole occasion that something went wrong.

" The Not So Holy Innocent," remarked Crook to his A.D.C., Bill Parsons. " Funny the brakes should go just that one day when he was in London. And how come that nut worked itself loose ? In my opinion nuts have their own Trade Union, never do a stroke more than they need. I've been driving a car for thirty years and I've never known that particular nut to work loose of itself. Next thing we shall hear is that the widow left a nice little prize packet, and Hubby inherits every penny of it. In fact, I wouldn't put it past him to have taken out a life assurance on the lady."

" One of these days," remarked Bill in his colourless way, "you'll find yourself in the dock on a slander charge."

But Crook said, " All things come to him who waits, and that cutting goes into *Tombstone Serenade*. Might be worth a packet one of these days," he said.

It was surprising how often his cuttings book had come in handy.

When new clients came, for instance, and started laboriously to tell their story they were apt to find that Crook knew all the salient details already, knew what the police thought, knew, too, that even the police can be wrong.

" Chap's a marvel," they had said when they had left his office. " Had it all pat, goodness knows how. Enough to make you think he's discovered how to travel faster than light and did the job himself though all the time you know he was right here in Bloomsbury Street."

Well, there it was. Mrs. Beryl Gardiner was dead and buried unobtrusively in a West Country cemetery, without even a stone to mark where she lay. " Have to wait three months," said the stone masons. " Let the ground settle." " I'll be back," said the widower. No, he said, he wouldn't decide anything at the moment, wanted to plan it out just the way she would have liked it. And that, whether the stone mason recognised it or not, was sweet Fanny Adams for him.

Crook, who had his own means of obtaining information and could probably have run M.I.5 with one hand tied behind his back, observed in his cheerful fashion that the widower could buy himself mourning made of cloth of gold out of the pickings. It turned out that the deceased had no living relatives ; such a lot of women who died suddenly, many of them soon after marriage, had no one to notice if they were living or dead. That was what you would expect, of course. The Smiths, the Landrus, the Gardeners whose names figure so prominently on the roll of dishonour like it best that way. It saves trouble if there's no one to question the deceased's will. And that's another thing worth noticing—there's always a will. Even if they've only been married a short time and haven't got their own roof over their head, there's always been the spare half-hour it takes to write out and sign a will. And, naturally, it's always the husband who benefits. If it wasn't, where would be the sense of them dying at all ?

That brought the record up to the early spring. Crook kept his eyes on sticks and his ears stretched, but several months were to elapse before he was actually pitchforked into the story, just before the end of Chapter Three.

I I I

FLORA

FLORA RANSOME, like the ill-starred Miss Benyon, was a spinster rather more advanced into middle-age, who had also inherited a legacy from an aunt, in her case in 1948. Unlike Beryl, she had no intention of opening a business. She had worked hard at various unremunerative employments since the death of her paralysed father early in the war, and when her Aunt Marian died, leaving her sole legatee, she gave away the clothes she had worn till she hated the sight of them, shook the dust of the latest boarding-house off her feet and moved in the luxurious up-to-date Parade Hotel at Sunhaven, prepared to enjoy as much of her life as remained to her.

Which, in the event, proved to be a good deal less than she had anticipated.

She bought a fur coat and a string of pearls and took to going about in taxis and private cars instead of standing in bus queues. She learned to play bridge, having discovered that this is an infallible entrée into hotel society, and thought of taking a trip round the world. But before she could put this tentative plan into execution she met a tall, dark, madly attractive man called Henry Grainger one evening on the marine parade, and married him within the month.

The Parade Hotel at Sunhaven was the acknowledged queen of that self-styled queen of watering-places. It catered for the middle-aged and elderly who were for the most part without family ties. It specialised in wealthy widows, but an occasional old bachelor, who had been a sad dog in his youth and was a much sadder dog now, pushed in there and had the time of his life, spinning yarns about the dear departed days when he was a young chap and England was England, and no nonsense about equality and Jack being as good as his master. They yarned and yawned (during the other fellows' yarns), and yarned again. (The number of elephants, rhinoceroses, hippos, tigers and the more savage breeds of horned cattle slaughtered by these old gentlemen would have filled a sizable number of zoos.) There were a few moneyed spinsters to whose ranks Miss Flora Ransome had graduated since her delightful and unexpected legacy six months earlier. It was like a country club—newcomers were severely vetted—a very high standard of bridge was played, and now and again one or two of the residents took a trip to the Continent, travelling in as much comfort as money could buy, and came back to say that winning a war didn't seem to be all it was cracked up to be. Look at the food you could get abroad, beautiful materials, nylons galore. When there was a by-election the entire company went down as one man to address envelopes at the Conservative headquarters.

Flora revelled in everything. She remembered at Seaview how those who had small rooms, practically attics on the fifth floor (no lift) were only given three prunes for lunch while those on the second floor, who paid thirty shillings a week extra, got six. And towels and sheets once a fortnight, and a conveniently forgetful proprietress when one asked for a new electric light bulb. She was an adaptable creature who might, given her chance, have become quite a passable actress ; she had done well in the amateur dramatic group of which she had been a member until poor Papa's paralysis got so bad she couldn't leave him at night. " It won't be for long, Flo," he had promised in his rusty voice, and he had gone on dying for nearly five years ; by which time the war had started and amateur theatricals were a thing of the past. But at the Parade she acted with the best of them. It was of course a disadvantage never to have had a husband ; but she made the most of father, who would have fallen out of his heavenly mansion with shock to see the noble adventurer he had become since his death. He had, it appeared, been a soldier of considerable distinction instead of a mildly popular colonel who had lived for years on half-pay, trundling between his home and his club until his physical collapse. Without actually saying so, Flora gave the impression that he had won practically every medal that had ever been struck.

" He must have been a wonderful person," said Lady Parrott, who looked so like her name you have to concede Providence a sense of humour. " He's positively the only man I ever came across who could be in three different parts of the globe at practically the same time."

Flora threw up her nicely marcelled head. " Oh, he was like those carriers' advertisements you used to see before all road transport was nationalised. Distance no object."

The only time these days she really felt at a loss was when the old termagants started rummaging out their dead and gone love affairs. She supposed she could have had the classic military fiancé who died on the way to

India or his naval counterpart who was drowned in his country's service, but she preserved the curiously un-stained romantic outlook on love peculiar to spinsters over forty. " Quite natural," said her brother ; " they're the only people who haven't had a chance of being dis-illusioned." If she had only known it her silence was more impressive than any amount of gabble. She was even credited with a past. On the whole, life was all right, except just now and again when a sense of the futility of the whole of her existence swept over her like a tidal wave drowning every scrap of assurance she had contrived to amass. Because—let's face it—Papa had been a very ordinary sort of fellow, and if she had managed to scrape up a husband from somewhere he would have got married again at the drop of a hat, since there are always widows quite glad to jump through the same hoop twice. Possibly he would have liked it better ; a man looked after by a spinster daughter is always faintly at a disadvantage. Someone's sacrificed her life to him—that's how he had felt about it, and the fact was he hadn't wanted the sacrifice. He would have liked to marry some jolly little woman with a bit of her own, and started off again when Charles was married and Flora not quite the girl she had been. Perhaps he had felt as tied by conscience as she had always pretended to be. The truth was, of course, no one had ever offered her the protection of his name and a wedding-ring—not even the protection without the ring, but that was much more understandable. Colonels' daughters don't go getting themselves mixed up with nasty fellows like that.

One afternoon she went to a film—by herself, as she so often did—and saw some magnificent shots of mountaineering ; she liked the brilliant technicolor, the heroic feats performed by virile young men all of whom were the colour of mahogany ; and just before the picture ended there was one shot of the mountains without a human being in sight, a wide dim stretch of Alps, dark in the dying light, a kind of desolate grandeur that held her dumb. As she came out, the picture still in her mind, she thought, Life's like that, a great stretch of untrodden rocky country, no landmarks, no signposts, darkness coming on and only the peaks ahead. There a man was like an insect, too small to be visible, pitting himself against the starkly inhuman universe. Life was like that sometimes, death, too, perhaps. She tried to imagine her own death, going out alone, the door slowly opening through weeks of illness, or flashing wide to let her through and then slamming behind her—whichever it was outside the darkness waited, no guide, no friend.

Sadness drenched her spirit. After dinner she looked round eagerly to see if anyone wanted a bridge four completed, but nobody asked her, and when she suggested making one up it seemed that the others all had engagements or headaches, which came to the same thing from her point of view. Because she couldn't sit like a mouldering statue in the big half-empty lounge she wrapped her fetching little fur coatee round her shoulders, and went out. It was better out of doors, a clear night, with a little topsy-turvy moon shining on the water and stars abounding. She crossed the street and leaned on the parapet looking down on the dark sea. She thought of the past and the future, remembering the bewigged creatures at the Parade and thinking that one day she would probably look like that, too. She was eternally grateful, of course, for the legacy only it had come a bit late. Woman's second blooming is always a hot penny, she had once heard someone say, but the flowers that bloom in the spring don't come back in—well, October— October merging into November at that. She had been brooding for some time when a light not far off caught her eye, a little red gleam, and the fragrance of tobacco smoke came wafting gently across to her. She turned her head, a little alarmed by the silent manner in which the smoker had approached. She saw a tall dark figure, as intent apparently on the black waters as herself. As she moved he said at once :

" Does my cigar annoy you ? "

It was a pleasant voice, and it seemed to sweep her loneliness out of sight all in a moment. It was extraordinary, a kind of sympathy seemed to spring up between them at just those few words.

" Of course not," she said warmly, and laughed. " Do you remember that music-hall song ? "

" I like to walk behind a man who smokes a big cigar ? " He laughed, too. " It all depends on the cigar, of course. I can vouch for this one, and I do know what I'm talking about. I used to be in the trade myself."

" How interesting ! Do tell me. I expect it took you all over the world."

" Pretty well. That's one of the reasons I went in for it, that and the fact that an uncle had a tobacco business. He had no son of his own at that time, and my father had the idea I might step into his shoes one day, but "—he shrugged—" *l'homme propose, le bon Dieu dispose.*"

" I know. I wonder sometimes what happens to all those dreams one has when one's young. Do they just disperse like your cigar smoke, and not leave as much trace behind them ? "

" It depends on how much you cosset them. If you lay them up in lavender you can uncover them years later."

" Rather faded," Flora agreed. " It's better of course do translate them into reality. What happened to the cigar business ? "

" Oh, my uncle unexpectedly married late in life and had twin sons within the year. I didn't see the fun of working like a black to support my infant cousins, and— well, I've always been a victim of wanderlust. . . ."

" How well I understand. Beyond the east the sunrise, beyond the west the sea. I remember when I was fifteen I wanted to be a pirate."

" I felt rather the same way myself." He forbore to add that this was one of the dreams he had put into practice.

" Sailing the seas with the Jolly Roger at the helm, a

law to oneself. I always meant to go round the world before I died, though I never quite knew how I should manage it."

"You've plenty of time," said her companion in rallying tones. "There are autumn crocuses as well as January ones, and a lot of people prefer them. Ever seen them growing in Switzerland or the Tyrol, a carpet of them ? "

"I must say," said Flora, neatly side-stepping the question, "it will be pleasant when we can travel again as we used. Winter on the Mediterranean, spring in the south of France, Switzerland in June—oh, dear, and all we can hope for now is a couple of weeks counting every franc and wondering if the value of the pound will have fallen before morning. I can see you've had an adventurous life. How I envy you."

. "All the same, the time comes when it's pleasant to have a harbour waiting your return and—someone on the shore counting the days. You live here ? Or——— ? "

"Oh, I'm in an hotel at present, but I can't tell you how tired one gets of hotel existence. You begin to wonder if you're a real person at all. Sometimes I think it must be rather like being in prison—oh, a very luxurious prison. But you're a name rather than a number, and everything has to be done according to routine."

He smiled in the darkness. A lot she knew of prisons ; he could have told her. He came a little nearer. This, he thought, was the goods. After a lifetime of adventuring you developed a very sensitive nose. You could actually detect the scent of money and luxury ; he could feel it wafting it across to him now.

"You gave up your own house in the war perhaps ? " he said.

"I kept house for my dear father for years, and when I lost him I didn't seem to have the heart to go on keeping up a place just for myself. Besides, the slump hit everyone, didn't it ? " She smiled radiantly in the darkness. She had nice teeth, and no thanks to Mr. Bevan.

" Oh, yes, I became rather a soldier of fortune myself for a time. Naturally, in the war one didn't want any luxury, but you can get very sick of cheap boarding-houses—not so much hard mattresses and poor service as the dreary companionship or rather the lack of it. Still, I suppose I shouldn't complain. I had no idea then of the wonderful piece of luck that was waiting for me round the corner. People talk as if money didn't matter, but the only people who say that are the people who've always had it, and so take it for granted. It's like health ; you don't think about it till you lose it."

" You were going to tell me about your piece of luck," he insinuated.

" Oh, yes, a legacy that I'd never anticipated from my Aunt Marian. Of course, when Father died my brother was the natural heir and since he was married with children, everyone thought it reasonable everything —well, practically everything—should go to him. Oh, he was very good about it, said of course I must regard his home as mine, but having been in charge of a household for years, I couldn't acclimatise myself to being—well, just a poor relation. And then . . . Have you any sisters, Mr.—— ? "

" Grainger. No, I'm an only child."

" I was only going to say that if you had and they were married, you'd probably be surprised that they'd chosen men who weren't your sort of person at all. I know psychologists tell you that men always marry women as unlike their own mother and sisters as possible, and I suppose the same is true of women. I mean, they marry people as unlike their brothers as possible. I did honestly try to like my sister-in-law, but she never attempted to conceal her contempt for me because I wasn't a married woman. Yet, when you think of the triumphs that have been achieved by the unmarried, in the cause of humanity——"

" Fortunately," said her new friend, " you don't have to consider her any more."

"I have dreams," Flora confessed; "quite unworthy snobbish dreams, in which my brother suddenly loses every penny, and they're all dependent on me."

Her companion seemed rather startled, but after a minute he said, "We must hope that's one of the dreams that stays in lavender till the end of time. Anyway, if Providence has suddenly turned a smiling face in your direction you shouldn't tempt it by even imaginary quixotry. I do hope you're enjoying your good fortune. I never could see any sense in being the richest man in the churchyard."

"Oh, I'm no miser," Miss Ransome assured him lightly. "I live at the Parade which is known as the millionaires' hotel—you're staying there yourself, perhaps?"

"No, no. I'm only here for a few days on business. I'm not at any of the larger hotels. A couple of rooms and good service suit me better. As a matter of fact, I came over to look at a house, but I doubt if this is quite the locality. I'm a countryman at heart, and I've a feeling that my nomad days are over."

"You mean you want to settle down? It sounds incredible to me."

"Does it?" He smiled and moved a little closer. "If you'd had my life you might understand my point of view. He travels fastest who travels alone—certainly. But there comes a time, inevitably, when you're ready to ease your pace and remember the universal goal towards which all this travelling is inevitably taking you."

"You haven't any family?" she ventured.

"None," he said decisively. "Since I lost my wife I've been quite alone."

"I'm so sorry," whispered Flora, a little embarrassed.

"I knew you were sympathetic," he told her charmingly. "I sensed it the moment I set eyes on you." He produced a cigarette-case. "How remiss I am. I should have offered you this before. Oh, but of course you'll smoke. There's something so companionable about a cigarette."

He snapped on a lighter, let its flame play sharply over

her before holding it to the end of her cigarette. He knew to a nicety the difference between rabbit gallantly pretending to be sable and the real thing, just as he knew which pearls were produced by the oyster's private enterprise and which by man's. As he had suspected, furs and jewels here were both genuine. He sighed happily. The time the place and the loved one all together, though his phrasing of the situation was more colloquial. "If ever I saw a sitting bird this is it," he thought.

"Yes," he continued, "the time comes when the notion of wandering for the rest of your days fills you with a kind of panic. You begin to long for the domestic fetters other men wear so lightly. After all, where does the nomad fetch up at the last ? "

"You should see the people at my hotel," exclaimed Flora incautiously. "I don't suppose there's a nomad among the lot of them, but sometimes I feel even I am not real, just a character in a story by Rudyard Kipling, one of a host of Kipling characters."

He smiled appreciatively. "All true blue ? "

"So blue it's contagious."

"Then—why not walk out on them ? You're free, white and twenty-one—and the world's wide."

She hesitated. "I suppose that's one of the reasons that one hesitates—the fact that the world is so wide, I mean ... One feels such—such a dot on the landscape."

"If one's alone—my point precisely. But—is it necessary to be alone ? "

He moved a little closer. Now they were standing side by side. It didn't seem possible she hadn't known of his existence half an hour ago. She thought of her favourite Mr. Browning. "But sudden the worst turns the best to the brave. . . ." Though probably it was ungrateful to think of the Parade Hotel as the worst. The point was— how brave was one ? She looked up and met her companion's eyes. His glance, companionable and understanding, seemed to fill her with a new courage. She took her fence at a rush.

"I don't know," she whispered. "Up to date it's always seemed to work out that way."

"And now?" His arm brushed against hers.

"I wonder," she said in a breathless voice quite unlike her normal deep tones, "if it was Providence that sent me out of that centrally-heated atmosphere to-night."

He knew then that his corner was as good as turned.

When Miss Ransome appeared in the cock-and-hentail bar, as the management so amusingly called it, of the Parade Hotel next day, accompanied by a most delightful and distinguished-looking man quite a number of heads turned in her direction.

"Brother?" hissed the Hon. Miss Audley to Mrs. Payson-don't-forget-the-E-Grahame.

Mrs. P. G. shook her head. "No. He came down once before. Not a bit like this man."

"Where did she find him?"

"Perhaps he's a new arrival."

"No. I saw all the new ones come this morning." She sat about like a social reporter watching people come and go. She knew exactly who had arrived and who had left. "Besides, he didn't bring any luggage." She rose and walked up the bar.

"Do forgive my interrupting," she murmured. "It's about the bridge tournament partnerships—I've been trying to get hold of you all day. . . ."

"A Mr. Grainger," she reported to the Hon. Miss Audley a few minutes later. "She says he's an old friend. Funny she's never produced him before."

"Co-respondent eyes," said Miss Audley gruffly. "She must have more in her than we thought."

After that all went as merrily as a marriage bell—and what an apt phrase *that* could be, reflected the self-styled Henry Grainger. He knew he had only to say the word, but he waited a little while. Some of the old cats had eyes in their heads, if Flora's were blinded by the thought of a conquest she had never dreamed she was likely to make.

But he couldn't wait too long. Already he had had recourse to a little jeweller's shop at the back of the town, where he entered by the side door and asked the proprietor how much he would be prepared to lend him on a handsome thin gold watch inscribed " For Henry from Beryl," and a date the previous year. Just a loan, he explained, while he waited for a remittance that had unaccountably got delayed. If it hadn't been for the inscription he could have got better terms ; women were so thoughtless about these things. (In just the same way Flora used to complain about people who would write their names in Christmas cards so that you couldn't pass them on next year.) Still, on the whole, it was just as well not to have that sort of memento lying about. Wives were notoriously curious creatures. Curiosity had killed other things than cats. Look at Bluebeard and those prying wives of his. You could really say they all committed suicide. An incurious wife could hope to complete her century—but there were so few of them about. And as to that he should know. Wives were his stock-in-trade. Within four weeks of meeting Flora Ransome, he had added another to his list.

IV

ENCOUNTER IN A RAILWAY CARRIAGE

THEY WERE married very quietly in London and spent their honeymoon there. It was a splendid fortnight of the best seats at theatres, meals at all the most exclusive restaurants and such an orgy of spending as Flora had not enjoyed since she first came into her legacy. Dear Henry's ideas were as expensive as her own. He positively encouraged her to buy a second fur coat. And he waved away her suggestion of something economical with a scornful hand. " You should have the best because it is the best," he told her. She emerged in a supple coat of summer ermine, and if he thought that a younger more lissome figure would have done its luxury more justice nothing in his voice or manner betrayed the fact. She bought one or two good pieces of jewellery also. " When you were Miss Ransome you only had to dress to please yourself," he reminded her playfully. " Now you must dress to please your husband." His wedding-present to her was a diamond and emerald ring, the stone not very large but of great depth and purity, set in a rose of small diamonds. It was a beautiful ring and might have graced the fingers of a marchioness. She wore it with pride and flashed it with a sort of innocent pleasure whenever opportunity offered.

" Now," said he, after she had presented him with diamond cuff-links and a watch quite as handsome as the one Beryl Benyon had given her bridegroom, " we must decide where we are going to live."

She was delighted to learn that he, like herself, had a predilection for a country home. London was all very well for a brief holiday, but you had to be a millionaire to live there with any comfort in these costly times. Together they searched the advertisement pages of the *Record* and the *Post*, eagerly marking down anything that seemed suitable. One in particular they both liked. It was a country cottage of character, with all modern amenities, electric light, up to the moment sanitation, telephone, an excellent garden, an orchard. They went to the house-agent—it was being offered jointly by a man in London and another firm on the spot—and obtained details. The price was rather high but the agent assured them it was an excellent investment. " With so many changes in our social and industrial life," he pointed out, " nothing is safe. We can't tell you how the trend of world events is shaping. Shares may fall like a stone through water, but if you have a house then you have at all events a roof over your head." There was a good vegetable garden. " I can see he means us to become vegetarians,"

32

remarked Henry as they left the office. " Still, we might as well look at it. It doesn't do to take anything at its face value, not when that face value is presented by a house-agent." They wrote that same night to the owner and were given an appointment to see the place forty-eight hours later. When the morning came Henry travelled down alone. Flora was bitterly disappointed ; she had looked forward more than she could say to going over their future home—she was convinced it would be their future home—with her husband, whom she still regarded as a cut between the Archangel Gabriel and King Arthur, but something she had eaten the night before must have disagreed with her, for she had a terrible night, sickness and pain that nothing seemed to stop. Henry was all attentiveness ; he wanted to send for a doctor at once, but Flora said, No, it was just a bilious attack. It must have been the mushrooms. Henry hadn't had any mushrooms. Henry said, Better send this chap a wire to say we can't come to-day after all, but Flora, fearful of losing their darling house, said, No, they couldn't possibly do that, a house of that character would be snapped up in a minute and Henry must go alone. If it seemed what they wanted they could go down together again a little later. So off Henry went, and Flora lay in bed and and resolved never to touch mushrooms again in all her life. She felt better after lunch and when Henry got back that same evening she was dressed and waiting for him in the private sitting-room he had insisted on their having. " Public rooms are all right for old married couples," he had said, " but when you're newly-weds you want a little privacy." Flora thought it perfectly sweet of him, and repressed a faint sense of disappointment. She wanted everyone to see them together. Still, there were meals, and sometimes they sat in the drawing-room for coffee, and of course there was a lot to be said for a sitting-room of your own. For one thing, it ensured incredibly good service, and as Henry liked to remark, What was money for but to be spent ?

While he was away the hotel sent in its account for their first week, and it occurred to her that it would be a nice surprise if she were to make her beloved husband a present of their entertainment for those first few days. She knew he hadn't very much money and, after all, husbands and wives should have everything in common. So she sent down a cheque and waited eagerly for dear Henry's return. He came back glowing with enthusiasm for the house, which he declared was everything they had hoped ; yet he seemed hesitant about buying it.

" The fact is," he said, " there's a snag. Oh, not in the house itself. We're not likely to find anything we like so well—it's almost too good to be true—the trouble is that the chap who's got it is going abroad for good very suddenly, and wants cash on the nail. One sees his point. He's closing his bank account here, and he doesn't want any trouble about trying to get money sent across to him later on. Besides, I gather he's got considerable commitments in his new environment, and will need all the cash he can scrape up. Naturally, I'd intended to raise a mortgage—that's the usual thing when you're buying a house, and there wouldn't be any difficulty about it. I called in on my brokers on my way back to get their advice, but they tell me frankly I should be selling at an immense disadvantage if I tried to raise that sum of money now. Everything's at sixes and sevens, not only in the country but in the world in general, and prices aren't likely to rise until they're more settled and goodness knows when that will be. I can only sell by accepting a considerable loss, and though no one likes chucking money about more than I do—

" Lots of money and pots of honey
Tied up in a five-pound note—

I do feel a bit disinclined to take such a step. It looks to me as though we'd better let this opportunity ride and hope that another as good—well, nearly as good, one doesn't come upon perfection twice in a lifetime—will turn up."

But Flora would have none of it. She felt in her bones that this was their house, the intended setting for their happiness. Henry needn't look so downcast, she would put up the money.

"But, dearest," protested Henry, smiling at her impetuosity, " this was going to be my marriage present to you. Not just a wedding present—we can only marry once—but a marriage present, because marriage goes on for all our lives. You can't buy your own present. It doesn't make sense."

"It makes much less sense to let the house go because of your silly pride. Anyway, I've got some stock due to be paid off almost at once and I shall have to do something with the money. What could be better than putting it into our house ? "

Eventually he allowed himself to be persuaded ; the money—£6,000—was to be placed to his account, he would pay for the house, and as markets rose he would recoup her outlay. It appeared that the owner would not be going abroad for about a month, and because they didn't want to prolong their stay at this very expensive hotel, and neither fancied living at a cheaper one, they shook the dust of London off their feet and went into rooms at Frampton-on-Sea—both liking the sea, for different reasons.

"I want you to indulge me in one more thing," urged Henry. "This house is to be a sort of surprise for you. I'm having one or two changes made that I hope you'll consider improvements. Yes, I know it was almost perfect, but almost isn't quite."

"What's the favour you're trying to ask of me, Henry ? "

"I want you not to see the house till these changes have been made. It's only a question of a week or two."

"I didn't know you could get anything done these days," said innocent Flora.

"Oh, well," said Henry in his lordly masculine way, "it's different in the country. People want to be helpful."

"So long as you don't get yourself into any sort of trouble, my dearest, I'll promise you anything you like." She knew she was besotted about the man ; she could refuse him nothing.

Well, she had possessed her soul in patience and now it seemed she was about to reap her reward. They had given the landlady notice, and she had said how sorry she would be to see them go. Flora knew it was more on Henry's account than her own. Henry was the sort of man landladies and servants love to serve ; they have a way with them. At the end of the week she would set eyes on the dream-house.

"Do any shopping you want before we leave here," her husband warned her. "You're going to Eldorado, you know, and there are no shops there."

She was spending one last day in town, having her hair permanently waved and her nails done with colourless varnish and getting a few country clothes, because she didn't believe you had to look like a gipsy or a frump simply because you didn't live in a town. A really good country skirt and some of those handsome brogue shoes that look so simple and cost simply pounds—and of course something for Henry. A handsome shooting-stick perhaps, though he never shot, or an umbrella with a silver band—her ideas were not very original. Still, there were delightful shops she could visit with this end in view —Fortnum and Mason and Dunhill—oh, between them she was bound to hit on just the right thing.

It was a perfect afternoon and she did her shopping more quickly than she had expected. Her permanent wave was a great success with none of the frizziness you got at the cheaper establishments. She confided in Mr. John, who had been detailed to attend to her, that she was going down to the country in a day or two, to live like a hay-seed.

Mr. John looked rather shocked.

" You'll come up for a set at regular intervals," he said anxiously. " And whatever you do don't let any of those amateurs cut it for you. The harm done by a bad cut . . ." His gesture seemed to intimate a disaster second only to a third world war.

Henry had promised to meet the train arriving at five-two, leaving Waterloo at three forty-eight. She could have caught the earlier one if she had hurried, but it was still so delightful to step on to a platform and find someone waiting for you that she trailed round the shops buying one or two more oddments and then got to the station in good time to settle herself comfortably in a first-class carriage. She thought she was going to have it to herself, but just as the guard waved a green flag someone came dashing through the loitering crowds who would travel on the next train and wrenched at the door of her compartment. A short stout man atrociously dressed in bright brown landed with a thud like a land mine. Flora's nose quivered and she looked away. The newcomer picked himself up, looked at the window, realised he was in a non-smoker, and produced a cigar.

" Nearly missed it," he offered in a cheerful tone. " I see this is no smoking, but I dare say you won't mind—your husband will have got you used to the smell. That's one of the advantages of marriage—for other people, I mean. These unmarried dames, they look as if a cigar was something you picked off the manure heap." And, really, if they came within range of many cigars like this one you couldn't blame them, Flora reflected.

She wanted to say she detested cigar smoke, but his ready assumption of her married state softened her. Besides, he looked such a—such a tough, it was probably as well to humour him. The train was the old-fashioned kind that doesn't have corridors, so she was stuck with the creature until the next stop at all events. Perhaps decency would compel him to get out and look for a smoker then, but she had a feeling that he wouldn't recognise decency, not that kind, if it came up and shook him by the hand. And she knew she wouldn't have the courage to change her carriage herself, in case he realised her motive and took it as a personal insult. She couldn't know that Crook was just as exasperated as she to find them fellow-travellers. It was bad enough having to go by train at all—the Scourge for once was out of commission—without finding yourself mewed up with a lah-di-dah dame for over an hour. For he remembered, if she didn't that this was an express and the next stop would be Frampton. One thing, he would dip his lid and depart like winking as soon as he got the chance. He didn't produce a newspaper as she had anticipated ; instead he stuck his horrible square-toed brown shoes up on the opposite seat and stared fixedly at a photograph of Lyme Regis. Flora opened her paper but could feel his gaze burning through it. She wished a ticket collector could appear, she was sure he hadn't a first-class ticket—in which assumption she was perfectly correct—then she realised that no one could interrupt them until the next stop.

Suddenly he spoke. " Well, you're not taking any risks, are you ? " he said, and there was a grin on his big pug face. " You could knock any chap out with that cudgel you're carrying."

She felt herself turn scarlet. " It's a present for my husband," she said.

" You're a brave woman. Me, I wouldn't put ideas like that into the head of the best husband in the world. Still, maybe it'll keep the cosh-boys off. They're like those chaps in the Bible—more blessed to give—crashers, I mean—than to receive. Even a cosh-boy might think twice if he saw that."

" That wasn't my idea in buying it. We are going to live in a very remote house in the country, and we shall do a good deal of walking."

" This craze for walking," said Crook good-humouredly. " If a man was a natural pedestrian he'd have been given four feet instead of two. What's wrong with a car anyway ? "

" Ask the government," flashed Flora. " We can't get a car, except at a piratical price that my husband won't allow me to give."

" Sounds a bit dim to me," commented Crook candidly. " Cottage in the country and no way of getting about but your own plates of meat. What's it like, really ? Bus once a week and no alternative but a hearse."

" A hearse ? " She sounded startled. " What on earth makes you say that ? "

Crook looked surprised. " We all come to it," he reminded her soothingly. " Whereabouts is this little love-nest of yours ? "

" Oh, I don't suppose you'd ever have heard of the place. You'd have to be a real nature-lover to appreciate it."

" You'd be surprised the number of places I have heard of," said Crook, taking no offence. " My work takes me all over the country, from castles to cemeteries. Now, I know everything's hunkydory with you at present, and let's hope it will be till the end of the chapter, but me, I believe there's a pattern in life, can't help believing it, seeing what I do. And even a casual meeting like ours, which is about as unexpected as you could look for, may be part of a chain. So to show there's no hard feelings just you take my card and if ever you should want a bit of help just remember the name—Arthur Crook."

" Nothing but a tout," thought Flora, curling up like a snail if you touch it. Selling something. She made no move to take the card.

" Go on," said Crook, " don't be proud. It won't burn."

Flora remembered her husband's words that morning when she was preparing for her journey. " Remember there are a lot of queer fish about," he had said. " I'm not sure I oughtn't to come with you." And he had urged her not to wear her fur coat or any conspicuous jewellery. There was a long tunnel, one of the black variety, between

London and Frampton-on-Sea and that gave train
brigands their chance. Now she stretched out her hand
ungraciously and grabbed the card, but she put it not in
her bag but in her pocket. As soon as this uncouth
creature was out of sight she would throw it away. She
couldn't imagine why he had given it to her in the first
place. Crook began to chatter like a magpie ; she gathered
that he was describing himself as a lawyer, but she didn't
believe it. Lawyers didn't pay the finicking attention to
appearance that they had done in—say—the time of
Arthur Wing Pinero, when they were unmistakable, but
they certainly didn't go about wearing the awful clothes
her companion sported without apparently any realisation
of how awful they were. Then she remembered there was
something called a Poor Man's Lawyer. He might be that
sort. But when she hinted as much to Crook he put back
his head and roared like any Nubian lion.

" Don't get me wrong," he pleaded. " Eighteen carat
gold's my standard, though I will take nine at a pinch.
But don't go mixing me up with a philanthropist any
more." His eyes, little pig's eyes she called them rather
unjustly, twinkled at her. " Any more than I'd confuse
you with the kind of person who'd expect to get advice
free."

Then at last they reached Frampton and she jumped
out of the train and hurried down the platform looking
for Henry. It was a shock to find he wasn't there. She
would have minded less if she hadn't been sure this Crook
person was watching her. " Now he'll think I'm one of
these gone-in-the-upper story spinsters who buy cudgels
to protect their virtue which I'm sure no one else wants.
If he'd seen me met by my husband . . ." She paused,
because Henry might have got tied up in some way and
be speeding towards her at this very moment in a hired
car. He wouldn't be pleased if he arrived to find her gone.
She was still waiting when the train drew out of the
station. At the window of the carriage she had occupied
Mr. Crook beamed at her and waved a hand the size of a

leg of mutton. "Odious creature," shuddered Flora, turning away. "I hope that's the last I shall ever hear of him." But as it happened it wasn't the last Crook was doomed to hear of her.

V

END OF A ROMANCE

ABOUT THREE HOURS after his wife's departure for London Henry received a telegram and when he had read it he said in a rather worried voice to Mrs. Robins, the landlady, " Look here, I've just had a telegram from these people at the house asking me to get there as early as possible. Their plans are changed and they have to go off sooner than they expected ; I must meet them because of getting the keys. Will you explain the position to my wife and ask her to come on by train ? I'll take all the heavy luggage, and just leave her small case, that she can manage without much trouble. There's a train at five-thirty she can catch from Durlston—I'll bring the car to meet her—I'm afraid it's rather a cross-country journey, but she'll arrive about nine unless the train's late. I can't get in touch with her because I stupidly forgot to ask her where she gets her hair done, and there must be about a couple of hundred hairdressers in London." Then he thanked her for her care of them both and tipped the girl handsomely, piled all the luggage in the car that, he said, he had bought as a surprise for Flora, and off he went. As soon as he was out of sight she remembered she hadn't asked him what the address was, but consoled herself with the thought that of course the lady would know it. By sheer good luck a Mrs. Martin came along that after-noon looking for rooms, liked Mrs. Robins' house, and arranged to come in next morning. Mrs. Robins put the girl to setting everything to rights and the time passed quickly enough until half-past four.

" What time's Mrs. Grainger expected back ? " asked the girl who was on excellent terms with her employer. They were sitting companionably in the kitchen, having a cup of tea.

" Well, I did think she'd be back by now," Mrs. Robins acknowledged.

" She'll never catch the five-thirty from Durlston if she isn't quick." The girl fetched the local time-table and checked up on London trains. " Next one arrives five-two," she said. " Say it's on time she'll hang about till five-ten or five-twelve if she's expecting him to meet her —no, she can't get the five-thirty." Her brow wrinkled. " That's a funny thing. I mean, he must have known she couldn't catch the five-thirty."

" Then she'll have to take the next one."

" If there is one. Where are they going ? "

Mrs. Robins had to confess she didn't know, but the girl sensibly looked up the time-table and found that the five-thirty went to the West Country.

" Can't be a through train because he said she wouldn't get there till nine. Wonder when the next one is."

" She can't stay here, we've got the room all ready for Mrs. Martin. Stella, you don't think there's anything funny about it, do you ? "

Stella considered. " Funny he didn't leave a letter, that's all."

" He couldn't let those others go off without giving him the key."

" They could have left it with a neighbour, couldn't they ? " Neither could imagine a life that didn't include neighbours on both sides.

It was nearly half-past five when Flora returned to be greeted with the disconcerting news that her husband had gone on ahead with the luggage in a car, and that it was impossible for her to catch the five-thirty.

" Oh, dear," she exclaimed, " how very unfortunate. I don't think people have the right to change their plans at the eleventh hour like that. What other trains are there ? " Together they hunted through the time-table. Flora was looking troubled. " Didn't he even leave me a note ? "

" He went off in such a hurry as soon as he got the telegram. Something about a misunderstanding, I think he said. You're sure this was the day they agreed on ? I mean it's so easy to make a mistake. . . ."

" I think it would be best for me to stay here to-night," said Flora, still uneasy, " and go down in the morning. There doesn't seem to be any connection that would get me there before midnight, and I don't like the idea of waiting an hour and a half at a wayside station. I suppose he was in such a hurry, my husband, I mean, that he didn't realise I couldn't possibly catch the five-thirty."

" I'm afraid you can't stay to-night," said Mrs. Robins. " We've done the room out for Mrs. Martin, the lady who's coming in to-morrow. Besides, Mr. Grainger's expecting you."

" What time did he leave ? " asked Flora, still following her own line of thought.

" About lunch-time. Well, say half-past twelve. He wouldn't even stop for a meal, said he'd get one on the road. He'd got to be there by four."

" I'll ring him up and explain," said Flora. " Haven't you some other room I could have just for this evening ? "

" Well, I haven't," said Mrs. Robins regretfully, " and that's a fact. Look, why don't you ask him to come and meet you at this place where you have to change. Then you could take the seven-twenty. You'd be there by nine —it's not as if there was someone the other end who couldn't be left, like a child or an invalid."

Flora thought that was a very good idea. The telephone lived in a little room at the end of the passage and she went along at once. Surely Henry must have arrived by this time. If he didn't like the idea of coming out this evening she could, she supposed, put up at an hotel, though privately she thought it rather disobliging of Mrs. Robins not to stretch a point and accommodate her for the extra night. Still, she knew landladies don't like their plans upset. Not surprising, she reflected, that so many of them are widows. Wives need to be far more adaptable. She had to wait a minute or two for the connection, and when she did get through the voice that answered her certainly wasn't Henry's. When she asked for him the stranger in a rather curt voice said, " You've got the wrong number, I'm afraid. Nobody called Grainger lives here."

" But—isn't that Manor Cottage, Felsworthy ? "

" Yes, it is, but——"

" We have just bought the house, my husband came down this afternoon. Naturally, we should have travelled together, but unfortunately——"

She got no further for the voice said, " I'm afraid there's been a mistake. This house has been bought by a Mr. Wyse. What name did you say ? Grainger ? Wait a moment." (There was a sound as of papers being turned over.) " It's perfectly true," the voice continued. " Mr. Grainger did come down and look at the house—but he decided it was too isolated for his wife. I gather she's a bit of an invalid." Then the voice broke off abruptly. " Did you say it was Mrs. Grainger speaking ? "

But Flora made no reply. She had dropped the receiver, didn't even hear the voice calling urgently at the other end of the wire. And presently its owner got tired of waiting and rang off.

Flora sat numbly beside the instrument feeling waves of darkness wash over her. It couldn't be true, there was some mistake, these things happen but never to oneself. Henry had told her he had bought the house—the darkness began to recede a little. Yes, he had told her, but he had also persuaded her to let him have the money—the cheque had been made out to him personally—he had prevented her from going to the house or having any communication with the owners. He had seen her off to London with a promise to meet her on her return. He was gone with all the luggage—oh, no wonder he hadn't wanted her to wear the fur coat or take any jewellery. Slowly the appalling truth forced its way into her shuddering mind.

Mrs. Robins, becoming troubled, came along the passage and tapped on the door. When no one answered she turned the knob. Mrs. Grainer was sitting there as white as a sheet. Immediately she thought, It's bad news. There's been an accident. " Whatever is it ? " she gasped.

Flora stared at her as though she had been a stranger. " Bad news ? " she repeated mechanically. " Oh, no." She struggled to her feet. " It's all right. Only—I shan't be going down to-night, after all." The sight of Mrs. Robins' face, avid with curiosity, restored her to her senses. " I can go to the hotel for the night," she said. " There are always rooms at a station hotel, and I shall be on the spot for to-morrow. There's an early train——"

" You mean the Durlston Hotel ? "

" Yes. Yes, of course." Whatever happened she must get away from here quickly.

" At least you'll have a cup of tea before you go," urged Mrs. Robins, but she negatived that at once. She must leave now, immediately, before she was tempted to confide in the woman. She knew what a cup of tea can do to you. Before she knew where she was she would be telling Mrs. Robins the whole story, and kind-hearted though she might be it would be more than you could expect of human nature if she wasn't thrilled and excited, even pleased in a sort of way. " Just like something in the Sunday papers," she would remark. And probably, when she was alone with Stella, she would add, " Still, what did she expect ? These old maids getting married in about five minutes, are asking for it in my opinion." So she said she had had some tea on the train, and of course she would have dinner at the hotel.

" You'll want a taxi," suggested Mrs. Robins. " And why not telephone the hotel and get a room ? "

No, said Flora, she wouldn't do that. There were plenty of hotels in Durlston. She would stop at one that looked comfortable. But she telephoned for a taxi just the same. " I can catch the six-twenty from Frampton," she said. " I shall just have time." She asked if she could go up to their room for a minute.

" Well, yes, you can," Mrs. Robins agreed a little grudgingly.

" Just to make sure he hasn't left anything. You know what men are."

" Stella and me have done the whole place out," the landlady warned her, but she went up just the same. The room had the anonymity of all furnished apartments. There was nothing whatever to betray the fact that she and Henry had been there. " I suppose," she said, turning away, " he didn't think to leave the telegram."

" Leave the telegram ? No, he didn't. Why ever should he ? "

She couldn't think of a good answer to that. Of course, he had sent it himself as soon as he was sure she was well on her way to London. He must have had this plan in mind for days, and yet only last night he had discussed with immense enthusiasm their plans for the future. The taxi came, she collected her little case and drove off.

" She did seem put out," said Mrs. Robins, closing the door. " But you can't blame him. Just a piece of bad luck. Oh, well, she'll get in at Durlston all right. The hotels are half-empty this time of year."

Flora paid off her taxi and bought a ticket for Durlston. She had no plans for the moment except to get away from Frampton as soon as possible. She couldn't, couldn't face Mrs. Robins again or anyone who had seen her and Henry together, and Durlston was as good a place to go as any. She booked a room at the hotel, left her case and saying that she didn't want any dinner, she was dining with friends, went out again. It was a little after seven o'clock, and the evenings were still light. She walked down to the cliffs and stood staring out at the cold sea. Henry had loved the sea : she remembered how they had once stood on this very spot watching the waters surging against the cliff-side, until she had shivered and turned away saying, " I don't believe I like the sea after all. It's so pitiless, so relentless, ebbing and flowing, absolutely unmoved by all the tragedy and misery it's caused. Think of the wrecks, the accidents, the drowned people. . . ." " Oh, come my love," Henry had rallied her, " you're getting morbid. Why, that's the very reason I do like it. Think of it, Flo, miles and miles of it as far as eye can reach and much farther, think of its power, its relentlessness. . . ." " That's what I hate," she had cried. " It has no thought for all the terrible damage it has wreaked. Think of the wrecks, the dead bodies, the man-eating monsters it conceals. It's so pitiless, yesterday's tragedy means nothing. . . ."

" But what a lesson to us," he protested. " That's where mankind goes astray. If you walk with your head over your shoulder you're bound to come to grief. Forget yesterday, live to-day, plan for to-morrow, that's the only gospel for the sensible man." And laughing, he added, " When I was a kid I had a pokerwork motto over my bed ; they were very popular ; all the arts and crafts shops of England sported them. Mine said :

> " ' Every day is a fresh beginning,
>   Listen, my soul, to the glad refrain.
>   Forget old sorrow and older sinning,
>   And puzzles forecasted and possible pain.
>   Take heart with the day and begin again.' "

And no one who knew his record could complain that he didn't live up to his belief.

To-night the water was stormy, beating up against the cliffs and falling back in black disorder, in a welter of creamy spray. Under these dark waters as she well knew the rocks waited. She thrust her hands into her pockets, for the wind was cold, and stood looking down while pictures of her past floated before her disillusioned eyes. She thought of her husband. With whom was he at this instant dining and talking ? What woman would wear her jewels, her handsome fur coat ? Oh, it wasn't surprising he had wanted her to buy the best. A motor cyclist and his young lady came chuffing up the steep cliff-path and saw her standing there.

" Coo," exclaimed the girl, " she didn't half give me a shock standing there like the Eddystone Lighthouse. Balmy, I suppose, poor old girl."

" I don't like it, Mavis," said the young man. " What's a woman doing there this hour of the night by herself ? Wonder if we ought to do anything ? "

" Don't be silly. What can you do ? Your trouble, Joe, is you want to put the whole world right. End up in Parliament, I shouldn't wonder."

She tried to persuade him that England was to some extent at least a free country still ; if the poor old sausage wanted to stand and stare at the sea she had got a right, hadn't she ?

But the young man wasn't reassured. He insisted on stopping the motor cycle and walked over to where Flora was standing.

" Excuse me, miss," he said. " Are you all right ? "

She turned in a flash. " All right ? Of course. Why shouldn't I be ? "

" Well, these cliffs, they're none too safe," he said awkwardly. " There's bin some nasty accidents. . . ."

" Are you afraid I shall fall over ? " She contrived an odd laugh. " Into that ? " She shivered. " It looks very cold, doesn't it ? "

" It would be."

" But fascinating."

He went back to his companion.

" Dotty, if you ask me," he said. " I don't like it, Mavis. Tell you what, I'm going to hang about a bit. She looks as if she's had some sort of shock, poor old girl."

VI

PROFITABLE DEATH

FLORA DIDN'T KEEP them waiting long. As though she
had made up her mind she turned and walked back to
the hotel. She had seen the last of Henry, of that she was
convinced. He might be anywhere now. Of course she
could go to the police, but how much good would that do ?
She didn't know the number of the car or its make, so
she couldn't hope to trace him that way. There were
ration books and identity cards, of course, but a man
who could treat a woman as he had done would be clever
enough to have alternative documents. Besides, heaps of
people managed without them for long periods—look at
the deserters, for instance. And then you could stay at
a hotel now for three or four nights without giving up a
ration book. He could go from place to place for months.
And even if she could trace him how much good would
it do her ? She couldn't deny giving him the cheque for
£6,ooo. It had been made out to him personally ; there
was the fur coat, but what did a fur coat matter ? She
wasn't bankrupt, she could buy another coat. What did
matter was that she couldn't stand the publicity attendant
on police proceedings. She felt thankful that Charles and
Janey were in Canada and likely to remain there for
months. Charles would be kind, but how could you tell
what he would be thinking ? Janey wouldn't even be kind.
Couldn't she see what he was after ? she would say. Why
does any good-looking man want to marry a woman of
fifty without any special looks or talents ? Oh, she had
been led up the garden path all right. In her imagination
she saw her picture all over the papers. It was a story she
would never live down. They had read about her at the
Parade, and what a nice dish of gossip she would prove

for them. Why, it could easily be that she wasn't even legally married. And at her age to be caught so easily by an adventurer, to fall off the tree straight into his hands. No, it wasn't possible. All the same—where was he now ? And with whom ? Telling the same tale to some other guileless fool ? She thrust her hands into the pockets of her coat. There was a bit of pasteboard there. That extraordinary creature she had met on the train. She could see his great red face split with amusement when he heard what she had to say. The duped middle-aged spinster has no friends. Other spinsters who haven't had her chances regard her with scorn. They know they would never have been caught like that. To the young she would be not so much an awful example as someone rather disgusting. Fancy thinking of getting married for the first time when you were nearly fifty. You should be resigned to your spinsterhood by that time. " I wonder how many of us there are," she reflected aloud, and a couple passing turned to stare after her. (Another of these goofy old girls, talking to herself because she couldn't find anyone else to talk to.) " We might form a club perhaps—the Dupes' Club, say, membership to be restricted to women who had been cheated by men. What an army of them there would be. Perhaps if one could see oneself as a member of an army one would mind less. Nothing's as bad in the mass as it appears to the solitary victim." She walked back into the hotel, her mind made up. She knew what she was going to do. She hated the thought, but she was resolved. There were alternatives, she supposed, but she rejected them all. Up in her room she started to unpack her little case. Just as well to find out how much her delightful husband had left her. Well, you couldn't say he had been lavish. Just her night-things, some cleansing cream, her sleeping tablets (and it was a mercy he had left those or she would have had to find some all-night chemist and buy some), a sponge-bag, a brush and comb. In one of the pockets she found a postcard. On it was printed in small, neat, capital letters :

"I AM SORRY TO GO LIKE THIS. IT IS THE ONLY
WAY. I CANNOT ENDURE IT ANY LONGER."

She sat staring at it, her cup of humiliation overflowing.
He might at least, she thought, have spared her this.
The words were well chosen. She could never show that
message to anyone. I cannot endure it any longer. But
what a good actor—what a superlative actor ! Why, she
could have sworn he liked being married to her. She
thought of that lean dark face close to hers, the beguiling
voice—oh, he could have coaxed a hippopotamus out of
its pool in a heat-wave. She made a gesture to tear the
card up, then changed her mind. She had visions of him
in their room at Frampton hunting for precisely the right
word. Someone knocked on the door and the chamber-
maid came in.

" Can I get you anything, madam ? "

" No. Yes. I should like some hot milk. Is that
possible ? "

" Certainly, madam. And what time do you wish to
be called ? And do you take morning tea ? "

" Yes, please." She was thinking fast. " I shall be
catching the London train immediately after breakfast.
Could you have my account made out for me, as I shall
have no time to lose ? "

Fortunately she had sufficient ready money to settle
the hotel bill. Strange hotels don't like taking cheques.
She counted the notes in her purse—seven pounds. When
the hot milk came she was undressed and in bed. " Now
where's my fountain pen ? " she wondered when the
chambermaid had gone. " I ought to write a letter."
She realised he hadn't even left her her writing-case.
It was rather a nice one. They had chosen it together at
Asprey's. Oh, well, it didn't really matter now. Come to
that, nothing mattered much. It had been a most
exhausting day, and the morning would do perfectly well.
She unscrewed the little bottle of sleeping tablets, began

to shake the pellets into her hand. . . . When the chamber-maid brought up her tea next morning at seven-thirty as arranged she had been dead for some hours. On the table beside the bed was a card on which a message had been printed in small, neat, capital letters :

" I AM SORRY TO GO LIKE THIS. IT IS THE ONLY WAY. I CANNOT ENDURE IT ANY LONGER."

This time the inquest did attract some attention. A doctor, hurriedly summoned by the hotel, said death was caused by an overdose of sleeping mixture. The tablets contained a small proportion of hyoscin, and there was a label on the bottle warning the patient that it would be dangerous to take more than two. Precisely how many the unfortunate lady had taken no one could tell, since no one knew how many tablets the bottle had contained when she arrived. But that it had been a fatal dose was evident. The proprietor was livid. With the sea so near it was intolerable that a would-be suicide should get his place a bad name by taking her own life under his roof, hiring a room simply for that purpose. No sense, in view of the message found at the bedside, pretending it was accidental death. It was a case for the police, of course, as suicides have to be. They traced her recent movements : Mrs. Robins gave evidence at the inquest. She had seemed troubled about her husband going on in advance. No, she hadn't got the telegram. Mr. Grainger had taken it with him. She couldn't give the address of the new house, but Mrs. Grainger had rung her husband up the night before, and had apparently arranged to join him next day. A queer factor of the case was that the husband didn't put in an appearance. Mrs. Robins' description of him as a tall dark man, clean-shaved, rather good looking, could fit hundreds of men. No one knew the number of the car and no car licence had recently been taken out in the name of Henry Grainger. The coroner said that in his opinion here was a clear case of suicide, but the responsibility lay with the husband. It seemed obvious that he had taken advantage of his wife's absence in London to go off and desert her. Inquiries were made at Manor Cottage, and the nature of Flora's conversation became public property. The reaction was just what Flora herself had anticipated. It was a dirty trick, of course, but . . . "This husband may consider himself a lion among ladies," said the coroner, who rather fancied his oratorical powers ; "but to any decent man he is nothing but a marauding wolf." The bit about the cheque came out too, of course. Crook, whose card was found among the dead woman's few possessions also had a visit from the police. But he couldn't tell them much. Why had he given her one ? Did he always give cards to solitary females who shared his compartment ? Crook said it was a hunch, and his hunches generally had something behind them.

The verdict was suicide while the balance of her mind was disturbed. Her lawyer settled up her affairs and promised to get in touch with the surviving relations as soon as he could. But even here Providence seemed on the side of the rogues. For the plane in which Charles and Jane Ransome were crossing Canada crashed in bad weather, and there were no survivors. The two children were minors and, in any case, scarcely knew their aunt. It was another dead end.

The detailed report of the inquest went into Crook's *Tombstone Serenade* under the heading of The Case of the Marauding Wolf. "Suicide my eye," he remarked to Bill Parsons. "That woman didn't mean to take her own life."

"You're wasted as a lawyer," said Bill. "You should have been a professor of mathematics. What makes you so sure ? "

"I went down and had a look-see at her belongings. There was no writing-case, no notepaper, no envelopes, nothing. Then where did that postcard come from ? Going to tell me she bought just one ? Come off it, Bill. It can't be done. And what was the sense of printing it ?

If you're leaving a suicide note you don't fake your hand-writing. It don't add up, Bill, and that's the truth. If she'd meant to put out her own light she'd have left a letter for the brother or the lawyer or someone. Besides, her pen was found in her bag. If she'd just written a suicide note, would she have put it away and then left the bag the other side of the room ? No, I'll tell you what this is, Bill, it's murder."

" How are you going to prove that ? " It was practically impossible to disturb Bill's calm.

" Oh, it ain't my case. But one of these days I might run across Mr. Marauding Murdering Wolf in the flesh. You know the sort of thing. The Wolf strikes again. If you ask me, he planned it all very neatly, got her up to town, then sent himself a telegram—that was for the landlady's benefit, of course—packed everything of any value and vanished into the blue. Even if they could trace the car he might have changed the number-plates. He'd got plenty of time. He left her her sleeping tablets. . . ."

" He couldn't be sure she'd use them that night."

" It was all Lombard Street to a china orange she would, and sooner or later she'd take the fatal ones. Oh, yes, that's what killed her. She took an overdose of hyoscin, but not because she meant to. He could sub-stitute a couple of deadly tablets—did you see the bottle ? Well, it was a tube, really ; the tablets come out one at a time, and they were a largish size. That was a bit of luck for him. If they'd been small ones, like aspirin, say, he couldn't count on her taking the two fatal ones first. But she'd have to take the top ones, and once they were down the long red lane that knows no turning it was sweet Fanny Adams for him. And there's another thing, Bill. Notice his initials ? H. G. That's the third time they've occurred in connection with a woman's sudden death. There was the girl who was accidentally drowned with a bagful of money that was never recovered ; there was the lady, newly-wed, who died in a car smash, and all her money went to the husband, and now there's Mrs. Grainger."

" And what do you do ? "

" If you mean, do I stick my neck out, the answer is No, I don't. I'm not a lawyer for nothing. I couldn't prove a thing. After all, there's no law to prevent a lady printin' her dyin' message instead of writing it, and the rest of the tablets are innocent enough, you can be sure of that. No, wherever this chap Grainger is, you can be sure he's grinning like a dog and runnin' about the city. Like that chap who sat in a corner and patted himself on the back. ' I've done it again,' he's saying, but what he don't realise and what'll bring him to the little covered shed in the end is the fact that Arthur Crook's on his tail now, and Crook always gets his man."

As for Henry, he lay low until he saw the result of the inquest. By this time he was so convinced of his luck that he had not really anticipated trouble, but all the same, once the unhappy lady who had gone by the name of Flora Grainger was underground, he drew a deep breath of relief. Now he could come up for air. Things had worked out once again as he had intended. Henry Grainger was as dead as his one-time wife, though no one was going to say, " Dust to dust, ashes to ashes," over his corpse. In his place a pleasant dark-haired gentleman with the beginnings of a smart little black moustache and whiskers, called Henry Gould, sat in a cottage in a remote part of the West Country, continuing his hobby of examining the histories of famous criminals. One of these days—and fairly soon—he was going to publish a book ; it would sell all right. That sort of book always did. People loved murder ; probably the cynic was right when he said that most people would commit one murder if they weren't afraid of being found out, and there was that chap, G. K. Chesterton, who said if they desisted it was because people would die so messily. Anyway, they liked to commit murder by proxy. Why, there was a club

ANTHONY GILBERT

somewhere in London whose members had only one thing
in common, an absorption in capital crime. He grinned
at the thought that perhaps one day he might be invited
as a guest speaker ; he could tell them a lot, and oddly
enough his advice would be the same as Arthur Crook's,
and both of them stemmed from Macbeth's Bloody Child.
Be bloody, bold and resolute. His private reservation
was, " Go easy on the blood." Accident was as simple to
contrive, and left no stain. In the meantime, he had not
done too badly out of his last adventure. He had got Flora
to give him an open cheque for six thousand pounds and
you could be sure there was precious little of that left.
He had bought the car and drawn considerable sums at
regular intervals that were now deposited in other banks
under various names. You never knew when you might
need a little money, and a spare name or two carrying an
account was a necessity to all adventurers. He had the
fur coat and the jewellery, which were worth another
thousand ; he could hock those at any time or sell them,
come to that, but he knew the wisdom of delay. These
apparent suicides and showing-off coroners only occasioned
a nine-days' wonder, during which it would be advisable
to lie low. But people tended to forget such affairs ; their
own concerns were infinitely more important and would
soon swamp their attention again. In any case, he could
afford to take it easy for a while. He could live for a year
on his gains from this last adventure ; but he was like a
best-selling novelist, who need never write another line
but goes on, though most of his profits accrue to the
authorities, simply because he can't stop. With St. Paul
Henry could say, " One thing I do." With him women were
always ultimately wives. They were not an indulgence,
a vice, a way of passing the time, a pleasure or a grief,
they were a vocation. As one man becomes an engineer
and another a doctor, so Henry became a husband. It
was his living. The knocking off of his various wives when
they had served their purpose was part of the routine, and
involved no personal dislike or revenge ; he was like a

woman who decides she is tired of a certain hat or dress, it has served its turn, it is out of fashion, it is blocking her wardrobe, it must go. So in turn went Greta, Beryl, Flora, so would go their successors for so long as he could contrive to evade the law. It was all perfectly simple, and his conscience never gave him a twinge.

Still, with the passing of Flora, even his enthusiasm had suffered a check. It was the first time he had really called attention to himself. He had been described as a marauding wolf ; the name he had been using had become dishonoured. This had never happened before ; either his identity had never come to light or he had been an object of sympathy. He had wanted to save Greta, but it had proved physically impossible. He had been miles away when Beryl died, and was instantly transformed into the heart-broken husband. Now he was branded as a cad, a man who took a woman's money and fled. But he consoled himself with the reflection that no one guessed he had also taken her life. At that stage he had never even heard of Mr. Crook.

VII

SARAH

HENRY MET Sarah Templeton in November in a London cinema. He had lain very low since the unfortunate Flora's death and, as he had anticipated, all the hoo-ha had died down months ago. If it had been a police case, if anyone had so much as whispered that perhaps Flora hadn't taken her own life, he would have been more careful still. The police have a tireless quality that is maddening from the criminal's point of view. But everything had gone off just as he anticipated, and after rusticating in the West Country, where he really had a cottage, a useful hideout when things became a bit too warm for his comfort, he brushed up his new moustache, put on his London clothes and returned to town. You could find solitary credulous women anywhere, but a big town was best ; in the country everybody knows everybody else's business. In London you can walk up a street twenty times and none of the people living in it will recognise you if they meet you face to face on your twenty-first peregrination. He had gone to a cinema that was showing a superlative French film in which the much-deplored Raimu was starring: among his accomplishments was an excellent knowledge of French. He could follow the actual dialogue instead of relying on the dubbing as most of the people round him were compelled to do. It was a very amusing film and particularly so if you could understand what was being said. It was easy to tell the non-comprehenders ; they always laughed a second too late. After a time he became aware that a girl in the adjacent seat also knew the language ; her laugh, gay and infectious, rang out at precisely the right moment. When the lights went on he turned to glance at her. She was about twenty-five, he judged, a dark handsome young woman, with a broad forehead and a beautiful mouth. True, the nose and chin indicated an obstinate temperament, but that did not trouble him. He had no definite plan in mind, as he drifted easily into conversation. He had had, as he put it, a fair sickener of elderly women, and he owed it to himself to have a little pleasure. Of course a penniless girl was no use to him professionally, but he liked her looks, and it shouldn't be difficult for a man of his experience to learn all he needed to know about her. Within a minute they were discussing the film ; though she didn't look the sort of girl who had to go about by herself. Lonely women were, of course, his stock in trade, but usually they were middle-aged or unattractive or had no knack of making friends even with their own sex. Sarah, he guessed, was here alone because she wanted it that way. When she rose to go at the end of the succeeding feature film he rose also. The rain was coming down in sheets when they reached the door and there was no hope of getting a taxi.

" It's only a storm," he remarked, eyeing the black skies in a very knowledgeable fashion. " I give it half an hour. If you've nothing better to do "—and here his charm showed itself all wool and a yard wide—" perhaps you would give me the pleasure of having some tea with me. There's an excellent refreshment room on the premises."

Sarah accepted at once. Some of the old girls he knew would have made a lot of fuss about paying for themselves ; others would have looked at him as if they expected to see the label WOLF spring up on his forehead in electric lights. Sarah said, " Tea ? Lovely," and went with him without demur. Across the table in a good light he saw that she was even more attractive than he had realised. She was what an earlier generation would have called top drawer, and she was obviously accustomed to the companionship of men. But she wore no ring and gave no indication that she was engaged or even expecting to be. He learned quite a lot about her at that first meeting, her name, her age, the fact that she was an orphan and an only child, and that she was a secretary for her daily bread.

" An architects' firm," she told him, " and as dull as ditchwater. All natty little villas or public halls about as decorative as swimming baths. And the partners are a perfect match. When I first went into an office about five years ago my aunt, my sole relative, who had made a home for me after my parents were killed in a raid, warned me to be careful about men, all in capitals, if you know what I mean. Some of these scaremongers should work in offices themselves. They'd soon lose some of their illusions. They get their ideas from the magazines or the lending libraries, where the employer's middle name is always wolf, and he's always dying to seduce the latest recruit. Mr. Rimington is the dullest of bachelors and his partner about as exciting as a pudding when the water's got in. Neither of them will ever see fifty again, and Mr.

Cope has a wife and six children. If you want to ensure your daughter or niece achieving a blameless old age, put her into an office."

He laughed at that and asked her why she stuck it.

" Oh, I shan't much longer. No, it's not what you think. I'm not getting married, but it's a mistake for a woman to stay too long in one job. With men it's different. It's their life-work (heaven help them—only most of them don't seem to ask for anything better so one shouldn't really waste sympthy on them), and they do have chances of promotion. A firm like Rimingtons would never dream of giving a woman an executive job."

" You're very hard on them," objected Grainger. " After all, as you've just said yourself, the men having put their hands to the plough don't on the whole look back, but how many women under thirty do you know who aren't secretly hoping to get married eventually ? They don't want to make any office their life-work. Employers, having some sense, are bound to realise that. They can't afford to give a department to a woman who may at any moment throw it all up and o p t for a wedding-ring. No, I know what you're going to say, that plenty of married women go on working, but that leaves the employer sitting on the fence. At any minute a wife may have to give up her job, at all events, for a time. Or, if her husband falls ill, she has to look after him ; even if she keeps on with her job her heart isn't in it. She's going to watch the clock, come as late and go as early as she decently can. Tom, Dick or Harry is going to bulk much larger with her than the most important client."

Sarah laughed. " I seem to have jumped right into a hornet's nest."

" But it's true," Henry insisted.

" Yes, I suppose so. All the same, it doesn't alter what I said at the beginning. It doesn't do to stick in a rut. Oh, I've seen them ; we've got one at Rimington's. She's a clerk and she's been there twenty years. As soon as she nears pension age they'll find some reason for getting rid of her before they become liable to give her a pension, and I don't care how well meaning this government is, people like Miss Sherren aren't going to be able to make do on the Old Age Pension."

" But would she be any better off anywhere else ? "

" She might have more fun ; she couldn't conceivably have less. Of course, the truth is there's no way of making money so long as you're working for someone else. You have to be one of the self-employed to get rich."

" Or go bankrupt ? "

" Well." Sarah sounded scornful. " You must take some risks in life." She looked the sort that would take her fences with a rush ; she might break her neck or she might arrive at the head of the field. He approved her style of dressing, good quiet clothes, very little jewellery but what there was, the real thing. That string of pearls she wore was small, but it had come from an oyster ; her one ring had a real stone in it. Nice shoes, handsome gloves—a pity she was only a secretary.

" I suppose you employ any number of women," Sarah suggested, taking a chocolate éclair without even asking him if he was sure it wasn't the one he wanted. That was how a woman should be ; he didn't like them humble. Humility might win you the Kingdom of Heaven, but it got you damn all in this world.

" Me ? Oh, no. I'm a writer. I spend most of my time buried in the country like a badger in its burrow. Then I come out for air and rush up to London for a short time."

" How lucky you are," said Sarah sincerely. " I suppose you do know you're the envied of all the wage-earners on earth ? To be master of your own time. And to live in the country."

" You like the country ? "

" My great ambition is one day to have a cottage of my own, a bit of earth to dig in and know it's mine, to make things grow, to see trees that aren't the property

of the L.C.C., and to have the right to prevent horrible
little boys throwing sticks to break the branches to bring
down chestnuts. Have you worked in an office, Mr.——?"

" Gould—Henry Gould."

" I'm Sarah Templeton. You didn't answer my
question."

" The answer is in the negative. To tell you the truth,
I doubt if I could stand it. I've lived on my wits in
various parts of the world taking any job that offered.
Now I'm fortunate enough to have a little money and a
cottage in the country, and I can please myself."

" What sort of books do you write ? "

" Actually, I haven't had one published yet, and when
I do it won't be fiction."

" Autobiography ? "

He smiled in a way she didn't quite understand.
" Perhaps. Look, oughtn't we to take advantage of a
break in the clouds and make a dash for it ? "

" Meaning that curiosity killed the cat ? " She laughed,
not in the least offended.

" And more than the cat."

" Bluebeard's wives ? "

He shot her a sharp glance, but her face was gay and
serene.

" To be frank with you, I've never had much sympathy
with them. I've always thought Bluebeard absolutely
justified in his action."

" You should be a barrister, Mr. Gould. You'd be a
godsend to homicides."

He pulled a face. " That Americanism. Isn't English
good enough for you ? "

" Murderers sound so much more sinister. Would you
really defend Bluebeard ? After all, he had killed a lot
of women."

" They brought it on themselves. If there was such a
creature as an incurious wife she might live to complete
her century." (This was a frequent line of his. He used
it on all his wives in turn.)

Sarah laughed again. " I'm sure you're a bachelor. No husband would dare proclaim such heretical views."

" That's very far-sighted of you." He beckoned to the waitress and paid the bill. " Do I see you again ? "

" Doesn't that rather depend on you ? " asked Sarah coolly. She hailed a taxi. " Can I give you a lift anywhere ? "

" In return for the tea ? Now you're all set to show me you're the independent citizen. What a pity. I like women so much better."

" And then," smiled Sarah, jumping into the taxi, " they say we're the illogical sex. Good-bye, Mr. Gould, and thank you for my tea."

The taxi drove away, leaving Henry on the pavement. The rain was over and a repentant sun turned the puddles in the gutter to blue and gold. Henry was smiling as he walked away. He had thoroughly enjoyed the encounter. He wondered if Sarah often came to the Luxor on Saturday afternoons. He turned up the following week a short time before the big picture, another French classic, was due to begin. But his luck was out. Sarah did not appear. He was about to leave when he heard someone say, " Mr. Gould ? " and there she was.

" I wondered if you would be coming," he said not attempting to disguise his pleasure.

" Oh, I came to the early house. It's cheaper. Also, you have the rest of Saturday afternoon to yourself. But you mustn't miss it," she went on as he fell into step beside her. " After all, that's what you came for."

" Now you're talking nonsense," said Henry smoothly. ' You know very well I came in the hope of seeing you again."

Sarah's heart was beating unaccountably as they came into the sunlit street. This part of London was looking delightfully sophisticated this sunny afternoon. A woman went by with two miniature apricot poodles.

" Where do we go from here ? " inquired Henry easily.

" I'm going on a Green Line bus into the country."

He looked amazed. " It'll be dark by the time you get there."

" It's not as far into the country as that. It's just struck half-past two. My coach goes from Marble Arch at a quarter to three. I'm going to Curlingham. Do you know it ? It's a queer little village just off the beaten track, with the reputation of being haunted. I shall have tea at a place called The White Owl, which isn't nearly so arty-crafty as it sounds, and I shall walk round the second-hand bookshop and spend much more than I can afford. It'll be quite dark when I come back, and I shall light a fire and pore over my conquests, my literary conquests that is. Quite soon it'll strike midnight and I shall wonder how it is that the hours fly when you're doing what you want to do and drag so when you're at work. But I suppose for you the opposite is the truth."

He walked with her to Marble Arch and when her coach arrived, he said, " Would it ruin your afternoon if I came with you ? "

" That's like the famous question : Have you stopped beating your wife ? " But if her words were not encouraging her voice belied them. He knew she had caught the contagion, that she wanted him to be with her. Well, that was nothing. He was accustomed to seeing women go down like ninepins before his treacherous charm. What was new was his own feeling. It was sheer waste of time, spending an afternoon with a girl who had to work as a stenographer to pay her rent, but he no longer cared. When he had mounted the coach and was sitting beside her he thought there was no place on earth where he would sooner be.

It was a most successful excursion. At the teashop the familiar process was repeated ; Sarah got twice the attention she would have done had she been alone, or indeed with any other man.

" I know what you are," she said suddenly. " I've been trying to think of the phrase for the last half-hour. A lady-killer."

This was so apt that Henry almost dropped his cup.

" That's not a very pleasant thing to say."

" Are you on the stage ? I feel like someone in a play, getting all the right cues."

Now she was laughing at him ; he could scarcely believe it ; immediately he felt his need of her intensified.

" Why do you waste your time in your architect's office ? " he asked sharply. " It can't be very interesting for you. You're much too talented. That old buster. . . ."

Sarah chuckled. " I wish he could hear you. And you should have heard him yesterday afternoon when I told him I wanted to give a fortnight's notice. He couldn't believe his ears. When at last I persuaded him that I meant it he said it simply proved that he was quite right about the unreliability of women. They were always wanting to move on, but when they reached a new place it wasn't really any better than the old. He said they were unstable, and he made it rhyme with Dunstable."

" And what do you propose to do next ? "

" I shall look for a job in the country. I did actually answer one advertisement—a farmer. Now that there are all these forms to fill in and P.A.Y.E. to do, a lot of them need secretaries, and I thought that might be quite interesting. But when I went down, having taken an afternoon off for the purpose, I found Mr. Farmer was working in a very small way, and Mrs. Farmer, a woman with a face like the back of a taxi-cab and a mind to match, really wanted someone to help with the chores. You can imagine the kind of thing. ' Of course, Miss Templeton, when you're not busy with my work you'll have no objection to lending my wife a hand.' I thought perhaps she ran the W.I. or the W.V.S., so I said cautiously what was her work, and it turned out she was one of those women who can't keep even the rawest of local girls, and there were four children under ten."

" So you cried off ? "

" To save them the trouble of saying I wasnt quite what they wanted. Oh, he wouldn't have minded, but the minute she set eyes on me it was perfectly obvious she wasn't going to have me about the place."

" Too much temptation for Mr. F. ? "

" None at all for me, I can assure you. If only you'd seen him. . . ."

They both laughed.

VIII

ENTERTAINMENT FOR A MURDERER

WHEN THEY GOT back it was quite late ; Henry proposed dinner, but Sarah said, " Come and have a snack with me. It's my turn to do the honours."

He accompanied her to her flatlet, one room and a kitchenette-cum-bathroom. He was astounded at what she could make of such a small place.

" It's perfectly charming," he said.

" I can do without it," she told him coolly, producing sherry and two fine cut-glass beakers. " I do think a couple of mouthfuls of sherry are ridiculous, don't you ? In the old days they used to have it in tumblers mixed with water."

" Not exactly my tipple," murmured Henry, accepting the glass she offered him.

" Water was more popular in those days. Do you remember Charles Lamb drinking gin and water ? "

She dished up an excellent meal, and how she did it on one ration book he didn't know. After dinner she asked suddenly, " What's this book you're writing, really ? Your own life story ? "

Again he shot her that sharp glance. Was there anything behind the apparently simple query ? She had him guessing all the time.

" Famous criminals, their methods, motives and mistakes."

" You should substitute murderers for famous criminals. Then you'd have the perfect alliterative title." She was laughing at him again. No, she couldn't guess what he was or she wouldn't be so calm, so amused.

" People like murder," he told her simply. " Look at the jam there is to get in when a man's on trial for his life. And there's an immense demand for that type of book—I'm happy to say—and the cases themselves are often quite fascinating. The Moat Farm Murder, for instance. Do you know that ? "

Sarah shook her head.

" An enthralling affair," he assured her and there was no doubting his enthusiasm. " A middle-aged woman of perfectly respectable antecedents, went to live in a lonely farm with a man of a different class, some years her junior and, as she very well knew, already married though living apart from his wife. His side of the bargain is easy enough to understand ; she had money and he had every hope that she'd turn all her affairs over to him."

" But she didn't ? "

" No."

" Good for her," said Sarah.

" Not really." Henry's tone was very dry. " He lost patience and one afternoon after a day's excursion he shot her as she dismounted from the trap. After that he forged her name systematically to cheques and went on for about four years until local suspicion was aroused. He was a rather conspicuous person, casting his favours before all and sundry—which proved his undoing. And then there was Wainwright, who shot his mistress because he found it too expensive to run two establishments, and put her body under the floor of his warehouse. He might never have been found out but for the fact that he went bankrupt and had to give up the warehouse. He tried to move the body to a safer place and was caught through one of the stupidest pieces of folly any murderer ever committed. That's what's so fascinating—not the crime

67

itself ; that's commonplace. People have been killing each other for passion or gain from the start of time. But why ? What motive has the murderer ? And more entrancing yet, what steps does he take to conceal his crime ? ''

Sarah looked a little perturbed. " I thought it was generally accepted that murderers were unbalanced people.''

" The law doesn't accept them as insane. As to being unbalanced—well, he that is without sin had better cast the first stone. You could say all artists are unbalanced because they devote a disproportionate amount of their time and vitality to their work, because it's the one thing that matters and they let normal considerations go hang. No, the truth is murderers are just like other people. That's their strength, really. Dougal was an amorous farmer ; Wainwright had an oil and colour shop and sang in the choir. It's believed that he was exceedingly fond of his wife and their children. Of course, cases like George Joseph Smith of the Brides in the Bath, do fall into rather a different category. He married half a dozen women and drowned several of them at different times and in different places, of course, in baths in lodging-houses.''

" But surely somebody began to put two and two together," protested Sarah. " I know coincidence has a long arm, but it's not an octopus.''

" Oh, they did—eventually. But if you're a person of no particular importance and your wife is drowned accidentally shortly after marriage—well, it's a tragedy, and the few people who know of it say, ' Poor chap, what bad luck,' but they've forgotten about it by breakfast next morning. That's the murderer's strength, you know, the fact is people are wrapped up in their own affairs. And then the tragedy took place in some obscure town, was reported in the local paper, and that's that. Six months later another bride is found dead in a bath, in a totally different part of the country, and the same thing happens. The odds are that the people who read the first report never see the second. They're not important enough to make the London papers, and so long as there's no suggestion of foul play they attract no attention whatsoever. That's what's difficult for people like us to realise. We're so tremendously important to ourselves and perhaps to half a dozen other people we don't appreciate that to the world at large we've no individual existence at all. We're just an item on a casualty list in a war. You've read them perhaps, but you don't differentiate one name from another, unless you happen to be personally concerned. You see my point ? "

" But the relations of the drowned women ? " persisted Sarah. " Didn't they think there was anything fishy ? "

" Suppose they did ? What could they do ? There'd be an inquest, a verdict of death by misadventure, and then a quick funeral. A few days later the widower's half across England. He hasn't got a home, just a couple of furnished rooms, taken by the week. The relations may have suspicions but unless they've something concrete to go on the police won't intervene. And when he marries the next time Smith, Jones or Robinson has a different name, is in a different part of the country. The trouble is that sooner or later he gets careless, swollen-headed because he's fooled people three or four times before. Smith reached the pitch where he didn't think he could be caught. He wasn't really hanged for murder, he was hanged for over-confidence, in a word, conceit. His last bride was actually drowned on her wedding night. She was the thirty-eight-year-old daughter of a clergyman who had been acting as companion—and that was a pretty poor job thirty-odd years ago—she was swept off her feet by the notion that any man wanted to marry her, and she went to the registrar's and her death within a few hours. That was Smith's undoing. If he'd waited a month he might have got away with it yet again, but no —he was the fellow the police would never catch. So you got the headlines BRIDE OF A DAY FOUND DROWNED IN A BATH, and one of the landladies where a previous bride had died in a similar manner got suspicious and in a minute the hunt was up. Once the police had their hands on him, of course, he hadn't a chance."

" Why not try a different way each time ? " inquired Sarah, awfully fascinated by the trend of the conversation.

" Because he was the chap nobody could catch. Besides, the police will tell you that a man always commits the same crime, year after year. You'd think that had been said often enough to warn criminals or intending criminals to try different methods, but no—on they go till they run their heads against a stone wall, and—well . . ." He spread his hands. " Oh, dear, what a gloomy conversation ! Only if, like me, you're interested, absorbed even in the springs of human behaviour, the subject is irresistible."

" But what was his motive ? Was he just a maniac like Jack the Ripper ? "

" Oh, no. Gain in every case. All the women had small sums of money and mostly he persuaded them to take out life insurances or took them out himself, always with a different company, of course. . . . The trouble is the average murderer isn't sufficiently imaginative. He doesn't look far enough ahead. If he could put himself in the position of the relatives—what should I think if the dead woman was my daughter, sister, grandchild ? And the police ? If I were Sergeant Poopstick how should I regard this ? He's got too many considerations—landladies, neighbours, casual acquaintances."

" What I don't understand," persisted Sarah, " is what they saw in him ? Apparently he hadn't much money or he wouldn't be taking these huge risks for small rewards. And if he was outstandingly handsome or brilliant he could scarcely hope to escape the headlines."

" It's a thing called charm, one little word, five letters. It's quite inexplicable. The oddest people have it. Remember Charles Peace, a hideous little wretch, almost revolting in fact, but the women swarmed after him like the rats after the Pied Piper. And—ever hear of Lucille Hillman ? "

Sarah shook her head.

" She was that rarer creature, the wholesale woman murderer. I don't mean there haven't been women murderers on a large scale before—there were Mary Bateman and Catherine Wilson to mention only two—but not many who were the female prototypes of Smith. She was a big woman, with no particular charm that an ordinary person would see, inclined to be heavily built with masses of thick black hair—she could have emulated Lady Godiva with no fears of an indictment for indecent exposure. It was little men who fell for her, and how they fell—right through the bottom of life. She was almost six foot tall, with very large beautifully-shaped hands, small black eyes, a big nose—nothing remotely resembling the conventional beauty. But she married one man after another, always small men, small in every particular ; in stature and in position. Travellers, tradesmen, clerks, and when she'd got everything she could out of them they just disappeared. Her undoing was the same as Smith's—over-confidence. Having disposed of five husbands she went to the police to ask them to find the sixth, who'd disappeared like all the rest. Her story was that he'd said he was being sent by his firm to Glasgow, and from the moment he left the house she'd never heard from him again. She told a very convincing story, and her landlady backed it up. ' A devoted couple,' she said. She'd mentioned on the previous evening that her husband would be going to Glasgow, and the next morning she was heard closing the front door about six-thirty after calling out, ' Don't forget to send me a telegram as soon as you arrive.' She met the landlady on the stairs and said, ' I've just been seeing Fred off. He's not sure how long he'll be away, but if he isn't back in a few days I shall go up there myself.' The landlady laughed and twitted her with being jealous. Mrs. Hillman (that's the name in which she was eventually tried, though of course she took on a new name with every new husband), said, ' Well, wouldn't you be ? He's ten years younger than I am, you know, and the girls are always after him.' The landlady said in court about a year later that the missing Fred had been a good-looking young chap and she'd wondered at the time what lay behind the marriage. Because the money was always theirs—she hadn't a bean. No, it was some sort of charm. She simply bowled men over. At her trial one of the jurymen refused to believe she was a murderess, and they had to have a second jury and a second trial."

" But she was guilty ? "

" Guilty as hell. Oh, yes, she did for Fred just as she'd done for the others."

" Did they ever find him ? "

" Well, yes, they did. I told you she always went for small men. When they arrived at their lodging she brought among her other luggage a large trunk, one of the big old-fashioned kind you only see in curiosity shops these days. She warned the chaps who took it away a few days after Fred's disappearance that it was heavy, it was full of books, her husband was a student. It was so heavy she had it sent by carrier to King's Cross Station, and thence it went across country to South Wales to await collection. And when no one collected it the authorities became suspicious for obvious reasons, and it was unstrapped and the lock forcibly broken open. It must have been a shock to the fellow who tipped up the lid. By that time there could be no possibility of identification. . . ."

" The clothes ? " suggested Sarah.

" My dear, there were no clothes. The police were informed, and they turned up their list of missing persons. It's one of the mysteries of contemporary life," continued Henry thoughtfully, " that it's possible for people to vanish absolutely and no trace of them ever to be found, with certainty that is. Relatives give information and the routine inquiries are made, but again and again that's the end of it. That fellow who was found burned to death in Rouse's car is an example. To this day no one is certain who he was. He was just a chap to whom Rouse had offered a lift. Even when the whole country was discussing the case his identity was never established. I suppose it's true that there are people who have absolutely no human ties. They've cut themselves off or been cut off—and when they die it's no more than a ripple on the face of the waters. It spreads for a minute or two, then it's gone, and there's nothing to show it was ever there. The waters are perfectly untroubled. Well, the police had a number of names on their files of missing persons and they got to work. It's ironical to reflect that if Mrs. Hillman hadn't over-reached herself by going to the police about her husband she might be alive still. But she'd given a description of him and it tallied roughly with all that remained of the unfortunate victim of the Trunk Crime. It turned out to be a poisoning case. This was several years ago when it was easier to get hold of poison than it is now. Oh, I forgot to say that she had told the landlady on the night before Fred was due to go to Glasgow that he'd been a bit sick and seemed feverish and she thought possibly he wouldn't be able to travel. That explained her coming down so early in the morning to see him off. She said he insisted on going against her judgment. When the case was referred to his employers they said no instructions to go to Glasgow had ever been given him. The general view was that he'd done a bolt— either couldn't stand married life with Mrs. H. any longer, or had gone off with someone else. Once the police were on the trail, of course, she didn't stand a chance. They traced her through the trunk."

" But they'd have done that in any case, wouldn't they ? "

" No. She thought of a good many things. As soon as she got to King's Cross she went out and bought a second-hand trunk as like the old one as need be—nobody's going to swear to the identity of a particular shabby black trunk—and travelled with it to Glasgow. Oh, yes, she went there ; she knew her movements might be questioned and she'd told the landlady she was going to Glasgow. When the police came to see her she showed them the second trunk and swore it was the one she'd had all along. But they found a man who remembered selling a trunk to a very tall dark woman on the very day Fred disappeared, and it wasn't difficult to identify her ; there were plenty of Mr. Hillmans, all as alike as two peas, but only one Lucille. And then, of course, the landlady remembered she hadn't actually seen Fred go, only heard her calling out her line about the telegram."

Before he left he said, " If I haven't alarmed you beyond measure by revealing my secret vice, as perhaps it seems to you, would you (assuming you're free to-morrow) come down to my cottage for the day ? It's a charming drive, and the cottage itself is mad but perfectly delightful."

" Lonely, I expect ? "

" Quite lonely enough."

" Set in a haunted wood ? "

He said with sharp annoyance, " You don't believe I have a cottage, do you ? "

" You wouldn't be inviting me to come if you hadn't. I mean, you'd look so silly when you had to confess you hadn't got one."

" I might be what you called me this afternoon—a lady-killer."

" But not without motive, and what motive could there be ? I don't stand between you and a fortune, I don't possess some guilty secret that you can't afford to have revealed, I'm not a policeman's moll. . . ."

Oh, she was maddening. He was tempted for one wild moment to tell her the truth. Then she might have if not respect for him at least a wholesome fear. The most maddening thing of all was she wouldn't believe him if he did tell her the truth. He was accustomed to women hanging on his lightest word ; he had never taken any interest in them, only in what they had. This girl hadn't a penny, he was wasting his time. But he couldn't tear himself away.

" Since you're so sure of my *bona fides*, will you come ? "
he asked, and she suddenly disturbed him again by saying
" You knew I was longing to see it, didn't you ? Yes,
of course I'll come."

When he had gone she went round clearing up the
place, washing the plates and the silver, polishing the
glasses, plumping up the cushions, so full of delight she
knew she would never sleep. It was ridiculous, this sense
of exultation and pleasure at the prospect of the morrow.
She had only seen the man twice, each time by chance
(unless he'd come to the cinema on purpose ; she couldn't
be sure ; certainly he hadn't waited for the film). She
knew nothing of his antecedents or his history ; he had
never mentioned a wife or any ties at all. " The Man of
Mystery," she said aloud, and then laughed for sheer
happiness. Her heart was leaping, she was full of joyous
anticipation. Her only fear was that to-morrow it might
rain.

Sunday, however, was one of those brilliant days of
sharp blue skies and a silvery tang in the air that often
occur late in an English autumn. The leaves on the trees
were crisply gold, there was a little wind, everything was
as bright as if it had been washed over during the night.
Henry came on time, and she ran down to meet him.
He also had had his misgivings. The only danger, he
believed, lay in allowing one's feelings to be involved.
A wife was a professional matter, something from which all
emotion should be divorced. He even thought, " It might
be a good thing for us both if she's changed her mind."
But he knew she wouldn't.

Sarah looked as gay as the morning.

" You wear the morning like your dress," he told her
as she took her place in the car beside him. She was
wearing the colours of autumn, chestnut brown, with a
bright orange scarf round her throat ; her smooth dark
head was bare and she wore no ornaments at all. As he
had promised, the drive was a beautiful one once they
had left the city behind ; they ran through country roads

with fields and commons on- either side, past streams glinting in the sun, stopped at an inn for lunch and half an hour later reached the cottage, that was shut off from the road by a pair of fine wrought-iron gates, set in a tall quickset hedge. The building was scarcely visible from the lane, an odd humped affair with one shoulder much higher than the other, with windows like peering eyes.

" How extraordinary," said Sarah, " since we came through those gates we seem to have left the entire world behind. I could almost believe that if I shut my eyes for a minute and then opened them again the cottage would have disappeared. How on earth did you find it ? It's exactly like a house in a fairytale."

" Houses in fairytales were always the scenes of misfortune," he reminded her. " They were mostly inhabited by witches."

" And haven't you a witch here ? Not even as a house-keeper ? You know, it wouldn't surprise me in the least to see a broom-stick fly over the house roof and vanish into the blue."

" As a matter of fact," he said a little reluctantly, " my housekeeper is—well, not a witch, but slightly rocky in the upper story."

" Just what I expected," said Sarah happily. " After all, an ordinary kind wouldn't want to live here."

" Why not ? " The sharp note snapped back into his words.

" Too lonely, too mysterious. No cinemas, no queues. Are those woods haunted ? "

" The locals think so. The whole countryside has the reputation of being haunted. There are parts of England like that. I stayed in one years ago where otherwise normal lorry drivers wouldn't come through after dark. It's all nonsense, of course. There are no such things as ghosts."

" Aren't there ? "

" You're not going to tell me you believe in them ? "

" I've never seen one, but—how can I say they don't

exist ? Other people have seen them. I might as well say I don't believe in the Pyramids because I've never been to Egypt. Is there any particular ghost associated with this cottage ? "

" If so, she's never troubled me."

" She ? "

" The ghosts they see hereabouts are always women. There was a case of a body found in the quarry some years ago. There was nothing to identify it beyond a ring on the skeleton finger ; otherwise, even the experts mightn't have been sure. But the locals will tell you with perfectly straight faces that she's haunted the woods ever since."

" Suicides are supposed to haunt the scene of their deaths, aren't they ? Isn't that why they bury them at a cross-roads with a stake through the heart ? "

" Aren't you confusing them with vampires ? " He opened the door and ushered her into the little house.

" What an extraordinary conversation this is. Everything about the situation is extraordinary. It's extraordinary, really, that I should be here. Already I begin to feel I've stepped into another dimension. I might vanish into thin air and never be seen again."

" It's not so easy to vanish these days."

" I was thinking," she said, walking over to the window and staring out at the wild neglected garden. " Suppose this were a film ? Suppose I didn't get back to London to-night ? Suppose you really were what you said you might be—a lady-killer ? Nobody knows where I am, nobody even knows I've met you. I didn't see a soul on my way out this morning, I'm self-contained, so to speak, no housekeeper, no porter. I could lie in your famous quarry for months. . . ."

" Your employer would miss you, your friends. . . ."

" Oh, yes, they'd miss me, they might even go to the police. But why should the police even connect me with you ? I've wondered sometimes how it is that people can disappear for months—don't the police keep a register of missing persons ?—and no one discover their whereabouts. But if they have some relationship in their lives of which no one else knows—it's what you were saying last night about the man who was found in the burning car. . . ."

" It all sounds very melodramatic," agreed Henry dryly ; " but as I haven't any intention of strangling you with your own scarf and humping you to the quarry, it's a bit beside the point."

Sarah laughed. " Yes. You see what your cottage does to me. All the same, it's fascinating. I wonder who built it here and why ? "

" You're forgetting one thing. The cottage was here before the forest. The building's more than two hundred years old ; when it was erected it was probably just a nice little house comfortably set among trees and fields. . . ."

" Not fields," corrected Sarah. " A blasted heath perhaps that someone decided to rescue. But why are there no other houses round about ? "

" There are—at least the skeletons of them. You'll find shacks in the woods that haven't been lived in for a century. No water, no amenities of any kind. But people did live in them once. This place was pretty ramshackle when I took it over. It seemed to me a perfect retreat for a man who wanted to escape from the world. Mind you, I couldn't live here perpetually. I really should go mad, though not necessarily in any violent way. But now and again when you want to be quiet and unnoticed, this is perfection."

She roamed at his side through the rooms of the cottage. It must once, they agreed, have been a single story ; then someone decided to improve it and built on some additional rooms. " This big room where I work is supposed to have been a barn once. They had them cheek by jowl with their living-rooms once upon a time. Then it was made part of the cottage, a slightly more modern kitchen was added, and later a bathroom and those rooms upstairs. There are three of them, and an attic. It's a very lopsided sort of house, isn't it ? "

" If you were a woman," said Sarah, " you'd know it was far better to be strikingly plain than conventionally pretty. This house may be odd, but it's unforgettable, while the country's dotted with cottages of character. Every house-agent in the land has dozens to offer you, but when you get there you find it's what's called a demi-bungalow, which is a bungalow with a sort of cocked hat atop, in which they've put two coffin-like bedrooms and a bathroom so small you have to go in sideways."

" What an enchanting description. I'd never heard it before."

" Oh, yes," said Sarah warmly. " A little while ago when Aunt Jessie died and left me a bit of money I thought I'd buy a cottage. I went all over the place. I was very credulous, for quite a long time I thought house-agents advertised properties they had, I mean that the properties really answered to the descriptions in their lists. Of course, I know better now. Jonathan and I looked at several."

" Jonathan ? "

" Mr. Rimington's Dogsbody, a very serious young man. We went out together occasionally—after I got Aunt Jessie's legacy and seriously thought of buying a cottage. He was quite sure I should buy a pig in a poke and needed advice, and as he's an architect he suggested coming in an honorary capacity. But he soon tired of it, and really you couldn't blame him. They were frightful." She threw back her head and sang out in a voice as bright as the sun :

" Long ago when I was young
I went to live in a demi-bung.

That was as far as we got—in the song, I mean."

They were sitting either side of the wood fire he had deftly kindled when he to his own amazement heard himself say, " Sarah, would you marry me ? "

She felt her pulses racing, the rich colour flowed into

her cheeks, she was really beautiful as she turned to face him.

" You've only seen me three times," she said in unsteady tones.

" Once was enough."

" You'll be able to get a secretary free," she went on in the same voice. " Oh, Henry . . ."

It had worked for her just as it had worked for all the rest ; she was infatuated with the man, would have done anything he asked. She desired nothing but to be with him wherever he went ; his past was unknown and she was content that it should remain so. She was madly, irrationally in love with a stranger. Wiseacres warned you against losing your head in these circumstances, but wiseacres only knew what was written in books. They didn't understand how the pulses raced and the heart leapt at the sound of a voice, the touch of a hand. So she whispered again, " Henry ! How could I dream—— ? "

How indeed, when he had never dreamed it himself ? Until, of course, ridiculously late in the day, she had spoken of her Aunt Jessie's legacy.

I X

THE HOUSE IN THE WOOD

JONATHAN TRENT was the man-of-all-work at Rimington, Rimington, etc., and knew more about architecture than the two partners lumped together. He was a square-built young man with a north-country directness, and more virtue than charm, just as Henry had much more charm than virtue. He remained with the firm for a number of reasons, giving himself the right to despise both Mr. Rimington and Mr. Cope. But he had begun without financial backing, had worked at anything and everything to pay his rent while he was a student, and had a shrewd idea that when old Rimington was gathered to his fathers (or retired on the ground of senility though Cope would put it more politely) he stood an excellent chance of being taken into the firm. When that happened they would turn out something more praiseworthy than their present deplorable output. He had the patience commonly attributed to Job and the ambition of Lucifer, with a fixed intention to avoid the disadvantages of both estates. He also had a strong personal interest in Sarah.

On the Friday of her departure from the firm he was waiting in the passage when she came from her final interview with the old man.

" Well ? " he said belligerently. " What did he do ? Kiss you on both cheeks and give you a present for a good girl ? "

Sarah's back went up like a cat, at least it would have done had she been a cat. " Since you're interested," she said clearly, " he told me what a pity it was young women didn't know when they were well off ; that there was no stability about the present generation, that they stayed in a job just long enough to learn their business and then, when they might be of use to their employers, instead of more or less of a drag, they walked out in search of fresh woods and pastures new. And he prophesied that in ninety-nine cases out of a hundred they were no better off in their new job."

" I didn't know the old boy could talk so much sense," said Jonathan admiringly. " What is this job you're going to ? "

" I've told you already, I'm going to act as secretary to an author living in the country." For some reason she didn't want to tell anyone she was going to be married until after the event. She agreed with Henry, who appeared to have strong views on the subject, that marriage was a personal affair, personal to the two people concerned, that is, and that all the publicity and fuss usually attendant on marriages was deplorable.

" Have you seen the place you're going to ? " Jonathan's voice was very grim.

"I have, and it's perfectly delightful. I fell in love with it on sight."

"And with the author, too, perhaps," commented Jonathan. "Did he say anything about a wife ? "

Sarah laughed. "Oh, she'll be there."

"Will be ? Do you mean you haven't seen her yet ? How do you know she exists ? "

"I saw her when I went down."

"I don't suppose you'll like working with another woman," said Jonathan disagreeably. "And she'll probably be as jealous as hell of you."

"She will not," contradicted Sarah calmly, and he thought her smile the most exasperating he had ever seen. "She took to me at once. We're going to be the best of friends."

"What does this chap write ? Has anyone ever heard of him ? "

"Biography. He's working on a book at present. And his name, since you're so anxious to learn it, is Henry Gould."

"I've never heard of him."

"You will," prophesied Sarah serenely (Crook said it was uncanny the way women could tell the truth without knowing it. It upset all one's sensible masculine calculations.)

"Well, I hope it's all right," muttered the young man.

"Why shouldn't it be ? "

"Because I don't believe you're safe to look after yourself. You've got a reckless streak in you, you leap first and look afterwards. You're always sure you know best, but the fact is you need someone to think for you. I've often noticed——"

"You're wasted as an architect," Sarah told him smoothly. "You're a born baby-sitter."

"That tongue of yours will get you into trouble one of these days. Whereabouts is this place you're going to ? "

Sarah suddenly fired up. "Is that any concern of yours ? "

"Of course it is. Good heavens, girl, haven't you realised yet that anything that concerns you concerns me, too? Why, from the start I knew you were the girl for me, but naturally I had to wait till I had something stable to offer you. Now Rimington's just given me the rise that makes it possible for me to think about getting married. That is, I've been thinking of it for some time, of course, but I've no intention of starting with a millstone of debt round my neck. Now, Sarah, swallow your pride and confess you'll be better off with me than with some long-haired writing chap no one's ever heard of."

Sarah gasped. "I could look at a violet a long time before thinking of you," she exclaimed. "Talk about modesty—you don't know how to spell the word."

"You're like all your sex—confuse modesty with false modesty. It wouldn't be modesty to pretend I'm not pretty good at my job. It's only conceit when you expect everyone else to take you at the same valuation. Though come to that," he added with that sturdy northern assurance she found so maddening, "they will one of these days, I can promise you that. Well, Sarah, how about it? Will you be engaged to me, for a start? Of course, we'll both have to work hard for the next year at least to get a home together. No instalment plan stuff for me—when I have a house it's going to be mine, not the property of some housing society, with tickets on the furniture because it's not been paid for. Personally, I call it downright dishonest. . . ."

"A tub-thumping baby-sitter," amplified Sarah. "Well, now you've got round to thinking of marriage you must start looking out for somebody worthy of your attentions. And if you're not too proud to take a little advice from a member of the despised sex, next time take the girl into your confidence. Women have the vote nowadays, you know; thev're no longer classed with criminals and imbeciles, and they do like to be consulted about their own futures. Oh, and be sure to send me a bit of the wedding-cake, won't you? I adore wedding-cake."

She turned and swept away down the passage, a tall dark defiant girl, a fool, of course, stubborn, conceited, self-sufficient, but for all that the girl he obstinately loved. He couldn't think just where the conversation had gone wrong ; he supposed she didn't like his offering her advice. But seeing that he was proposing to marry her, surely he had some rights. There had been a time in that blessed period when women didn't think they owned the world, when they had felt honoured by an offer of marriage. It wasn't as if he were old or maimed or feeble minded. There was nothing against him but his poverty and time would cure that.

Sarah went back to her flatlet and instantly forgot about him. Rimington and everyone connected with it belonged to the past ; she had done with them all, or so she thought. It was the small hours before she went to bed. Henry was calling for her early next morning and they would be married before a registrar, as soon as the office opened, and then they would go back to Goblin Cottage and spend their honeymoon there. Sarah couldn't imagine why newly-weds wanted to rush abroad or go to some great vulgar hotel at a seaside resort the instant they were married. Get to know each other in your own home and then go abroad when you're familiar with your companion's fancies and foibles. That was her idea. Besides, there was the book. They were going to work like the proverbial blacks on that and when it was done and dispatched to the publisher, they could go abroad, to the French Riviera, say, and for the first time in her life she would see oranges and lemons growing on trees. To date she had never seen them except in a greengrocer's shop window or on a barrow-boy's stall.

Punctual to the moment, Henry turned up next morning driving a very handsome dark-blue car that had made a considerable hole in poor Flora's six thousand pounds. They were married with immense dispatch by Henry's local registrar. Sarah went through the ceremony in a dream. Henry slipped a gold ring on her finger, and when they were once more in the car he said, " Now I'm going to give you your engagement ring. It's putting the cart before the horse, but I hope you won't like it any the less for that." Taking her hand in his, he slipped on her finger a very pretty affair, a small square emerald set in a rose of diamonds.

Sarah was enchanted. " Oh, Henry, how clever of you to guess that emeralds are my favourite stones."

He smiled. They had been Flora's favourite stones, too. Women either loved or hated them ; if they didn't like them it was because they were superstitious, thought they were unlucky, being green. The ring looked very beautiful on his bride's well-shaped hand ; the sun shone, the trees moved eagerly in the light wind—altogether a perfect morning for a wedding. Even he couldn't ever remember a better.

They drove companionably in silence for a time. " Penny for your thoughts ? " suggested Henry after a while.

" Who called the place Goblin Cottage ? I mean, it's so bogus—like fairies at the bottom of the garden."

" There are worse things," Henry assured her. " I don't know who christened it."

" I suppose we could change the name if we liked."

" If it gives you any satisfaction, my love, change it by all means. But I assure you it won't make any difference. To the locals it will always be Goblin Cottage."

After lunch the day underwent a sudden change ; the sun vanished, dark clouds covered the sky and by the time they reached their destination the rain was falling in a steady stream.

Henry, however, remained as cheerful as a grig. " There's one thing about driving through rain," said he. " It makes the fire and the lights at the other end all the more inviting."

But when they reached Goblin Cottage it was black as night ; no welcoming lamp gleamed in the window, no fire cast its ruddy gleam on china cup or polished table ; it was, thought Sarah, with a sudden shiver, like a house of the dead.

" What the hell ? " muttered Henry, bringing the car round in a splendid sweep in front of the modest front door. " What's happened to Mrs. Truelove ? I told her we should be down to-day and should want dinner. She doesn't sleep in, of course, but she comes every day except Sunday—when I want her, that is."

He produced a latch-key and opened the door ; the hall was square and black ; the narrow staircase stretched up into obscurity ; a bat dashed itself against the shadowy window of the sitting-room ; somewhere in the invisible woods a bird sent forth a high piercing note. Henry struck a light and kindled the lamp standing on the hall table. Sarah started for a moment ; she had forgotten there was no electricity. The next moment, however, her husband had snatched up a cheap envelope lying beside the lamp and addressed in a careful scrawling hand.

" Can you beat it ? " he exclaimed, passing the enclosed sheet over to her. " Mrs. Truelove has seen the ghost. It came up to the kitchen window in the dusk and beckoned to her. According to her theories that means a death in the house, and I suppose she wanted to make sure it shouldn't be hers. It's a nuisance," he added, taking the letter back and tossing it into a waste-paper basket, " because by this time she'll have spread the news all round the village, and no one will come within half a mile of us."

" What do you suppose she really saw ? " questioned Sarah.

" The great white owl that lives in Baker's Copse. I've seen it myself sometimes at dusk. I admit it gives you a shock till you realise what it is. It seems to appear from nowhere and hangs in the sky, a mighty white apparition, but if you wait an instant it turns slowly and flaps into the darkness again. Oh, depend upon it, that's what Mrs. Truelove saw, though she'll never admit it."

" Perhaps she believes the owl is the ghost of someone who died in the woods."

" I wouldn't put it past her." He walked into the sitting-room and stooped to put a match to the fire. " Thank goodness it's laid. It wouldn't have been much fun going out in this weather to look for wood." The fire caught quickly ; the flames shot up and painted the walls with a cheering ruddy glow. Henry drew the curtains on the rain, the darkness and the bats. Sarah, catching the infection of his energy, followed him into the kitchen. They lighted a big oil-cooker and put on water for tea ; Sarah found cups and plates, Henry opened a bread-crock, said, " Not even a half-loaf. Thank heaven I brought a good deal of stuff down from town."

They had a cheerful meal sitting beside the fire. Henry opened a tin of ham, and produced a sliced loaf. Sarah made toast, and Henry produced a bottle of whisky, to keep out the cold. Sarah wondered whether any bride had ever enjoyed her wedding dinner so much as she. Afterwards they washed up together with hot water from a huge black iron kettle. Henry, who was clearly going to be a handy husband, got the big stove going—" Oh, I've had experience with furnaces," said he—and soon the little house seemed warm and cosy. In the kitchen hung a calendar of Windsor Great Park and the King's deer. It hadn't been torn off since last month.

" Oh, they never look at it," said Henry cheerfully, crumpling the out-of-date leaf in his hand. " A pretty picture donated by the butcher ; and next year it'll be cows and roses—don't ask me what the connection is— an offering from the dairyman.

" In the morning," he continued, " I'll go into Kings Benton—no, I can't, though. It'll be Sunday. Well, we'll makeshift for a day or two and see what chances there are of getting help on Monday morning. Not that I'm too sanguine myself," he added candidly. " We're at the back of beyond here, half a mile off the high road, and there's no bus nearer than two miles. We couldn't get a married couple by offering them quarters, because there isn't enough work for a man to do here, and he'd be too far from any job of his own."

" A bicycle ? " suggested Sarah, but he shook his head.

" Not on that gravel slope ; it would cut the tyres to pieces. Ah, well, we can but hope for the best."

Clearing away and washing up with her husband, and afterwards unpacking and preparing the bed for the night gave Sarah such happiness as she had never dreamed. She had often heard that brides were nervous and tongue-tied on their wedding night, and for some reason the thought of Jonathan Trent flitted unbidden through her mind. You would never see him taking these minor upsets with the casual gaiety and philosophy Henry displayed.

" How lucky I am ! " she thought. And so in a way she was, but not for the reason she would have given you.

X

THE GHOST IN THE GARDEN

ON MONDAY MORNING, after an enchanted week-end, Henry set out for Kings Benton, saying that he would drop in at the post office, which was also the grocer, baker and tobacconist, to say nothing of selling shoes, haberdashery, aspirin, castor-oil and running a lending library, to inquire what chances there were of some local woman giving a hand.

" Stick about the house till I come back," he advised Sarah. " Just on the chance that someone looks in, and, if so, grapple her to your breast with hoops of steel. Even a half-wit would be better than nothing, and we're not likely to get anyone else. They don't mind loonies in this part of the world ; you'll see 'em all over the place at harvest-time, earning a bit extra for tobacco or chocolate."

She had a busy morning arranging her store cupboard —Henry was going to buy a lot of stuff at Kings Benton

—and she prepared vegetables for dinner and characteristically ate a sandwich from Saturday's ham herself, and several times she ran to the window to see if some mysterious figure was climbing the path ; and she listened hopefully for the telephone. Perhaps Henry would ring up ; it would be pleasant to hear a voice in that silence. But nothing happened until almost four o'clock when she heard the sound of the car returning up to the drive. She ran out to meet it.

" No luck," said Henry quickly before she could ask. " The worthy lady at the registry office said all the women were going into the factories—they're having a production drive here, and some of the war-time factories are being reopened—she couldn't even offer me a half-wit. I spoke to old Mrs. Potts at the post office, I thought someone might come if only out of sheer curiosity, but she wasn't very sanguine either."

For the first week or two Sarah remained optimistic ; everything was turning out so well she convinced herself that a *bonne-a-tout-faire* would suddenly drop from heaven. She tried to convince Henry, too, but he only laughed. He seemed to be in the right of it ; nobody came, the front-door bell never rang. Sometimes the silence seemed rather overwhelming, as if they were people in a legend enclosed in ice and snow or shuttered away from the rest of the world by a bell of glass. But there was so much to be done she had little time to be lonely. She was accustomed to keeping her own small flat in apple-pie order, and she took great pleasure in keeping this house spick and span. " When women complain they don't like housework," she told Henry once, " it generally means that they don't like having to spend every minute away from their job doing chores. When housework is your job you can take a pride in it and really enjoy it. I've always wanted to be able to spend half a morning arranging flowers and leaves, but there was never the time. Now I've got all the time there is." She sighed with bliss.

She soon mastered the oil-cooker, and she and Henry

would go out in the car buying provisions. Henry was in some ways as fussy as an old maid.

" If you want the best you must select it yourself," he insisted. " I've never understood these men who let someone else select a wife for them. Of course, you'll get what used to be called block ornament in my young days if you're content to ring up the butcher and ask him to send along whatever he's got."

They didn't shop in Kings Benton, their nearest town ; he said it was a poor place and they could do better by going a little farther afield, and since this involved a longer ride and more of her dear Henry's company Sarah never objected. Henry had expensive tastes, but could be careful over trifles, and he liked the best of everything. " It's there on the dish," he would say. " Someone's going to have it. Why not you ? "

He didn't care about gardening ; she never saw him lift a spade or trowel, but he explained that he really hadn't the time. When he had done his share of the chores, brought in the wood and the coal, stoked the furnace and polished his own boots, he had his book to write. If Sarah had been a little inclined to laugh at his literary pretensions before she married him, she knew better now. The man was not merely interested in his work, he was absorbed. Sometimes he would talk for an hour on this case or that, assessing motives, pointing out mistakes, explaining what in similar circumstances he himself would do. " Of course," he would always end up, " I have the advantage of profiting by another chap's mistakes, or should have, if I thought of taking to murder." He said the British public was unreliable, few people were sufficiently cool-headed to be completely just. A man taken on a capital charge was largely at the mercy of the jury, and as for them, they were twelve ordinary men and women with no particular qualifications.

" You've probably noticed that there's very little sympathy for a wife-murderer," he said. " Have you ever wondered why ? In the nature of things you'd expect half your jury at least to have experienced the sour side of married life, and that should make them lenient. But, of course, in actual fact it works just the other way. Their argument is, ' Well, I've had to put up with Sal or Molly or Daisy all these years and I haven't laid her out with a chopper or dunked a spoonful of poison into her morning tea—why shouldn't this chap take his medicine like the rest of us ? ' It's a kind of jealousy, really. They can't stand the thought that you, the fellow in the box, may go free, not only free of the major penalty, but free of those maddening domestic ties that hamper other men."

When the housework was done she would type a fair copy of his manuscript.

" You have very gruesome tastes," she told him one day. " In fact, I feel I'm rather brave to have married you at all."

" How so ? " asked Henry, looking surprised.

" You know so much about the surest way of disposing of an unwanted wife."

He threw his arm around her shoulders and stooped his handsome dark face to hers.

" Operative word being unwanted," he reminded her.

" All the same, copying all this stuff for you does make me realise how ridiculously easy I've made it for you. Do you know, I haven't written to a soul since we came here ? I was never much of a hand at writing letters, and now there doesn't seem to be time."

" Well, what would you like to do about it ? " inquired Henry. " Shall we give a cocktail party and you can invite all your London friends and your relations, of course—— ? "

" I haven't any of those. As for friends—it's queer how marriage seems to take you into a new world. When you look over your shoulder the gates are closed. I have got friends, of course, but they don't seem to have any part here. Perhaps it's living in this isolated place. Perhaps living in the country does that to everyone. Of course," she went on thoughtfully, " one usually does it with wedding-cake, break the news, I mean, if one hasn't had a reception or a public ceremony, but we never seem to have thought of that."

" Didn't you tell your Mr.—what was the chap's name ? "

" Rimington."

" Rimington, that you were getting married ? "

" I didn't tell anyone, not even Jonathan. I suppose there was no reason why I shouldn't. In fact, I think I meant to, only it turned out he rather wanted to marry me himself—in his own good time, of course."

" You must save him up for your second choice," said Henry pleasantly. " All the same, I don't want to roast before my time, so perhaps we could keep our secret a little longer. These young lovers are so impetuous, and he's probably a dead shot with a poisoned dart. I'll tell you what, let's get this book out of the way and then we can have a real honeymoon, starting at Claridges and continuing in the south of France."

" You do say the sweetest things," hummed Sarah.

And for the moment, that was that.

It was a short time afterwards that an incident occurred that gave Sarah her first stab of uneasiness. It was so unexpected, so, it seemed, out of character.

One afternoon Henry was working on his book in the room he called his den, that looked over the garden. He worked with his back to this wilderness, and no wonder, thought Sarah. It gave her uneasy conscience pangs to see its tattered state, the paths overgrown with weeds, the lawn unmown. She would have mowed the lawn herself but there was no mower and to cut it by hand at its present stage was unthinkable. It had grown far too long and rank. On this particular afternoon when everything was illuminated by a wintry sun and for the first time the spirit apprehends the footsteps of spring, be they never so far distant, she wandered out resolved to begin on a magnificent clearance scheme. For years now she had longed for a garden ; there was nothing to be done in front, a narrow herbaceous border and that pocket-handkerchief of grass that Henry cut with a pair of shears, though that, she reflected, could do with a little attention again. She walked past the dead sticks of the chrysanthe-mums, the black plants that defied identity, and came upon a one-time rockery at the garden foot. Her first thought was, " What a strange place to put a rockery, where it can scarcely be seen from the house, and con-sidering the condition of the garden, you wouldn't be likely to bring any visitors this way." It seemed to be the work of the veriest amateur, a collection of rocky oddments put together rather clumsily with no thought for how the flowers planted there would grow. Whoever had made it had tired of it a long time since, for a bundle of tree-cuttings lay across it, and some withered swathes of grass. Someone, it was clear, had been using it as a dump, and she thought it odd that anyone should trouble to bring rubbish all this way when there was a rubbish heap, that a more skilful gardener would have used for compost, not far from the kitchen entrance. Sarah had always had a particular feeling for rock plants, the minute daffodils and pansies, the miniature juniper trees under which only a Lilliputian Elisha could have concealed himself, the aubretia, the tiny toad-flax, and all those plants that make such a brave show in miniature. She began her work by tearing away the dead faded grass, and pulling at the sticks and discarded withered branches. She had almost uncovered the surface when she heard footsteps behind her and an instant later Henry came bursting through the trees.

" What the devil is this ? " he cried, evidently in a great passion. " What on earth do you think you're doing, Sarah ? "

She looked up, amazed and shocked. " Why, Henry, it is simply that I thought I would clear some of the rockery. It looks so very untidy, and I've always longed to make a rock garden."

"You'll please leave it alone," he said, still white with some emotion whose nature she could not altogether identify. "If you must go digging there are the flower-beds and we can see those from the house. There's no sense," he added, speaking more calmly, "wasting time clearing up this bit of the property. No one ever sees it."

"I'd thought of that," Sarah agreed. "It did seem to me extraordinary that anyone should think of putting a rock garden here. It's been a half-hearted job, anyway. I can't see any trace of plants. It's as though someone collected the rocks and then got tired."

"Or realised he was wasting his time."

Henry stooped and picked up the spade that was lying on the ground.

"All the same," said Sarah in a more cheerful tone, "there was no need to terrify me out of my wits like that. Anyone would think you had a body concealed there."

He sent her a long considering look. Then he said slowly, "As a matter of fact, I have. I had a dog—Rover was his name—a big black brute, no special pedigree, I dare say, but he meant a good deal to me. I was alone here and things weren't working out too well, and he was my sole companion." He stopped abruptly.

"He died?" suggested Sarah.

"He was shot. Some brute of a keeper said he was raising the pheasants."

"Pheasants here? I shouldn't have thought you could preserve in this wilderness. Besides, where's the house? I mean——"

"It was some distance away. We used to walk a good deal. Yes, I suppose Rover might have disturbed their damned birds. He was such a big chap, could jump any fence. I was warned once, and I said I'd keep him away and I did for a time, and then one afternoon I wasn't thinking particularly where we were going, and suddenly he went off like the wind and I saw him go over. I bawled to him, but the shot came almost the same moment."

He clenched one hand into a fist and struck it repeatedly into the palm of the other. " No sense telling me the chap was within his rights. Perhaps he was. But he killed my dog. No one's got a right to take life, have they ? I got him back here, and the deuce of a job that was, and I buried him there behind the trees. I couldn't leave him *there*, but I went back for the car, and I—this seemed a quiet place, I didn't often come here. I found those rocks and shoved them in and then covered everything over. I don't like men who're sentimental over animals, shove up little tombstones and rhymes, but—well, now you begin to understand what I felt when I saw you well on the way to uncovering him. It would have been a shock for you, too," he added more considerately. " You mightn't have thought at first that it was a dog."

" I shouldn't have expected it to be anything else," mused Sarah. " I mean, people have to be buried in churchyards. I'm sorry, Henry, I never dreamed—you didn't tell me——"

" I don't talk about him ; and I've never had another dog. Don't want one. Can you understand that ? "

" I see you probably wouldn't want another straight away, though I've often been told you should get one immediately. But it seems a pity to do some dog out of a happy home. After all, even happily married men often have more than one wife."

He laughed abruptly. " You know," he said, " I think it's time you thought about tea." He looked over his shoulder. " I suppose if we're going to do anything to this garden we ought to think about ordering plants. Do you know anything about gardening ? "

" I've always longed for the chance."

" I believe it's a very expensive hobby. Still, we must think about it. And after tea there's a lot of stuff ready for you to type, if you're sure you don't mind being my unpaid secretary."

" You know I love it." She went into the kitchen and put on the kettle. She had had a shock ; Henry's voice had been so angry, so—apprehensive. Well, of course, she argued, he thought I might have a fit if I suddenly uncovered bones, might not realise what they were. By evening she had put the incident out of her mind ; but it didn't stay forgotten ; it lurked at the back of her consciousness. She didn't think about it again, but it was like some accident that leaves a scar. You forget the accident until your eye falls on the scar and memory reasserts itself.

The days passed very rapidly with work and gardening and drives, and almost before they knew where they were Christmas was upon them.

Henry suggested that they should go to an hotel for a few days. They had not been able to attract any local labour, and he said they didn't want to spend the whole time in the kitchen. Sarah agreed readily enough, and they went to Barsett in Mereshire to an hotel who made Christmas a whole-time job. A beautifully illustrated programme was given them on their arrival ; luxury motor-coaches were provided, and their days were arranged for them. They went to the meet, they were taken over one of England's historic houses, they had a dance each night, with a floor show, they went to the pantomime at a nearby seaside town ; not a moment was left unaccounted for. On the day before they were due to return Henry drove Sarah into Beachhaven ; he said they might as well escape from the crowd for an hour or two. They were walking along the parade when a young man on the other side of the street saw them and suddenly stiffened and turned to stare after them.

" Sarah and her long-haired author ! " he thought. " Staying down here. But why have I never seen them before ? Perhaps they're only here for the day." He himself was spending Christmas with his widowed mother, this being the family feast, and though they made a tremendous fuss of him, two widowed sisters sharing a house, he found it all pathetic and rather unreal. Coloured decorations and cards along the mantelpiece seemed to him out of place in 1950. While he watched them the couple paused beside a long blue car, and Henry opened the door. Jonathan, whose sight and memory were alike excellent, noted the number, XYZ5001. He wondered at what hotel they were staying and, on an impulse, got into his own little boneshaker (barring Arthur Crook's Scourge, it must have been the oldest car still on the roads) and followed at a discreet distance. Luckily, Henry was in no hurry or the pursuer would have been outpaced at once. The car drove away from Beachhaven, turning inland, and the little black rattle-trap followed it faithfully. When it stopped at the big hotel the couple got out. Jonathan parked a little farther down and walked into the hotel bar. At the far end he saw Sarah and her companion, who was ordering drinks. He wandered out again and stood irresolutely in the hall. Sarah had said the chap was married but there was no sign of a wife. The hotel clerk came up and asked politely if there was anything he could do. Jonathan said, " I believe a friend of mine is staying here. I wonder if you can tell me. His name's Gould, Mr. Henry Gould."

The clerk said, Yes, Mr. and Mrs. Gould were staying here ; he thought they had just come in. Jonathan said, Thanks, and he would ring up, and stormed out. Mr. and Mrs. Gould—so that's what Sarah had come to. Of course, there was plenty of gilt about the chap, you only had to see the car to realise that. He stopped beside it, and his fingers itched to be on the steering-wheel. But who would have thought Sarah would be swayed by such a consideration ? The fact that she might really be Mrs. Gould never passed through his mind.

After that Christmas week, Henry went back to his book and Sarah started making something of the garden, but she didn't get very far because about a week afterwards she slipped on a frosty day and her hand came down on the prongs of a fork, which pierced the flesh. Henry said, at once, " We must get a doctor," but Sarah said, " No it's not serious, only inconvenient." It was inconvenient all right ; she couldn't lift and carry and washing-up became almost impossible.

"We really must get someone to help if we pay her a king's ransom," said Henry, and he went into Kings Benton next morning to pay another visit to the lady at the registry office. But still no one came ; the next few days were wet and Sarah sat hopefully listening for the sound of the front-door bell. But it never rang. After four days she took advantage of Henry's temporary absence to telephone the registry herself.

"We don't mind paying high rates," she said, " it would only be for a short time, but it is absolutely essential that we find someone."

To her amazement the woman at the other end said, " I've sent two people to see you, Mrs. Gould, and they both came back saying they could get no reply."

"No one's been here," said Sarah in amazement. " I've been indoors all the time, listening for the bell."

"Perhaps," said the voice rather frostily, " the bell is out of order."

"It's very recent if it is," Sarah retorted. " It was ringing all right last week when the postman came."

After she had rung off she walked down the long quarter-mile path to the gate. The bell seemed all right, but of course she was too far away to hear if it rang in the house ; when she got back she started to look for the indoor connection. Although there was no electricity in the cottage this bell had been rigged up with an electric battery. It took her some time to find the place, which was under the low dark stairs, and when she came to examine it with the aid of a torch she saw why it didn't ring. Someone had placed a small wad of paper between the clapper and the bell.

XI

DAFT LIZZIE GIVES A WARNING

SHE STOOD STARING at it, a prey to sudden misgivings. This couldn't be an accident ; the paper had been placed there deliberately—but why ? Henry coming in surprised her still staring at it.

" What is it ? "

" The bell." She nodded her head. " It's been plugged up."

" Good lord ! " said Henry. " I clean forgot. The other day when you were out, someone rang and I sweated down to the gate to find the Church Army asking for contributions. I was damned busy at the time and they got nothing but short shrift from me. When I came back I wedged the bell, thinking we were expecting no one, and I clean forgot." He began to laugh. " I wonder how many noble visitors we've missed."

" We've missed two women sent from the registry," said Sarah crisply. " They came all the way out, as it happened for nothing."

" Who says so ? " His voice was scornful.

" The woman who runs it. She sounded rather aloof, and I suppose one can hardly blame her."

" Meaning you blame me ? My dear, it's unfortunate, but surely my work is more important at the moment than anything else ? It is our living."

" It's on your account I want to get someone in," said Sarah. " You have to leave your work so much—besides my not being able to type your stuff with this wretched finger."

" Well, it's unstopped now," said Henry soothingly. " I dare say, darling, they wouldn't have been any good. Nothing but a half-wit would want to come here."

" A half-wit who could wash up would suit us very well."

She moved towards the telephone.

" What are you going to do ? "

" I'm going to explain to Mrs. Kent that the bell was out of order, but we've had it put right now and will she please send along anyone she can ? "

" Oh, I shouldn't bother," said Henry easily. " She'll send them along anyhow. Besides, I want the telephone for the moment."

By the time he had finished with it it was too late to get in touch with Mrs. Kent, as he reminded her, for it was early closing day in Kings Benton. Next morning when she was out on a casual stroll, a woman driving alone in a car stopped to know if she wanted a lift. " I'm going into Kings Benton," she said. Sarah fortunately had her purse in her pocket and said at once that she would be delighted. When she reached Kings Benton she went straight to see Mrs. Kent, and explained the position, without going into details.

" I thought perhaps if you had someone whom I could interview it would save a long journey," she said.

" I've only got one woman," said Mrs. Kent doubtfully, " and I don't know if she'd be willing to come. She might be along this morning—she's a bit—you know . . ." She touched her forehead.

" Does that matter ? " asked Sarah. " I mean it won't prevent her sweeping a floor, will it ? "

Mrs. Kent became confidential. " There's some thinks it's an advantage ; can't get their minds off their work, you see, not having any minds in the first place."

" And you think she might be in to-day ? "

" She comes in most days. Whatever have you done to your hand, Mrs. Gould ? "

" Oh, I damaged it on a fork. It's taking rather longer to heal up than I expected."

" Doctor seen it ? He should. I'll tell you what, why

don't you go along and see Dr. McKay while you're waiting for Daft Lizzie ? That's what they call her round about," she added a little apologetically.

" Will he see me without an appointment ? "

" If you're not a National Health patient he will. Always a mistake to let a thing go, I say."

This seemed to Sarah good advice, so off she went and saw the doctor.

" Should have had it seen to before," he told her. " Where d'you live ? "

Sarah told him. " It's rather out of the way," she acknowledged.

" Goblin Cottage ? Yes, I know the name. A fellow called Grey had it a few years back, tall dark chap with a beard—a bit artistic. But he didn't stay long—reputed to be haunted."

" Oh, we don't believe in anything like that," Sarah told him cheerfully. " Anyway, we have each other. Perhaps this Mr. Grey was a bachelor."

" You tell your husband with my compliments he'll be a widower before he's much older if the pair of you aren't more careful," said McKay brusquely.

Sarah bridled a little and began to explain how busy Henry was.

" Be busier still without his right hand," McKay suggested.

Sarah laughed dutifully and returned to Mrs. Kent's Registry, where she found that Daft Lizzie had arrived and was waiting for her. She proved to be a tall woman with mouse-coloured hair drawn off her face and the most appalling squint. When she looked at Sarah the girl automatically glanced at the window as if expecting to see someone trying to climb in. But, of course, there was no one there.

" Now, Lizzie," said Mrs. Kent, " this is Mrs. Gould. She lives at Goblin Cottage and——"

" It won't be for long," said Lizzie in a deep sepulchral voice. " They never stay long."

"I explained it wouldn't be for long." She began to describe the nature of the duties that had to be done.

Lizzie looked at her steadfastly with one eye and watched the door with the other.

"You can hear them of a night," she confided, "crying fit to make your blood run cold. No rest for them as died out of their turn."

"Look," said Sarah desperately, "I'm not interested in ghosts. I don't believe in them."

"Walk with their toes turned in," said Lizzie. "You can see 'em of a night rising from the places where they were cast with no tombstone to keep them down, floating among the trees, knocking on the windows. Wanting you to come out to them, and then they can take you away with them. Never you go out after dark, lady, not in them woods. It's not safe. There's a mort of graves there as none knows of. . . ."

"I really don't think my husband would agree to employing her," Sarah told Mrs. Kent. "She is so very odd."

"You're from London, aren't you?" said Mrs. Kent briskly. "I thought as much. You don't understand country people and their ways. I expect most of them would seem daft to you. Well, if you don't want Lizzie I don't suppose I can find anyone else, and from the look of it, you'll have to rest that hand for some time yet."

"I should have to ask my husband," said Sarah indeterminately. "I know. I'll ring him up and ask him to come over and take me out to lunch. There's nothing to eat in the house anyway, except a bit of cold ham, and we shall want that for supper."

Henry, answering the telephone, said in astounded tones, "Where do you say you are? Kings Benton? How on earth did you get there?"

"I was going for a little walk, it's such a lovely day, and a woman in a car offered me a lift. I thought I might as well see the agency myself, and, Henry——"

Henry was trembling with such rage he could scarcely

hold the receiver steadily to his ear. "Another time you propose to make an excursion perhaps you'll let me know," he said.

Even over the wire his anger was evident. "You were busy," she began.

"You could have left a note."

"I didn't know I should be so long."

"I take it you took a purse, gloves. . . . Exactly. Do you normally take those just for a walk in the woods? I've been wondering what on earth had happened to you."

"I thought I ought to have my hand seen to, while I was here. Henry, I'm sorry if you've been worried, though you know I often do go for a bit of a walk when you're working, but I've heard of someone who might come and work for us for a while, and I thought if you could come in and meet me we could have lunch together and find out what you thought."

The receiver shook in his hand ; he was silent for a minute. Then he said, "Where are you speaking from ? The Kings Arms ? You'd better wait there for me. You'll have to be fetched home anyway."

She heard the receiver slammed back on to its rest. She wondered if he had really been afraid or if he was simply infuriated because she had disturbed his plans. She wandered round Kings Benton filling in time looking in the shop windows. This might be an opportunity to buy something for Henry's birthday. She so seldom found herself alone except at the cottage. The thought, slipping lightly into her mind, left her vaguely uneasy. Now she paused to think of it, this was the first time she had been out anywhere alone, except in the woods, since her marriage. It was sheer coincidence, but all the same, it seemed odd. She put the notion, that there was anything deliberate about the situation, from her ; but though she could push it to the back of her mind she couldn't blot it out completely ; it went to join other minor suspicions. Henry's alarm (there was no other word for it) when he found her digging in the rockery ; his laughing but still quite definite suggestion that she should refrain from writing to any of her former acquaintances until after the book was finished. " The truth is I'm as isolated as if I were in a prison," she told herself. " In fact, in a prison there would be the other prisoners, and the officers and visitors, when I qualified for them." Here there was just Henry—not even a Mrs. Truelove, most likely not even Daft Lizzie. It wasn't that she really supposed there was anything wrong, and she was a million miles from the truth, it was just that it did seem a little unusual. But perhaps husbands always seemed a little unusual ; she had never had any experience of them until now. Henry was right at all events about Kings Benton. The shops were few and poor. She knew he hankered for a gold pencil. " Don't ask me why," he had said. " I just have a fancy for one." There was a jeweller at the corner ; she glanced at the name over the door. Hansard, which for some reason seemed unusual too. She glanced in the window, but it was full of gimcrack stuff, what she called cracker jewellery, and though she went in to ask for a gold pencil it was without surprise that she found they had nothing to show her. The stationer combined his office with a toyshop and a post office, and here again she found only goods of a cheap quality. At the florist she paused and bought a buttonhole. After all, a meal out with Henry was something of an event. Diogenes could hardly have loved his tub better than Henry appeared to love Goblin Cottage. Then she turned into the Kings Arms, an unexpectedly comfortable inn, and ordered Henry's favourite martini and a glass of sherry for herself.

When Henry arrived she had another surprise ; he was as tranquil and gay as you could wish.

" You think of everything, Sarah," he said, when she indicated the glass in front of the empty chair. " The perfect wife ! " He took her hand under cover of the table. " Sorry I pulled down the roof as they say nowadays, but you gave me a fright. I didn't know you wanted to come into Kings Benton, or naturally I'd have brought you. Who was this woman, by the way ? The one who gave you a lift ? "

" I've no idea," said Sarah. " Just someone passing who saw me and asked if she could take me anywhere. She said she was going to Kings Benton herself, I can't imagine why, unless she has friends living on the other side of the town."

" And you didn't stop to think how you were going to get back, I suppose ? "

" There's a car-hire service—I saw a notice hanging out at the garage as I came by."

" That seems rather wasteful when we have a perfectly good car in the family. Hallo, someone been looking at your hand ? "

" I thought I might as well see a doctor as I was here."

" What did he say ? "

" Oh, just what you'd expect. Be careful of it for a while, keep it bandaged—he's given me some stuff to put on it—don't use it more than you can help. That's why I feel it's important to have this woman even if she is a natural, just to do chores till it's quite right again."

Henry frowned. " She'll bang about outside my door when I'm working," he objected.

" She's much more likely to bang on the window and insist that she has seen a ghost. She's quite batty, you know. She looked at me like a bird of ill-omen and croaked, ' You won't be there long. They never stay long.' " She laughed. " Let's have another drink."

" What on earth did she mean by that ? "

" I suppose she meant nobody could stick the cottage for more than a short time. How long have you had it, Henry ? "

" I bought it two or three years ago, as a *pied-à-terre*, really. No, I suppose no one could live there for any length of time, it's so remote. We're only there till I've finished the book, and that won't be long now, but it's a place to store one's things, and escape to from time to time."

The second round of drinks came, and she said laughingly as she lifted hers, " Escape from what ? The madding crowd ? Personally, I rather like it—the crowd, I mean."

Henry gave her a sharp look, but said nothing.

As they were drinking their coffee after lunch Henry said in a decisive tone, " You know, darling, I've been thinking about this lunatic of yours. I really don't think she'd be any good. And we shall be leaving ourselves so soon it's hardly worth trying to get someone into our ways. I'll give you a hand—I shan't be busy much longer —and as soon as the job's finished it's hey for the sunny south. Or, look here," he went on quickly, seeing she was about to raise an objection, " I'll have another shot at getting Mrs. Truelove to come back to us."

" She sees ghosts, too," Sarah reminded him.

" Only after dark. We needn't keep her then. We can look after ourselves in the evening, and she never slept in."

" Oh, well," said Sarah, " I can see you've made up your mind. I'd better let Mrs. Kent know. We don't want her to keep Daftie hanging about all the afternoon if we're not going to consider her."

" The fact is, I don't like the sound of her. You never can tell with these lunatics when they're going to have a violent turn. The moon affects a lot of them, and there are too many carving-knives at the cottage for me to be quite easy in my mind. It's not myself, because I'm working all the time and I should hardly see the creature, but you'd be with her in the kitchen. No, on the whole, darling, I think not. Look, you let Mrs. Kent know she's off, and I'll fill up the car with juice and we might as well go for a drive. It's a nice afternoon, and there'd be no chance of doing any more work to-day, anyhow."

In the car he was his usual charming self ; a golden morning had faded to an afternoon of melancholy beauty, with leafless boughs standing black as charcoal against a grey silk sky. A light wind wrinkled the water of a pond where willows bent languidly to their own reflections ; a few leaves not yet dislodged by winter hung like fragile gold pendants from a bush ; two magpies in glossy black and white went shrieking up a field.

Henry spoke of the future. " It's a nuisance about currency restrictions," he said. " It does put a period to one's holidays, but if I'm lucky with this book I don't see why we shouldn't go to Paris, say. for a few days now, and a little later go on one of those cruises to a hard currency country. Are you a good sailor ? I noticed an advertisement only this morning about a six weeks' cruise to the Gulf of Mexico. That 'ud be something to look forward to, if you like. I'm beginning to think I've kept my heiress cooped up too long."

" Heiress ! " she scoffed. " Aunt Jessie's bit of property."

" You've never told me what it is you inherited."

" A little business in north London. A man called Duncan is my tenant, such a nice little man. He had a very hard struggle to hold on during the war, but now I think he's getting his head above water."

" Probably making a packet," said Henry coolly. " I hope this lawyer of yours sees to it you aren't diddled."

" He pays his rent regularly. You can't expect him to do more."

" How long has he got the place for ? "

" His lease is up in March. I expect he'll want to renew."

" Ever thought of selling ? "

Sarah looked surprised. " I don't think he could afford to buy."

" He's not the only pebble on the beach. I doubt whether property will ever be worth more than it is to-day. In fact, I think the tide's beginning to go out. If you get a good offer it might be worth seriously considering it."

Sarah looked uneasy. " I shouldn't like to turn Mr. Duncan out. It's his living."

" Still, you're not a philanthropic association, are you ?

If you do want to sell you can always offer him first refusal. If his business is worth anything he can raise a mortgage with a building society. If they won't back him the odds are he's no tenant for you. Now, Sarah, don't stick your chin out like that. I know it's a perfectly charming chin, but—well, you do have to think of yourself, don't you ? "

" I have you to think of me," said Sarah simply. " Mr. Duncan hasn't anyone."

" And then women talk of their ability to run the country ! " Henry turned his eyes heavenward in mock dismay. Eventually Sarah agreed to put her husband's suggestion before Mr. Fair and they passed on to other topics. But a new suspicion was forming in Sarah's mind. Perhaps Henry was running short of ready money. She had never troubled herself with thoughts of his financial circumstances. It's the duty (if not the privilege) of husbands to have money. Any wife could tell you that.

They came back to Goblin Cottage to find the postman's van coming down the lane.

" Thought I'd got the bird for the second time to-day," remarked the cheerful young postman—he had only been on the round a little over a year. " Registered parcel. Tried this morning, but I couldn't get any answer."

" I must have been working," said Henry in a casual voice. " And if the tap was running we can't always hear the bell."

He took the parcel and signed for it.

" I'm glad to have this. It's the early part of my book back from the publishers. They asked to see the first chapters," he added explanatorily to Sarah as they walked towards the house, having garaged the car. " They may want some changes made." But he was frowning. " I've put a lot of work into this book. I hope they don't want any drastic alterations. It's a strange thing, Sarah, but when I've finished one section, one man's story, it's like closing a door behind me—a door with an automatic lock. I can't get back. Yes, if they want any but the most superficial alterations in the manuscript I shall tell them to omit the whole chapter."

It was clear that all his attention now was given to consideration of his book.

"I don't see why they should want any changes," she said soothingly. "Would you like tea or is it too near dinner?"

"I'm always ready for a cup of tea, and when it's ready for me, my dearest, I think I shall have a little surprise for you."

He said this in a voice so mysterious and complacent that she turned to look at him in surprise.

"What have you in your head now?"

He laughed.

"It won't be in my head much longer. Now, the kettle, Sarah, you can manage that with your bad hand, can't you?" Then he laughed again, more triumphantly. "Thank heaven you did ring me up. If you'd brought a maniac back here I don't think I could ever have finished my book and we should both have gone bankrupt."

She disappeared into the kitchen to fill the kettle and lift it on to the stove. She heard her husband go upstairs as she opened the bread-crock and brought out a farm-house loaf. Henry's appetite always surprised her; he could eat an enormous tea and by half-past seven proclaim himself famished. "Breakfast's a long time ago," was his favourite remark. "No, don't tell me we had lunch, we had a snack. Some people," he would add, "need very little food when they're writing but, personally, I'm always starving when my work's going well."

She was cutting the bread and butter when she heard a door upstairs close and a key turn. It puzzled her for a moment; but she had plenty of other things to think about. Toast burns the instant you take your eyes off it and Henry hated his toast burnt.

When she carried in the tea-tray her husband was sitting in his accustomed chair. He stood up and took the tray from her, and as she poured out the tea, he put his hand in his pocket and produced a little box.

" For me ? Oh, Henry, how delightful. I do love surprises."

" An unbirthday present," he confirmed. She removed the lid and could not repress a gasp at the sight of the diamond brooch nestling in its cotton-wool bed. " But— this must have cost a fortune—and it's not even my birthday."

He made a large gesture. " What's money for but to spend ? The fact is, darling, I had rather a guilty conscience about bawling you out when you rang me up. You must forgive me. Writers are like that. They get completely absorbed in their work, transported to another world. When the telephone went I scarcely remembered who I was or where." She thought, " But he said he was worried sick about me." " So while you went round to explain to Mrs. Kent we wouldn't have Daftie I strolled along to Hansards, the jewellers. I'll be honest with you and say I only meant to pass the time, but I saw this in the window and it was absolutely irresistible. I couldn't help thinking how wonderful you would look in it—or rather, how wonderful it would look on you."

He took it from its box and pinned it into the front of her dress, thinking as he did so how much more at home it looked on her than it had ever done on poor Flora, its original owner.

" In Hansards ? " Her voice was flat with non-comprehension.

" The jeweller on the corner. Perhaps you've never noticed it. It doesn't have anything out of the way as a rule, which made it all the more surprising that I should find this. Well," he added indulgently, " don't you like it ? " He thought her breath was taken away by its beauty and obvious costliness.

" It's the loveliest thing I ever had," she said slowly. " If possible, it's more beautiful than my ring. I shouldn't have thought you would have found a brooch like this in a little place like Kings Benton."

" Tell tell you the truth, I was rather surprised myself." From his manner he was candour personified.

After tea Henry went back to his work and Sarah escaped to the kitchen. There was some mystery here that troubled her more than the facts appeared to warrant. She asked herself why she should be so disturbed. Henry had given her a magnificent present. Yes, but why had he told her a deliberate lie about it ? That brooch had never been in Hansards' window nor, she was convinced, inside the shop. He had had no other opportunity of buying it to-day, therefore, he must have bought it or acquired it on some previous occasion. Perhaps he had been keeping it for a particular event. But it wasn't like a bunch of flowers or even a bottle of expensive scent. She was no great connoisseur of jewels, but she knew a brooch like this would run well into three figures.

Then she remembered the sound of a turning key. Possibly it had been in the house all along. But in that case why make such a mystery about it ? Why make her such a handsome present at this particular time ? It was not as though they had had any serious disagreement or as if he was trying to coerce her into something. For the moment she had forgotten about Mr. Fair and the property in north London. Then her thoughts moved on another stage. She saw them both standing beside the postman, who said, " Tried to leave this parcel this morning." And Henry commenting lightly, " Oh, I suppose the tap was running." But the tap hadn't been running. It had been one of those clear crisp mornings when sound carries easily on the golden air ; she had stood by the solid front door listening for the roll of wheels, for in this outlying bit of countryside the post came in a van. She had heard it coming along the lower road, heard it slacken, and then after a little while go on again. She had expected nothing in the way of letters herself, so she had not hurried for the moment. When she had gone down to the gates of Sussex ironwork that Henry locked at night to keep out possible tramps and burglars there had been nothing in the box, and she had been surprised, for she was sure she had heard the van draw up by the gate. Now that little perplexity was cleared away. There had been no letters, only this registered parcel, and when he got no reply he must have driven off again.

" But if the bell had rung I should have heard," she insisted to herself.

If the bell had rung ! She opened the kitchen door and moved softly along the hall till she stood by the staircase. Between the clapper and the bell someone had again inserted a little paper wad.

She hurried upstairs to the bedroom and sat down on the bed, surprised to find that she was shivering. It was perfectly clear now—Henry had replaced the paper, but why, why ? " Because I don't like being disturbed when I'm working," he said. But this was a very new development. He had been working just as hard before Christmas and the bell had not disturbed him then. No, that couldn't be the explanation. He had some reason for not wanting the bell to ring. " Though as I always answer it . . ." She paused. Was that the answer ? He didn't want her to go to the door. But why not ? Whom was he expecting ? The answer was—some applicant from Mrs. Kent's agency. " He doesn't want a third person on the premises, doesn't want a stranger. But that's absurd. He's nothing to hide." She sat there for a long time. What conceivable reason could he have ?

" If we were living in sin and didn't want anyone to know of my existence," she thought on a shaky laugh, and stopped again. Suppose that was the reason ? He had always made a point of taking her to some place other than Kings Benton when he took her out ; when he learned this morning that she had arrived there under her own steam he had been furious. But why ? Why was he afraid of them being seen there together ? There seemed only one answer to that, though it took her a long time to reach it. What if he had been living here with some other woman known as Mrs. Gould, what if that other Mrs. Gould were still alive, if her own marriage was no more than a sham—if that were true then no wonder he hadn't wanted them to be seen together in some place where he was known, where heads would turn, elbows nudge, voices whisper. And—jumping a farther step—would not that explain the diamond brooch? It might have belonged to the real Mrs. Gould. But if this fantasy was true where was the woman? Had she left him? And if so, why? And why leave her jewellery behind?

Henry's foot on the stair brought her quickly to her feet. " Keeping an ecclesiastical fast ? " inquired his voice as he opened the door.

She glanced at the watch on her wrist.

" Is it time to think about dinner ? Why, I've been in a reverie, Henry." For the first time she felt the need to dissimulate. " I was thinking of my brooch," she said. She saw a pleased smile cross his face.

" Some advantages in having a husband, eh ? " He threw a careless arm round her shoulder and stooped to kiss her. She repressed a desire to draw back, to cry out, " Whose brooch was this ? What happened to the previous owner ? Why did you tell me it came from Hansards ? And why, oh why, did you stuff up the front-door bell ? "

Of course she said none of these things, and a minute later she was running downstairs to prepare their evening meal. But setting the vegetables to boil, laying the table, bringing the sole they had bought at Kings Benton from the larder, she felt fear come to stand beside her and touch her with a cold implacable finger.

XII

NIGHT IN GOBLIN COTTAGE

AFTER THAT she was never again entirely free from a sense of Fear's presence. She could urge nothing particular against her husband, but she had the feeling of someone who, believing himself secure in a castle, has seen the door swing open and realised that there is no key that will ensure absolute security. She brooded a good deal on the question of the brooch. Other details came into her mind and try though she might she could not dispel her doubts. She would resolve to forget them, but the mischief had already been done. Once she surprised them both by saying unexpectedly, " Henry, am I really your wife ? "

Henry dropped his knife and cracked a plate. " My dear Sarah, have you taken leave of your senses ? Or am I to treat this as a joke ? "

" No. Actually, it wasn't. But—there is something a little sinister about our life here. I mean, we're like people who don't exist except for each other. It seems strange, we get no letters, we see no neighbours. If we walked out of the cottage to-day, locking the door behind us, who would notice the fact ? "

" What's behind all this ? " inquired Henry, sounding exasperated. " You never suggested before that you were feeling lonely. After all, it's only for a short time."

" It's not exactly being lonely, it's feeling somehow I've stopped being a real person. I don't exist for anyone except you, do I ? "

He smiled, with that heart-breaking charm that had won her heart at their first meeting. " And you don't find that satisfactory ? "

" Oh, Henry, it isn't that. It's just——"

" Yes ? "

" Well, I've been thinking—oh, I must sound absurd,

don't be angry, but living this secret sort of existence, I did begin to wonder if—as I said at the beginning—I really am your wife."

He said dryly, " I can assure you I've no other. When did these doubts begin ? "

" I don't know. I dare say it's being alone so much. And then—the fact is I had a letter from Mr. Fair this morning."

" I wondered if you were going to speak of that."

She thought, with the familiar stab of misgiving, " So it's true, I can't have any secret to myself." But she said with an assumption of liveliness, " He wrote about my property. He's going to ask Mr. Duncan about buying the property, though he adds that he can't safely recommend any more profitable investment and he's not sure that this is really the best time to sell. Then he adds that I haven't made a will since I married and suggests it might be a good thing to do. Naturally, I should leave everything to you, and in the odd way things do there came into my mind the thought that if I said, To my husband, Henry Gould, and by a thousand-to-one chance you weren't my husband—like Eugene Aram reversed "
—she felt she was becoming confused and struggled for an air of composure she was far from feeling—" well, you mightn't inherit after all and it would all go to the government, as I've no other relatives," she finished breathlessly.

He seemed to weigh that carefully. Then he said, " You're sure you're feeling quite yourself, Sarah ? "

She laughed in an uneasy fashion. " I suppose I must sound quite mad. Perhaps it's the cottage. Still, we shan't be here much longer, shall we, not now your book's so nearly finished ? "

" Oh, no," he said, " not much longer." But although he smiled she felt no corresponding lift of the heart. The reassurance for which she had conscientiously striven eluded her again. " Who is he, this man I've married ? What is he ? He never speaks of the past ; he might be one of those creatures suddenly born into life full-grown. Did he ever have brothers and sisters ? What was the first Mrs. Gould like ? " He had said once casually that he had been left an orphan at an early age but where he had been born, his father's profession, his own early upbringing, of these she still was in absolute ignorance. " As a matter of fact," Henry went on, " it would probably save a lot of bother if you did make a will, and it's the normal thing to do when you marry."

" Have you made one ? "

" Of course. Do I seem such a neglectful husband ? " His smile came out like sun after thunder-cloud, and she warmed herself gratefully in its glow. " I made one immediately we were married. Naturally, you're my sole legatee, for what that may be worth. Actually, I've taken out a life assurance, too. I think all men who can't leave their wives well provided for owe it to them to do that."

" Oh ? Do you think I ought to ? You wouldn't be very much richer if I died suddenly, you know."

" Well, we can talk of that some other time. Or see what Fair thinks. And if you're writing letters," he added, " you might get in touch with Bensons and ask them to send us some of their travel leaflets. We may as well let them do all the work. And we shall have to decide where we're going to go. I'm actually on the last chapter, so there's no time to lose."

In the excitement of making these arrangements she contrived to forget her fear ; writers were known to be temperamental people ; Henry had a phobia about the bell ; there was nothing sinister about it, she assured herself. As for the brooch—well, he had had it and decided to make her a present. If he said it came from Hansards that was probably because he thought she might be averse to the idea of wearing another woman's jewels. He was a widower when she married him, and presumably the first Mrs. Gould had had ornaments of some kind. It was even possible that the emerald and diamond ring had belonged to her ; but she scouted the idea. No man would make the same ring do for two betrotheds—she meant not the man she married.

The leaflets came and she pored over them with delight. Henry was shut up in his room most of the day. Her hand, having had attention, was healing at last ; she went round, already beginning to put things in order for their departure.

" Henry," she said one day, " I believe I ought to get another suitcase. Mine's very shabby. I've always wanted one of those patent ones that take six dresses on hangers."

" Don't do anything in a hurry," said Henry. " I may be able to help you there."

" Where did you put the suitcases when we came here ? " she went on.

" In the attic. You don't want them fetched down yet, surely ? We aren't going for a week at least."

" I like to have it by me, then I shall know what else I need. Don't bother, I can get it."

" I'll bring it down presently," he said. " The attic door doesn't latch properly, I have to keep it locked. I haven't got the key on me at the moment."

" I've never been up there, have I ? "

He laughed. " There's nothing to see, just a sort of loft full of rubbish. As a matter of fact, I must sort out some of the things or we'll get moth in them."

Well, that was all right, wasn't it ? The box was in the attic, and he hadn't got the key by him. That night she heard his feet on the stairs and he came in carrying her case. " I thought there might be something up there that would do for you," he said ; " but they're too shabby. We'll get your case when we go up to town and make final arrangements for the trip."

The book was finished now and—her hand really healed now—she was typing at full stretch to get it done. They arranged to go to London together to deliver the manuscript, visit Bensons and do some shopping.

" We might even spend a night in town," she said.

" It's ages since I saw a theatre, and I'd get my hair done at that place in Gresham Street. We can't have the French thinking how dowdy English women are."

" An excellent idea. I'll write to Fishers Hotel for rooms. It's the most comfortable place in London."

" I've never been there."

He laughed gently. " Well, you were an unmarried girl. I'm not sure they'd have let you in. You know, when we're in France I might get some data about French criminals, a companion book to this one."

" Oh, you ! " said Sarah in affectionate exasperation. " Do you ever think of anything besides murder ? "

The letter to Fishers was written, a note went to Mr. X of Bensons announcing their intention to pay a visit on the following Tuesday, and Sarah had an appointment with M. Julien. " Early to bed," said Henry. " I'll bring you your milk. How about taking an aspirin tablet ? "

She didn't want one, but she wanted to please Henry. The fears of the past weeks receded like mists melting in sunlight ; how foolish she had been to suspect his motives. These last few days he had been so lover-like her own feeling for him had flowered anew. He brought the milk and the tablet, and she took them both and settled down to sleep.

But history repeats itself. Flora hadn't been able to accompany her Henry to his fictitious cottage, and Sarah had to stay behind when hers went to London. For during the night she had an attack of sickness and internal disturbance, and although she felt much better by morning she could not face the thought of the long motor drive. Besides, she knew men hated women to feel off colour. Henry said doubtfully, " Well, look, shall I stay with you ? I can put Musgrave off, I suppose." Musgrave was his publisher.

" No, I shall be perfectly all right. Besides, you must go to Bensons. I'll take things very easily."

" Are you sure ? I'll get the fire going and leave you plenty of logs. How about food ? "

She shuddered. " I shan't want much."

" Well, I'll put the milk and some bread and an egg ready, so you needn't hang about in a cold kitchen. Now take care of yourself. The fact is I've been letting you do too much. What a selfish brute I am ! "

It was very quiet when he had gone, and she revelled in the silence. It was wonderful to be able to relax, to know that for several hours you needn't move. Probably Henry was right, she had been overdoing it. She spent most of the day by the fire, stirring herself occasionally to add an extra log ; she needed little food, and she decided not to think about supper ; there were plenty of tins in the larder. About four o'clock she got up and made up her face again, swept the hearth and put tea ready. Henry was lunching with Musgrave and going to Bensons. So far as she knew he was doing little else, so he might very well be back by five o'clock. But the clock struck five, then six and still there was no sign of him. She made herself some tea and sat by the fire, a rug round her shoulders, warming her hands on the flowered cup. She was sitting there thinking of nothing in particular when the telephone rang.

It was Henry at the other end of the line. " That you, dearest ? How are you feeling now ? "

" Oh, much better, thank you. It must have been something I ate. Where are you speaking from ? "

" I'm still in London."

" Henry, you are going to be late."

" That's just the point, my dear. By the worst luck conceivable the car's broken down, and the chaps at the garage can't get it done before morning. Some spare part that's not available apparently, though they swear they'll get to work on it first thing to-morrow. Now, I've been looking up trains, there's not a hope of my getting down to-night, but—look here, you'll be all right. You're not nervous of being alone in the house for one night, are you ? "

119

" No. No, of course not." (After all, why should she be ? No one had attempted to break in in all the weeks they had been there, why should anyone choose to-night of all nights ? Nobody would know she was alone.)

" That's the girl. Lock the front door—never mind about the gates—it's too wet to go traipsing down there, at least it's wet here. How is it with you ? "

" I don't know. I hadn't looked out."

" You sound a bit done in. Oh, darling, what wicked luck. All the same, if you take my tip you'll go straight back to bed. You haven't got up, have you ? "

" Well, just for a little. I don't like being in bed in a house by myself."

" You go straight back and take some milk and biscuits or something with you. And take a couple of aspirin and go right off to sleep. Before you know where you are the door will open and I'll be standing on the threshold. Now don't bother about anything. By the way, the jaunt's all fixed and you can start packing as soon as I get back to-morrow." Then the pips went and he called, " 'Bye, darling," and she heard him hang up his receiver.

She moved slowly into the hall, stood looking up the stairs stretching blackly away to the upper floors and wished passionately for the first time that they had electricity. How reassuring to press a switch and see light leap up illumining the upper landing, dispersing the shadows. A lamp was warm, but it threw vast shadows. Not, of course, that there was anything to fear. All the same, she ran quickly to the front door and turned the key in the lock ; she fastened the bolts, too, and then went to the back. She had to go down a narrow passage to reach this entrance and to her horror she suddenly found herself transfixed a few yards from the door. Why on earth couldn't she go on ? There was nothing between her and the back door, except the kitchen, whose door stood open. Yet she felt herself turned to stone. Who knew what might be lurking behind that half-open door ?

All day the back door had been unfastened, anyone might have come swiftly stealing through the woods and into the garden, slipping through the orchard to enter the house and prowl noiselessly in the kitchen.

"The longer I wait the worse it will become," she reminded herself, and made a little rush down the rest of the passage. No one jumped out at her from the darkness and an instant later she could be ashamed of her momentary panic. The wind was rising ; she could hear it trampling through the orchard, banging the heads of the creeper against the walls, shaking the doors in its violent grasp. She shut herself into the living-room, but hands tapped on the window and voices called. She knew this was only the wind, but the room swiftly became uninhabitable. She made herself enter the kitchen, collected the ingredients of a simple supper. Then she went up the stairs into their bedroom. This struck cold and she wished she had thought to light a fire earlier. She went down and fetched up an oil-stove that she kindled, and then sat in an easy-chair watching the circles of light reflected on the low ceiling. Slowly the air warmed ; she went softly to the window ; outside everything was quiet except when the wind lifted again. She thought she saw a light bobbing among the trees, and was stiff with dread, but a moment later she was sure it must have been her imagination. She set the milk in a pan on the top of the oil-stove ; it would take an eternity to heat, but it didn't matter ; she had all night to wait, all night, all night. She kicked off her shoes and put on warm slippers, took off her dress and wrapped herself in a dark woollen house-coat. There were two doors to this room, one leading to the passage and another into the bathroom that was also Henry's dressing-room. She locked the first door—there was no key to the other—and lay down on the bed with the eiderdown over her. Twice she got up and crept to the door and twisted the knob to make sure she had really turned the key.

"How do women live alone in the heart of the country?"

she wondered. " They must have some quality in their compositions that's lacking in mine."

Yet she wasn't naturally a coward ; she had spent the war in London, done fire-watching, helped at a relief station in Bermondsey where the bombing had been intense ; and all day long she had stopped at work except when the look-out man gave a warning that the enemy planes were overhead, when she descended to the shelter with everyone else. " I'm perfectly safe," she told herself in perplexed tones ; " absolutely safe." The milk boiled over without her noticing, and she jumped out of bed to remove it from the stove. She had made some egg sandwiches, found a tin of biscuits. She began to think back to the war days, the fear of fire, and at once she was questioning whether she had really damped down the fire sufficiently. Had she put the guard right round the hearth ? What if a spark leaped out on the rug and was even now smouldering ? This old house would burn like tinder. She wrapped the eiderdown round her shoulders and put the tray aside. When she opened the door the house was pitch-dark ; she took her torch and went resolutely down the stairs. She had closed the door of the living-room and when she opened it there was scarcely a glow in the hearth, but she went across to make certain that the slack she had heaped on the flames was really damp. She came back irritated at her own weakness, entered the room, shut and locked the door and turned towards the bed. Then she thought for a moment her heart stopped beating ; for the door between the rooms was ajar and she could hear the sound of heavy breathing. The lamp and stove combined gave too little light to illumine that black doorway. Besides, whoever stood there was waiting for her to come nearer.

" Who's there ? " she said in a low, tense voice. " Who are you ? "

The door opened another inch or two ; the breathing grew more pronounced. Then a sharper gust swept through the house and the door slammed violently shut.

Then she knew it was only the wind, only the wind, that had blown the door open ; as for the breathing, it had been her own panic-stricken respiration. She crossed the room and fixed a chair under the handle. Then resolutely she got into bed.

Five minutes later they started, the sounds overhead. Tap-tap, tap-tap, like a code. For the first moment she believed that the sound existed only in her imagination ; the cottage must be empty. How could anyone have entered without her hearing, or, having entered, climbed the stairs unheard ? These old houses were all alike ; there was always one creaking stair whose identity no one knew except the person who lived in the house and used it every day. There were only two people who knew the house with sufficient intimacy to avoid the treacherous stair, herself and Henry, and whoever was upstairs it could not be Henry, who had just telephoned her from London. Tap-tap, tap-tap, on it came a regular beating movement, as though someone swung a little hammer in time to some movement. She lay frozen with fear. The room above was the attic, that locked room into which during her stay at the cottage she had never penetrated. She supposed that a more curious woman would have insisted on seeing the inside of this place, but it had never seemed to her of any special interest. Henry had taken her suitcase and hat-box on the day following their arrival, and put it upstairs. The junk-shop he called the room, and said one of the reasons why he could never live comfortably in a modern flat was there was no space for the rubbish that all normal families collect. Tap-tap, tap-tap, the sound went on interminably until, feeling her senses would collapse if she remained quiescent in her room any longer, she left her bed, wrapped a shawl round her shoulders, for it was bitterly cold in this exposed dwelling on such a night, and cautiously, as though a hundred ears waited to register her smallest sound, turned the key and emerged into the passage. The sound was perfectly audible here, was not, as she had wildly hoped, something she had imagined, and it came from the locked room at the head of the stairs. She hesitated, then mounted two steps, and all the while the tapping continued. Stair by stair she crept up into the dark ; until she was standing outside the door. Then she suddenly began to laugh on an unsteady note ; the noise, after all, was only due to the wind flapping some invisible object against the wall or floor. She knelt down and tried to peer through the keyhole, but although there was no curtain to the window she could see nothing clearly. Only it seemed to her horrified eyes that she could discern some pale object swaying gently to and fro. It had the shape and size of a human body. She shrank back, then turned and bolted back to her room, where once again she locked the door, hurled herself into bed and lay there quaking. The darkness, the solitude, and the fear that enveloped her transformed the normal world into a place of fantasy. She opened the drawer of the cupboard beside her bed and pulled out a phial of sleeping tablets ; she crammed two of these into her mouth, swallowed a little milk and almost at once fell asleep.

XIII

ENTER A BIRD OF PARADISE

IN LONDON Jonathan Trent was dining with his great-aunt, Lady Mary Close at Fishers Hotel. The old lady was one of the few remaining landmarks of a bygone age : very small and neat, with the tongue of an asp and the face of an angel, one of her lovers had said in the golden days before the first world war, she had all the charm and toughness of a work of art. She was on her favourite subject, the probable marriage of her favourite young man.

" You're twenty-eight, my dear boy," she said, " and you'll soon be twenty-nine. Heaven knows I'm no sponsor of early marriages ; let people look in all the shop windows

before they make their choice, unless you're one of the incredibly fortunate few who see what they're looking for on their first excursion. But an unmarried man of over thirty is all wrong. He's inclined to argue, I've got along so far without marriage, why not a little longer, and thirty becomes forty and forty becomes forty-five, and then the world's saddled with another elderly maiden gent who's no good to anyone—God, man or woman. Besides, it's not fair to your children. They don't want an old man to tote around on the fourth of June——"

" You're forgetting, Aunt May, in our enlightened world the fourth of June isn't going to have any more significance than any other day. My sons, if I have any, will go to the sort of schools that will fit them for the lives they're going to live. Anyway, I belong to what you're pleased to call the fortunate few."

" My dear Jonathan, I'm delighted to hear it, but why on earth didn't you tell me before ? "

" Because it's one thing to make your choice and another to secure your objective before someone else gets in on the ground floor."

A wine-waiter stole up and refilled the old lady's glass.

" Well, my dear, if the girl was stupid enough to prefer someone else you must make another round of the market," said she decidedly. " I must say," she added in changed tones, " I hope the lady you're staring at so pointedly isn't your choice."

Jonathan dragged his eyes away from a striking-looking woman rather gaudily if obviously expensively clad who was dining with a dark good-looking man on the other side of the room. " Aunt May," he said persuasively, " you're a pet here, aren't you ? I mean, you came here as a little girl and you've been coming here ever since. They'll do anything for you, won't they ? "

" Are you asking me to blackmail them ? "

" I'm sure there's nothing you'd like better. No, but— Aunt M., you see that chap opposite with the outsize bird of paradise."

" A very neat description, dear," the old lady approved.
" And a very taking type," she added thoughtfully. " The
gentleman, I mean."

" You're telling me. Aunt May, can you find out who
he is ? "

" Is he someone you know ? Personally, I should say
he was the direct lineal descendant of Bluebeard."

" A very neat description," he riposted. " Aunt May,
last time I saw that chap he was Henry Gould staying at
an hotel in Barsett."

" With the Bird of Paradise ? "

" No, with Sarah. My girl."

" Dear me, what a lot of licence young people have
these days. Still, I believe it's quite often done, and no
one thinks any the worse of it. We were less blatant in
my day, but we didn't live mollycoddled lives for all that
—er—in what capacity was your young woman staying
with Bluebeard ? "

" They were registered as Mr. and Mrs. Gould."

" Then presumably she was his wife ? "

" She left Rimingtons to take up a job as his secretary."

" She may have married him afterwards. It's a thing
secretaries often do. Invaluable, you know. I don't think
you need glare at the Bird of Paradise like that ; she may
wear a wedding-ring, but I don't think Bluebeard gave
it her."

" I never thought that Sarah might have married him,"
acknowledged Jonathan slowly. " Do girls of twenty-five
marry chaps like that ? "

" Girls of twenty-five or indeed of any age are usually
quite bowled over by chaps like that, as you call them.
You may not appreciate it, Jonathan, but a man of that
type can usually do anything he pleases with women.
Watch him—his technique is impeccable, but of course
it's more than technique. It's something magnetic which
can't be acquired. Even I, though I'm an old woman,
can feel it all across the room. You mustn't blame your
Sarah if she did make a fool of herself with him. I

remember Jock Marling, when I was a girl ; they said he was responsible for more broken marriages than any other man of his generation. None of the husbands could see what the women saw in him, but the women knew ; it's like radio-activity, though I'm sure I don't know very much about it, except that it's very dangerous and quite irresistible."

" If that's Mrs. Gould," said Jonathan flatly, " where's Sarah ? "

" I can find out if they've booked as Mr. and Mrs. Gould," said the old lady rather doubtfully. " As a matter of fact they've made a mistake for once. As a rule, the clientèle here is irreproachable."

A little later the information he wanted was hers. " Mr. and Mrs. Henry Gould from a place in Mereshire. Is that where your Sarah went ? "

" I don't know. She simply said she was going into the country with this chap."

" And she's not written."

" Not a line."

" And you ? "

" How could I, without an address ? "

" No inquiries at all ? "

He said reluctantly, " I went round to the house where she had what she called a flat and I call a furnished room, but the woman there said there was no forwarding address and, anyway, there hadn't been any letters. People don't write much nowadays except to relations," he added. " They use the telephone."

After he had left Fishers Hotel he walked irresolutely up and down the streets. No sense going back yet, he wouldn't sleep. No sense going to a news reel, they were practically all over anyway. He went into a bar to get a drink and as he swung the door the voice of the barman pealed out, " Time, gentlemen, time. Glasses, please. Glasses, if you please." So he walked out again. He had digs in Bloomsbury, and as he walked up Bloomsbury Street he saw a light burning in a top floor. This wasn't a residential house, and he thought, " Someone's working late." And then he saw the number—123—and remembered that Arthur Crook had the top floor, and on an impulse he rang the bell and started to climb the endless stairs.

Crook didn't seem in the least surprised to see him ; Jonathan reflected he probably wouldn't be surprised if a unicorn poked its head round the door.

" Make yourself at home," he offered, opening his shabby cupboard and producing a bottle of beer. " Having a bit of trouble with the slops ? "

" If I told him I'd committed a murder he wouldn't turn a hair," the young man decided. He never seemed to change, was always the big boisterous fellow in bright brown clothes and even brighter boots, with a brown billycock and a check overcoat, thick red hair that never went grey and eyebrows to match.

" Go on," Crook encouraged. " Spill the beans. Or were you just feeling lonely ? "

" I've been dining with my great-aunt," offered Jonathan.

Crook pushed some cigarettes across and helped himself to a cigar. " They say the happiest man in the world was born an orphan on a desert island."

" Very short-sighted," said Jonathan, lighting a cigarette and forgetting to smoke it. " Everyone should have ties. Otherwise they're liable to get lost."

" You lost someone ? "

" I don't know."

" Don't let me hurry you," said Crook politely.

When he had heard the story he said, " Your auntie could be right ; she might have married the chap."

" Then why was this other woman masquerading as Mrs. Henry Gould ? "

" Maybe she is."

" You mean . . ."

Crook leaned forward. " I mean it was Christmas when you saw these two together. Christmas is six weeks back.

Your Mrs. Henry Gould might be under the daisies by now. Now take it easy, boy, I didn't say she was, I'm just pointing out that it's possible both ladies have a right to the title. Happen to notice if your girl was wearing a wedding-ring ? "

" She wore a very handsome emerald and diamond ring, I remember."

" Notice the design ? "

" A square stone, not very large but a good colour, set in a rose of diamonds. How does that help ? "

" Well, the lady you saw to-night wasn't wearing a similar ring ? "

" No. What's that got to do with it ? "

" May have a lot to do with it. Looks like your girl's still got it, though, mind you, there's no proof. What was this chap like ? "

" My great-aunt May said he was full of magnetism, and any woman would be attracted by him. He was pretty tall, dark—not bad looking, if you admire the type. . . ."

" Clean-shaved ? "

" A dark moustache, one of those natty little affairs that look as if they've been picked off a counter."

" And his name's Henry Gould. I wonder. Look here, when did your girl go off with the gent ? "

" She left us—oh, November. What difference does that make ? "

" Could make a lot. First thing, of course, is to find out if there's a marriage certificate. You didn't get the name of the place where this chap's living ? Mereshire's a sizable county."

" No. But I can tell you something. He had a car at Christmas, and I got the number. Now if that car is in a London garage——"

" Be your age," suggested Crook pleasantly. " Who do you think I am ? The police ? I can't go round demanding car numbers. Fishers Hotel, you said ? There's a garage on the corner there, an all-night one. You got a car ? "

" I call her that. She's parked at Rawsens. I didn't

take her round to Fishers. They'd probably have refused me admission."

Crook stood up. " Get her out. We're going places."

Jonathan knew him too well to argue. " Such as ? " he said as they walked down the stairs.

" The garage on the corner of Fisher Street. What's wrong with your car ? "

" Nothing."

" There'd better be. We're going into that garage."

" Petrol ? " suggested Jonathan.

" No soap. That wouldn't get us inside the garage. Well, if there's nothing wrong you'd better park her there for the night. While you do your bit of argy-bargy with the chap on duty—persuading him it is a car, I mean, and has a right to a place—I'll take a peek round. I know that garage. No lock-ups."

It was Crook's contention that the simplest way was generally the best. He was always trying to impress this on criminals who wanted him to prove their innocence and produced the most involved skein of alibis, enough to hang themselves forty times over, he said.

At Fishers the man on duty said he wasn't sure there was any room. " Always room for a little one," said Crook. " Suffering cats, you take some risks here, don't you ? "

" Risks ? "

" A hold-up gang could clean up a packet just by slipping something over your head and going off with this little lot. If they spaced it out no one would take much notice." He walked round the garage.

" Look here," said the man rather aggressively, " what's your game ? "

" I'll tell you," said Crook, with a handsome gesture as of one flinging all his cards on the table. " I'm a private snooper, see ? Matter of fact, I'm a lawyer. You ask anyone. Ask the police. What I want to know is if you've got a car here, dark-blue Napier, number XYZ5001."

" Why d'you want to know ? "

" Because if I win my guess it's no right to be here at all." He jingled the money in his pockets.

" Stolen, eh ? "

" Not exactly. Owner's no right to be here either."

He pulled out his wallet. Five minutes later he and Jonathan left the garage.

" So it's the same man. That's point one. Point two— we'll find out from Somerset House if there ever was a marriage between—what's your girl's name ? Sarah Templeton ?—and this chap, Gould. Point three—any note of a Mrs. Sarah Gould dying before her time. Point four—has Henry Gould married anyone else just lately ? Don't look so startled. Lots of chaps do. It's a sort of profession. Why, I'm on the tail of a chap now . . ." Then he stopped dead. " Suffering cats ! H. G. again. Your luck was in when you walked past my place to-night and saw the light burning—or I hope it was. One thing, Mr. Henry Gould's luck is out."

Somerset House confirmed a marriage between Henry Gould of a London address and Sarah Templeton ditto. The marriage had taken place on the day following Sarah's release from her employment at Rimingtons. There was no record of any other marriage that seemed to fit the villain. There were other Henry Goulds, of course, but none of them of the right age. Working by his own particular methods, Crook discovered that the car in Fishers Garage had been registered in the name of Henry Gould during the previous summer. He turned up *Tombstone Serenade*, and confirmed that it had been bought at approximately the same time as Mrs. Henry Grainger had been found dead in her bed. He read the account of that inquiry with renewed care. The dead woman wore a wedding-ring but no other jewellery. He wondered if it would be possible to establish the fact that she had at one time worn an emerald ring with a diamond rose setting.

" Of course," he reflected, closing his record, " any chap with any sense would argue that a man doesn't pass on jewellery from one wife to the next, but history shows that that's exactly what he does do. That was what got the gossip going about Samuel Dougal. The locals noticed that the lass of the moment was wearing stuff that had belonged to Camille Holland. It might be a line, though we'll be a long time on the road before we trip the fellow up. He's an expert at his job and it's the amateurs who are easy prey. On the other hand," he reflected, " he's been at the job so long he probably thought it was fool-proof." Still, the engagement had been opened. True, he wasn't definitely commissioned to hunt out Sarah Gould who had as much right as anyone else to stay hidden if she wanted to. The operative words were the last four. If she wanted to. And though he didn't want to scare his young friend he felt in his bones that Sarah was walking on very thin ice. Henry G. (Gould, Gardiner, Grainger, Grant) never let a wife's existence stand in his way, and to date, he had never put a foot wrong. " Only," thought Crook with majestic simplicity, " he's never had Arthur Crook bowling to him before."

XIV

BLUEBEARD'S CUPBOARD

AT GOBLIN COTTAGE the new day dawned golden with hope ; a soft wind sang in the trees, the morning light lay in gleaming panels on the cottage walls. Sarah woke late from a heavy sleep to wonder why her husband wasn't beside her. Then recollection returned. He had been kept in London because of a broken-down car ; he would be returning to-day. As for last night's panic, that now seemed absurd. There had been a high gale and it had blown something loose in the attic ; those had been branches not hands tapping on the window. She went downstairs and made herself breakfast on a tray ; she was hungry, she discovered, and pulling her house-coat round her, she went into the larder for bacon and bread and tomatoes. There were some cold potatoes, she found, and she fried those, too, and brewed coffee, and took everything upstairs. Breakfast in bed was a luxury she couldn't often enjoy ; only when Henry was away. After breakfast she smoked a cigarette, then dressed slowly, putting on a suit Henry particularly admired. To prove to herself that she was this morning completely free from care, when she had washed her breakfast things, she went up to the attic and, kneeling down, peered through the keyhole. The room was full of the morning light. To-day at all events, there wouldn't be a shadowy corpse swinging slowly in the wind.

All the same she got a bit of a shock, for there was indubitably something light hanging from a hook or rail ; her limited view didn't allow herself to discover details. But it wasn't a body, it was a woman's dress—more than one dress. You might have thought Henry Gould kept a second-hand clothes shop. She swivelled a bit so that she could see a little more of the room, and discovered various pieces of luggage, some poor and shabby, some quite handsome.

" What on earth is Henry doing with all those ? " she thought. In the distance near the window there was even a domed black trunk.

" Just like a thriller," she reflected.

" Bluebeard's wife ? " said a voice behind her, and she leapt up so quickly that she twisted one ankle and had to catch at the wall to keep her balance. Her husband was standing half-way up the stairs, and though his face was as bland as his voice she knew at once that he was furious.

" Henry ! How you startled me ? I wasn't expecting you back yet."

" Obviously not. You know my views about Bluebeard's wives," he went on in the same pleasant conversational voice. " They broke a contract and the penalty was—

execution. Well, then, what right had they to complain ?
Bluebeard, if you remember "—he was mounting the
stairs slowly as he spoke and now he stood beside her—
" told his brides that they had the run of the house with
the exception of one room, and if they tried to pry " (and
on that last word his voice assumed a deeper, more
terrifying note) " the result would be death. We love
women—how can we help it ?—but we do have to
acknowledge their weaknesses. In the fairytales, my dear
Sarah "—and here he took her cold hand in a firm grasp—
" the prince promised everything to the half of his
kingdom. Bluebeard went further—everything except
that one room, he said. And they weren't satisfied.
Greedy, wasn't it ? And foolish. Oh, very, very foolish."

Sarah threw up her free hand and covered her mouth.
She felt that at any moment she would scream.

" A waste of breath, my dear," Henry assured her.
" There's no one to hear—only the ghosts and the ghoulies
that live in the wood."

" How quietly you came in," Sarah whispered.

" I thought you might still be asleep."

" No. I felt so well this morning."

" So well you thought you would pry out my mystery."
She contrived a terrified, breathless laugh. " Is it a
mystery, Henry ? I thought it was last night. I was so
frightened. . . ."

" Frightened ? "

" Yes. It was being alone in the house, I suppose, and
the wind shouting round the corners and banging the
glass ; and suddenly something began tapping from overhead, from this room. Oh, it seems fantastic now, but last
night it was different. Things are at night. I crept up in
the dark and I could hear the sound though I didn't know
what it was. Oh, I was terrified out of my wits."

" You thought I'd left you alone with the ghost, I
expect. Go on, my dear."

" I went back and locked my door and took a sleeping
draught. This morning when I woke the sun was shining

and I felt a new person. So, to assure myself I wasn't afraid any longer, I came up and looked through the keyhole."

" I don't quite follow," suggested Henry. " Why should that prove you weren't afraid ? "

" Because last night I saw a white shadow, like—like someone hanging. I told you I felt hysterical. To-day I knew it must have been imagination, and I came up to prove I was neither afraid nor crazy. All the same," she added, recovering a little spirit, " you did contribute to the sense of mystery. Why keep the door locked as if you had some skeleton behind it ? "

" Why does one ever lock a door ? " He drew her towards the head of the stairs and slowly began to descend. Her hand was held in his like a vice, but it was as cold as ever. " I'll tell you. Not so much to keep skeletons in as to keep curious folk out."

" But why, Henry ? What was the sense of making such a secret of it ? "

" Do you know," said Henry in a conversational tone, " the percentage of men who get tired of their wives ? You'd be surprised to hear how high it is. And do you know why ? Because women have so little sense. They want so much. They don't like a man to keep anything to himself. His money, his name, his home, they're not enough. They have the present and it's up to them how much of the future they can keep. But they want the past, too. That's the mistake women make, Sarah."

They had reached the foot of the stairs and he drew her into the sitting-room.

" Now I'll tell you what's in that room," he said. " It's full of things that belonged to my mother." The anti-climax almost made her giggle. But she managed to repress the impulse. " After she died it was my task to go through her things, sort them, distribute them. She didn't leave a great deal, not of value, that is, just clothes, a few jewels, personal possessions, her luggage and so forth. That was during the war. She was killed during a raid on a night when I was away from home. A direct hit. It's been in my mind ever since that if I'd been there I might have saved her. Of course, common sense says that the only result of my being there would have been there'd have been two casualties for the ambulance instead of one. Afterwards I had her things packed into her cases and stored them. I couldn't sort them, for one thing, there wasn't time and for another—well, I couldn't do it. Afterwards when I got this place I had them brought down here and put in that room. I got as far as unpacking the stuff, hanging it out—and there I stopped. It's been there ever since."

Sarah said in shaking tones, " But I didn't know, Henry ; I didn't know. Why did you never tell me ? "

" Because I didn't talk about her to anyone. Isn't there anything in your life that you want to keep private ? But no, women have no reticences. Worse, they can't respect the reticences of the other sex." He dropped her hand and moved away. " I'm sorry to have spoilt your mystery, my dear Sarah. If you had waited and asked me . . ."

But Sarah said nothing. She had seen the fatal flaw in his explanation and for the first time she was in desperate fear—not the sort of fear that had tormented her last night, which had been a fear of the unknown, but a concrete fear of the man she had married and who, she realised now, she had never known at all.

Rather unexpectedly Henry seemed to think that the subject could now be considered closed. He began to tell her about his trip to London. What his publisher had said, some small alterations that must be made, and then he added, " By the way, I telephoned Mr. Fair—had you remembered you had an appointment with him ?—and explained you weren't well. He said he would write, but if there's anything you want to see him about in person there'll be another opportunity before we go abroad."

Sarah pulled herself together. " Yes, I think I ought

to see him, both about the property and about making my will. I'm sure I ought to do that before we go to France. I don't want to sound melodramatic, but accidents do happen—aeroplanes crash, cars overturn, and it seems silly to leave things in the air when it's so simple to tidy everything up."

" Of course, you can do that part of it by post. As for the property—well," he shrugged, " it's yours, and naturally I don't want to influence you to go against your own wishes. It's anybody's guess how long property will retain its present inflated values, and no one can foreshadow what steps the Government may take in regard to private businesses. I think you should consider your own interests to some extent, and remember that official compensation is unlikely to reach the figure you could get for the place now before any compulsive scheme is brought in."

" I must talk to Mr. Fair," Sarah agreed. " Did you do anything about our tickets ? "

" Oh, yes, everything's in train. Bensons are seeing to that. As a matter of fact, we must see about getting your passport altered now that you're a married woman. I meant us to do all that yesterday, but we've plenty of time in hand. That's the best of being one's own employer."

He went back to his room presently with the manuscript he had brought back from London, and Sarah sat down to write letters. She saw now what a fatal mistake it was to lose touch entirely with your past. Nobody even had her address ; it seemed incredible that during the weeks since her marriage she had never even wanted to write to anyone. Now she faced the fact that she had no intimate friends. Her marriage seemed to have cut her off ; now and again she had had an impulse to scribble a line to one of her fellow-workers, but the secrecy surrounding her marriage had always stopped her. And then she had never felt the lack of company—Henry had provided all she needed. She still had a little time in which to repair her mistake. She took up her pen and began to write to Jonathan Trent.

Henry came in unexpectedly as she turned over the page. "Busy?" he asked.

"I thought I might as well write to Mr. Fair at once."

"A good idea. Give me the letter when it's finished and I'll post it with mine. What are you saying to him, by the way?"

"I'll show you when I've finished. It's all perfectly straightforward." She took up the pen she had laid down when he entered and wrote quickly. "That disposes of my will. Now I want your advice about my property." Henry sauntered across the room and looked over her shoulder. She felt the pen shake in her hand. Then his came down on her shoulders.

"Poor Sarah!" he said. "I believe I really alarmed you this morning. You mustn't take it all so seriously. But it's quite true what I told you, men hate to feel they're being spied on. Possessiveness, that's a woman's fatal mistake. All the same, I've been in the wrong, too. I should have spoken of her before; we might go through the things together one of these days. I never could stand the thought of doing it alone, but with you—if I'd had any sense I'd have packed the whole lot off to some home for decayed gentlewomen, only—I couldn't endure the notion of some old scarecrow wearing *her* things. You do understand?"

And Sarah, her eyes fixed on the wall ahead, said in a low voice, "Yes, Henry, I do understand."

He stooped and kissed her. "Poor darling! Terrified of being alone in the house last night and then frightened out of her wits in broad daylight by her own husband. Finish your letter and we might go for a bit of a drive."

As soon as he left her alone she took the sheet of writing-paper and put it in the fire. Whatever happened, whatever happened, she must not let him guess she was writing to Jonathan. As for what was in the room upstairs, she was as much in the dark as ever, only she knew his story was false from start to finish.

When he came back she showed him the letter she proposed sending to the lawyer, and he said, " Excellent, excellent." And then he laughed, and added, " I shall have to take great care of you for the future, shan't I ? History's full of men whose wives have come to an untimely end just after signing a will leaving everything to their husbands. The detective story-writers have a lot to answer for ; they've made married life even more complicated than, in fact, it is."

A laugh accompanied the words, but she could only summon up the flimsiest of smiles. Her confidence was undermined ; he had deceived her once ; for all she knew he had been deceiving her from the start. More than ever did it seem to her important to establish contact with some outside person, but now she became aware that all her actions were the subject of a secret and tireless scrutiny. Did she produce pen and paper Henry was certain to come along in a minute or two to ask with husbandly curiosity, " Who's that to ? " She had too much sense to tell him she was writing to Jonathan ; he might insist on seeing what she had written, and how could she let him see her *cri de cœur* ? He was always at hand, always on the watch. " I'll post it," she might say, but when the letter was nearing completion he would be waiting in the hall or strolling casually in the garden. " Something for the post ? Give it to me. I'll put it with mine." In the hope of putting him off the track she wrote a long gossipy screed to a fictitious Miss Elsie Blake, and gave her husband the letter to post.

" Who's Miss Blake ? Have I ever heard you speak of her ? "

"Just a girl I used to work with in London. It's rather on my conscience that I've never written to her all this time."

She was sure that Henry steamed open the envelope—she had fastened it very lightly on purpose—but if he did it wouldn't help him. It was the usual young woman

scrawl, how lovely it was to live in the country, what fun
it was to be married to Henry, how jolly to be going
abroad next month. How about a meeting in London after
their return ? Or perhaps a week-end at the cottage. As
she anticipated, Henry posted this ; she hoped that would
calm his suspicions. The following day she wrote a
desperate note to Jonathan and, tucking it inside her
dress, walked down to the gate. Once a letter was dropped
in the box just down the lane it could only be recovered
by the postman ; but when she reached the gates she
found they were locked. She could scarcely believe it ;
she caught them and shook them violently, thinking they
must somehow have become stuck. But no, there could
be no doubt about it. They were locked. She was a
prisoner, and she had no doubt that this was deliberate.
She was still standing staring at the lane, that for her
would have spelt freedom when she heard a movement
close at hand, and a voice said, " Hallo, Sarah. Something
for the post ? "

She shook her head violently. " No. I just thought I'd
go for a little stroll."

He laughed. " There's nothing very attractive about
the lane, I should have thought. Why not go a little way
into the woods, though be sure you don't get lost.
Perhaps "—he smiled with an affection that was as false
as it was cunningly assumed—" it would be best for me
to come with you."

Clearly she could advance no reason for preferring her
own company ; Henry kept up a cheerful flow of conversation. It had been decided that he should include one
or two new cases in his book to bring it to the necessary
length. " We're having a number of photographic repro-
ductions," he explained. " Of course, that puts up the
expense to the publisher, so he's got to charge a good
price for the book. People expect a fat book for fifteen
shillings, and he thinks another fifteen to twenty thousand
words would be an advantage. I've chosen for one, at all
events, the case of Mary Richards. You remember it, I

dare say ? " He chatted on, immensely enthusiastic.
" All my crimes have this in common," he pointed out ;
" they all deal with domestic crimes. Husbands whose
wives have become obstacles, wives who have to get
rid of husbands to make way for lovers—that's the sort
that's always fascinated me."

" Henry," interrupted Sarah, " why did you lock the
gate ? "

" There have been a number of robberies lately in the
neighbourhood—oh, quite small affairs, I grant you, but
there's a tendency for these chaps to carry arms—yes,
and use them. When I'm working you're particularly
vulnerable. One of these fellows might break in one
evening and harm you before I could get on the scene.
When you're alone——"

" I never am alone," said Sarah in the same, flat, level
voice.

" Most wives would appreciate that. Of course, I like
to keep my eye on you, make sure you're all right. I told
you I should have to be very careful, now I know I'm
your legatee."

This constant surveillance grew in intensity as the days
went on, until there seemed scarcely an hour, night or
day, when Sarah was not aware that she was being
watched. She would be standing in the hall and suddenly
glancing up would see her husband, remote and still as a
shadow on the upper floor ; or, sitting in the dusk in the
living-room, she would put out her hand for the matches
and another hand would drop a box into hers. The first
time that happened she gave a little scream.

" Henry, how you startled me ! "

" Wasn't that what you wanted ? "

" Yes, of course, but—I didn't even know you were in
the room."

" Perhaps I was a cat in a previous existence. I've
always admired that sleek stealthy way they creep up to
their victims, wait a moment and then pounce. There's a
sort of poetry about it."

"Perhaps that's why I've never liked cats," said Sarah, with a shiver of repulsion.

Once, waking in the small hours, she saw that her husband had left his bed and was examining her writing-case ; he held each envelope up against the flame of a candle, then, when it was obvious that it was empty, threw it down again ; he leafed carefully through a packet of writing-paper, shook out the case apparently seeking something in the lining. He even produced a small hand-mirror and held it over the blotting-paper. Sarah lay, terrified and appalled ; she knew she must make no sound. She tried every conceivable ruse to get in touch with Jonathan. When Henry took her for a drive she would have the letter tucked down in the bosom of her dress ; surely, surely this time she could find an instant of privacy during which she could slip it into a box. But Henry watched her like a lynx. She could, of course, have made a dash for a box and thrust the letter defiantly in, but in that case she was certain that Henry would pack up the cottage within twenty-four hours and incarcerate her in some place where no one would find her. She did not at that time think of him as a professional husband who had no scruples about ridding himself of outworn wives ; she simply thought he was mad.

He told her lightly that, thanks to the extra work on the book, they must put off their holiday for a little longer, and he had written to Bensons to that effect. Sarah didn't care. She was resolved that, come what may, she would never leave the country in his company.

X V

ALL HOPE ABANDON YE . . .

ONE AFTERNOON he went out without her, and she felt this might be her hour of deliverance. When she was sure he was well out of the way she rushed to the telephone and lifting the receiver asked for Rimington's number. The operator asked not only her number but also her name, which seemed to her unusual, but she had never lived in the country before and imagined this must be a local regulation. She heard the ringing of the distant bell, then silence. " Hallo," she said. " Hallo." " Trying to connect you," said the voice. " Hold on." Her heart beat in her throat. Even if Jonathan were out she could leave some message, somehow convey a sense of urgency.

" Sorry, no reply," said the operator's complacent country voice.

" There must be," she protested. " Oh, please try again. It's a firm. There must be someone there. Well, then, get me the supervisor." There was a long, long pause ; then another voice said, " Supervisor speaking. I am afraid your number is out of order." And the bell clicked and the fog closed in.

She thought desperately. It was perfectly obvious what had happened. Henry had given instructions that none of her calls were to be taken. But what excuse could he give for that ? That she was unbalanced ? Even that was possible. Another thought struck her and she telephoned to the nearest inn, standing about a mile away, where she knew a car could be hired. But when she gave her name a man's voice said, " I'm sorry, but the car's out. Won't be back till to-night. Sorry, I'm sure." She thought if this went on much longer she really would be mad. Obviously Henry had left her no loophole.

Henry came back in excellent spirits. " Anyone ring up ? Or call ? "

" How could they call ? You left the gate fastened. Besides, there isn't anyone."

" I don't think I'll bring you back here after our holiday," he said. " I believe it's too solitary for you. If I weren't so busy perhaps it would be different, but you've too much time on your hands. You sit and brood. If you had something to occupy yourself——"

" There's been your typing," she whispered.

" Perhaps that's not the best possible thing for you. My interest in it is sheerly professional, as I've explained to you, not so much who did it, as that's generally obvious from the start, but why ? How ? To me it has a scientific excitement, but I'm afraid it's rather a morbid way for you to occupy your time. One domestic tragedy after another, one more wife who couldn't make the grade. That's how it must seem to you. I ought to have thought of it before. No, when we get back we'll set up in London for a time. Perhaps in due course you'll have more duties." " He means children," she thought, appalled. " Oh, no, that final horror at least let me be spared." Later in the evening he said, " It's odd to think, isn't it, that if we hadn't chanced to sit next to each other at that cinema a few months ago we might neither of us be here ? A. P. H. is right. Do you remember those lines of his— ' It's the little things that matter, don't you see ? ' "

The next morning when he came up with the letters he was looking puzzled.

" I'm afraid your friend, Miss Blake's, changed her address."

" Miss Blake ? "

" Yes. Elsie. You remember writing to her the other day ? The envelope's come back marked ' Not known.' "

" I suppose she's changed her job," said Sarah with affected carelessness. " She might have left a forwarding address, though."

" Women don't always, do they ? I mean, you didn't. You didn't, did you ? " he repeated.

" No. No, I didn't. For all I know mail has been piling up for me ever since. Perhaps I ought to write to Mrs. Winter and ask her."

" We might go round in person when we're in town next week. She'd probably be glad to know you're happily married and we're both having such a good time. Did you get that last piece of typing done ? Good. It was a fine stroke of business I did when I married you, wasn't it ? A wife and a secretary rolled into one. I

think you deserve a day off. We might go into Redmondstone and lunch at the White Hart. It's famous for its
food, even in these days. Put on your best bib and tucker
and we'll start quite soon."

When they got to Redmondstone he stopped the car in
a street of residential houses. " Just want to stop off here
for a few minutes," he said. " I've got an appointment."

" Who is it ? A dentist ? " For she had glimpsed a
brass plate by the gate.

" Not exactly. A doctor. I thought as we were going
abroad it might be a good notion to get a clean bill of
health apiece before we start. When were you last
overhauled ? "

" Oh, I'm never ill," she disclaimed hurriedly.

" Ah, they're the people who give the doctors the most
trouble when they do collapse. It's like the people who
never have toothache or only a twinge now and again,
and then find with a shock when at last they are driven
to a dentist they've got to have the whole lot out."

" He won't be able to see us without notice," Sarah
protested.

" That's all right. I made an appointment. I told you
just now. You're beginning to be forgetful, my dear. I'm
afraid I've worked you too hard. A holiday's just what
you want."

" Oh, Henry, no. Really I don't want to see a doctor.
You go in. I'll wait in the car. You needn't be afraid I'll
drive it away "—she contrived a tremulous laugh—" I
don't know how to drive."

" Oh, I think we'd better both go in now I've made the
arrangement. If there's nothing wrong with you you
won't take up much of the chap's time." He took her by
the elbow as she reluctantly stepped out of the car and
guided her through the gate.

Dr. Forbes' receptionist said the doctor wouldn't keep
them a minute, and put them into a waiting-room with
an elderly man who looked at them keenly.

" Sit down, my dear," said Henry kindly. " There's

nothing to be afraid of. The doctor's not your enemy, nobody's your enemy, except perhaps yourself." He caught the eye of the man on the farther side of the room, and it seemed to Sarah that a meaning glance passed between them. Again she contrived that uneasy laugh.

"Of course he's not my enemy, I realise that. I don't know why you should say such a thing. It's simply that there's nothing wrong with me."

"Of course not," he soothed her. "It's just a formality." And then the door opened and a troubled-looking, middle-aged woman came in.

"Oh, dear, Herbert, I hope you haven't got tired of waiting. I feel a wreck, an absolute wreck. He's such a very unsympathetic type. Are you waiting to see him?" she added to Sarah. "I warn you, he doesn't believe a word one says, not a single word."

The receptionist came back and murmured something to the elderly man, who muttered an incoherent explanation and disappeared.

"They all hang together, men do," complained the older woman. "Do you think I don't know what he's telling my husband now? 'Just her imagination,' he's saying. He as good as told me so to my face. As if it could be imagination. I tell you, I'm being poisoned. I know it, but nobody believes me. They're all in it, Herbert and that nurse and the new cook, too, I dare say. It's awful to be a woman, defenceless, absolutely at the mercy of unscrupulous people." She stared tragically at Sarah. "You're wasting your time if you expect any sympathy from him," she said.

"Oh, I don't think that's what my wife's here for," said Henry in his pleasant way. "She's quite sure she's got nothing wrong with her." And he smiled, showing fine white even teeth. Then Herbert came moodily back to collect his wife, and the receptionist took Henry and Sarah into the doctor's consulting-room.

Sarah would have preferred to see the doctor alone, but it was clear that Henry had no intention of permitting this. Dr. Forbes was a man of medium height, with a pale rather flat face, a bald head, round brown eyes and a sallow complexion. He extended a large well-kept indifferent hand and invited Sarah to sit down.

"I should make it clear," said Sarah quietly, "that this is just a routine check up because we're going abroad, and my husband thinks it's a good thing."

"Quite," said the doctor in a voice as indifferent as his hand-clasp.

He made a casual examination then, sitting down and putting his hands together, he asked, "What about these dreams of yours, Mrs. Gould?"

"Dreams?"

"Yes. Your husband tells me you have very violent dreams. I wonder if you can account for them in any way. It's quite clear they're undermining your health, and we can't hope for any improvement until we've traced them to their source."

"I don't have bad dreams," said Sarah flatly.

"And then this feeling of enmity. You don't deny that you suffer from that? That you imagine every move your husband makes is in some way a threat to yourself? You do feel—insecure, don't you, Mrs. Gould?" She saw instantly the hopelessness of her situation. Suppose she said, "Yes, I do. I don't feel safe with my husband any longer," what reasons could she adduce to support such a statement? That Henry was unkind, threatened her physically? No. The doctor was waiting for a reply.

"Yes," she acknowledged. "I do. But I think anyone who was watched from morning till night would feel the same. I know just how a mouse feels waiting inside its hole knowing that every time it puts its nose out the cat's waiting to pounce."

"That sounds like a guilt complex, Mrs. Gould. To begin with, why this passion for escape?"

She said boldly, "I could talk to you more easily alone." And Henry stood up at once.

"Naturally, my dear. It was just that I thought my

presence might give you confidence. I'll wait in the next room, doctor."

"Dr. Forbes," said Sarah, as soon as she had heard the second door close, " it's perfectly clear to me that my husband has already told you his side of the story. He's given you the impression that I'm on the verge of a nervous breakdown."

" And I think he's right," said the doctor in his colourless voice. " I think, Mrs. Gould, you are on the verge of a nervous breakdown."

" If I am it's because of him, it's because I'm followed and watched at every turn. The gates of the place are locked and even if I walk down to them Henry sees where I've gone and comes after me. I can't get a long-distance call to London—the excuse is that there's no reply—but of course there's a reply, it's a busy office. If I ring for a hire car it's gone out. If I want to go for a little walk Henry says he'll come, too. If I lie down for a bit I can hear him listening outside my door. When I open it he calls from below, ' Coming down now ? Shall I put on a kettle ? ' If I want to write a letter he looks over my shoulder. ' Who are you writing to ? ' ' What are you saying ? ' Oh, I don't suppose that's what he told you. . . ."

" On the contrary, Mrs. Gould, that's exactly what he told me. The reason why he wanted me to see you was to see if I could trace the source of this antipathy you've developed for his proximity."

" I haven't developed any antipathy. But—is it unreasonable to wish to write a letter without being overlooked ? "

" Ah, yes," said Forbes thoughtfully. " Letters. I was coming to that. Your husband showed me a letter you'd written to a Miss Elsie Blake. I understand Miss Blake was a friend of yours in London."

" An acquaintance," amended Sarah, but to her horror she felt herself beginning to shake.

" Quite. Where did you meet her ? "

" At—at my work."

" You didn't tell her you were getting married ? "

" I didn't tell anyone."

He caressed his long bony chin. " I wonder why. Try and tell me, Mrs. Gould. Most women are proud of being married. There must have been some reason why you wanted to keep it a secret even from your friends, even from your family."

" I have no family."

" Ah ! " He nodded his bald head. " Your friends then ? This Miss Blake, for instance."

Sarah sat thinking. Why had she kept so quiet ? " The truth is," she said at last, and paused.

" Yes, Mrs. Gould. The truth is——"

" The truth is people are so curious. They want to know where you met and how long ago and what do you know about him, and the fact was I'd only met my husband very recently and I knew hardly anything about him. I suppose in a way it seemed to me more romantic not to say anything."

" No," said Dr. Forbes thoughtfully, " I don't think you kept silent because you thought it was romantic. I think we're beginning to track down the guilt complex. You felt, whether you realised it or not at the time, that there was something of which your friends would disapprove. You didn't feel able to justify yourself. But after you were married—you didn't write then ? "

" There were so many other things to do."

" But now you suddenly feel you want to let people know. This Miss Blake, for example."

" Well, it suddenly seemed to me rather silly, and— well, suppose anything happened to me nobody would know."

" By anything happened, do you mean something fatal ? "

" Y-Yes."

" Had you any reason to suppose anything fatal would happen ? "

" I was alone in the house one night when my husband's

car broke down and he was kept in London, and—I got a scare. I thought someone had broken into the house."

" And had they ? " Nothing shook this man's impenetrable calm.

" No. It was the wind, but—it made me think that I could die there like a rat in a hole and nobody would know."

" Your husband would know. Mrs. Gould, I put it to you that you are suffering from a persecution mania. You are convinced that there is a plot against you. Oh, I dare say you were happy enough with your husband at first, but—tell me, were you very surprised when he proposed ? "

" Yes, I was."

" Why ? "

" I'd known him such a short time."

" Is that the only reason ? "

" What other reason could there be ? "

" I put it to you that you were surprised because you weren't accustomed to popularity. You're how old ? "

" Twenty-five. Nearly twenty-six."

" And yet you had no intimate friends. No one in whom you could confide the truth about your marriage. No one to whom you felt the need to write after your marriage. Of course, I don't know yet why that should be so. From your general appearance one would assume you would be reasonably popular. Perhaps, though, you had some emotional shock whose consequences are now only manifesting themselves."

" I had nothing of the kind," said Sarah crisply. " And I never had any sense of being—unwanted."

" You were left an orphan at a comparatively early age, I understand ? "

" My Aunt Jessie looked after me. I wasn't pushed into an institution."

" And you had a great affection for her ? "

" She was very kind."

" But you didn't care for her as you would have cared for your mother. Perhaps you hadn't many opportunities

150

in her house of making friends. When you were older and independent that sense of inferiority remained with you. You had acquaintances, no doubt, but friends——"

" Why should you assume I have no friends ? " inquired Sarah desperately.

He leaned forward ; he shook the square white envelope in her face. " If you had real friends, Mrs. Gould, there would be no need to write to a fictitious lady called Elsie Blake. Your husband, who is seriously troubled about your condition, made a point of getting in touch with the landlady at this address, only to learn that no Miss Blake had ever lived there. He also contacted your late employer, but no one in that office had ever heard the name. Now, Mrs. Gould, I can do nothing unless you are frank with me. Isn't it a fact that Miss Blake has no actual existence, is simply a figment of your imagination ? "

" Yes, it is true, but Henry—my husband—gave me no choice." She tried to explain her reasons for writing to the non-existent Elsie, but they sounded so poor and improbable that she broke down. She felt that in another minute her control would give way altogether. She saw that this was exactly what Forbes anticipated.

" Why won't he leave me alone ? " she exclaimed. " That's all I ask. Not to be followed, not to be watched."

" He feels responsible for you," Forbes told her, " for anything you may do in a moment of despair or——"

" You mean he thinks I might kill myself ? Oh, I see, I see." And to her horror she began to laugh. She laughed and laughed. She didn't think she would ever stop.

XVI

PREPARATIONS FOR A JOURNEY

SHE STOPPED abruptly, feeling like someone who has risen from the depths of a wave to survey the unfamiliar landscape ; she had indeed the sense of being completely out of sight of land ; look where she might there was no hope, no security anywhere, just the waters of despair washing all about her. The doctor had obviously summoned his receptionist, for the woman now stood in the doorway, with bent brows and an alert look on her face.

" You think I'm mad, don't you ? " said Sarah clearly. " Let me tell you this. You'd be mad, too, in my circumstances. You asked me, doctor, if I felt safe. Of course I don't feel safe. What I want is to leave Goblin Cottage, go back to London—I could work again—my husband can't want me to stay with him any longer, the marriage was a mistake, I see that now——"

The doctor interrupted in his unhurried colourless fashion. " You can't break up a marriage so easily, Mrs. Gould. Besides, your husband has a great sense of responsibility for you. In law he is responsible."

" This is 1950," she reminded him. " I was responsible for myself before I married, earned my own living. . . ."

" No doubt, no doubt, but you weren't a sick woman then."

" I shan't be a sick woman once I'm away from the cottage. You don't know what it's like. You've never lived there. It's like being watched over by an eye that never sleeps, knowing your smallest movement is noted. You're a doctor, you know the mind to a large extent governs the body, you must realise nobody could stand that sort of strain."

" My dear Mrs. Gould, many women would be grateful

for a husband who was so concerned for their welfare. It's quite out of the ordinary."

" Yes," agreed Sarah in a peculiar voice. " That had struck me, too. Why should he be so concerned ? As for being responsible, I'm not a pauper, I have property of my own, I could get along all right."

" It's only fair to tell you, Mrs. Gould, that in your present state it wouldn't be fair to yourself or the community to allow you to—to run your own life. What I'm going to suggest to Mr. Gould is a thorough change. . . ."

" I don't want to go abroad," she said quickly. Abroad where she knew no one, where she could be completely cut off from her past, where her future would be nobody's concern.

" I think perhaps you are right there. No, I propose a complete rest."

" You mean in an hospital, or—"

" That would depend on your husband, of course. . . ."

" All right," said Sarah. " Only—don't let me go back to the cottage. I shall do something desperate if that happens."

" It's very unwise to make these threats," the doctor told her. (Was it possible for any human being to be so utterly unmoved in the face of human suffering and terror ?) " Naturally you must go back with your husband for a few days while arrangements are being made. And I do counsel you to try and pull yourself together. You're a young woman, you're in excellent health physically, and when you consider the number of people who have to endure physical disabilities, poverty, loneliness, who really do command our pity, you may be ashamed to spend your time thinking so consistently about your own imaginary troubles."

Hearing this, Sarah felt she really would go mad on the spot. " Imaginary troubles ! " she gasped. " You say that because you don't understand, you don't know. . . . I don't want to be a bother to anyone. I just want to have my liberty. . . ."

" Liberty," said the doctor sententiously, " has to be earned." (How on earth had Henry contrived to find a man so perfectly attuned to his purpose ? His usual luck, she supposed.)

She made another attempt.

" I don't want to appear unreasonable," she said. " Will you let me get in touch with my lawyer—Mr. Fair of Bishopsgate ? He'll assure you I'm a perfectly normal person."

" There's no obstacle to your writing to him," said the doctor.

" There is. There is." To her horror she heard her voice rising again. " I'm not allowed to post any letters."

The doctor lifted his brows. He picked up the envelope addressed to Miss Elsie Blake.

" That was different. He wouldn't think there was anything dangerous about that."

" Dangerous ? " He opened the door and Henry came in.

" It's no good, doctor," broke in Henry. " She's got this obsession about someone plotting against her. Why, she even began to think we weren't really married. I did ask Mr. Fair if there was any family history. . . ."

" You asked him ? You mean, you've been behind my back. . . ."

" My dear girl, you had an appointment with the fellow for the day we were going to London, and lawyers don't like having their appointments broken at virtually no notice. I thought it was the only polite thing to do to have a word with him myself."

" You talk as if it were my fault I couldn't go to London. I couldn't help being ill."

" Ill ? Now, come, my dear, you know very well you weren't ill. Why should you be ? You were as fit as a fiddle the night before."

" I was ill," she persisted. " I was desperately sick."

" Oh, you felt ill, but there was no real reason for it. I wasn't ill, we had the same food. Surely the doctor's made you understand that it's some buried fear—you don't want to meet people——"

" Why shouldn't I ? "

" You've not once suggested going up to London, meeting a friend, asking anyone down. Why, the only person you've written to, except your lawyers, is the fictitious Miss Blake."

" Who is it you wish to write to, Mrs. Gould ? " inquired Dr. Forbes. " Perhaps your husband could get in touch for you."

She was about to mention Jonathan's name when a new thought struck her. If Jonathan stood in Henry's way—well, so much the worse for Jonathan. And what right had she to involve him in the muddle she had made of her life ?

" I'd like to write to Mr. Fair," she said dully.

" Well, of course. Or see him yourself. I'll take you up to town, only it's no use making a definite appointment because you work yourself into such a state you're not fit to travel next day."

" I could go this afternoon," insisted Sarah.

" He may not even be there."

" We could telephone."

Henry glanced across to the doctor. " I see no harm in that," he said. " The post office is just across the High Street."

The receptionist came forward rather fussily to help Sarah into her coat. The doctor and Henry disappeared into the corridor. Sarah turned in desperation. " Will you do something for me ? You look as if you had a kind face."

" If I can, Mrs. Gould," said the woman primly.

" There's a letter in my bag. Will you post it ? Oh, I don't know how much you've heard, but there's a plot against me. If someone doesn't help me I really shall go mad. After all, if I'm writing to another imaginary person it won't be any harm. And this time it isn't, it isn't."

" I'll post it for you, Mrs. Gould."

Sarah didn't know whether to believe her or whether she would simply pass the information and the letter on to her employer. But she had so little to lose that the chance must be taken. Besides, even the cold-blooded Forbes might be impressed and forward the letter, and once Jonathan knew of her predicament he would come down and help her. In the midst of all her distress and terror she clung to that belief. Snatching up her bag, she rummaged in the roomy pocket at the back where the letter had been. " Don't let anyone see it," she implored.

" I've said I'll help you, Mrs. Gould. Where is it ? "

Sarah dropped the bag on to a chair. " I don't know," she said tonelessly. " It isn't there any more."

" It must be if you had it when you started," said the nurse tranquilly. " Perhaps you didn't put it in that pocket."

" I did. I know I did. Oh, what can have happened ? " She answered her own question. " Of course, he must have it."

" He ? "

" My husband."

" He's coming back now," said the nurse. " You can ask him."

" Ask what ? " said the doctor, returning to the consulting-room.

Blandly the nurse betrayed Sarah without the quiver of an eyelash. " Mrs. Gould mislaid a letter. Perhaps she dropped it in the waiting-room."

" Of course I didn't," said Sarah in a hopeless voice. " How could I when it was safely in my bag ? " She turned to Henry who had followed the doctor into the room. " You took it, didn't you ? Of course. When the doctor was examining me."

" Yes," agreed Henry without the shadow of a blush. " I took it, and it's a very good thing I did. A letter like that could bring you into court, you really must be out of your mind, Sarah. In danger of your life, indeed. How on earth do you suppose you could support such a contention in court ? Anyone would think I was planning to poison you."

" Oh, no," said Sarah. " You're much too clever for that. If anything happens to me the jury will believe I was responsible—one of those murders by accident you're so fond of. Where is my letter ? "

" My dear, you don't imagine I allowed a dangerous document like that to remain in existence for an instant ? It's in the fire. Did it occur to you to wonder what would happen if someone opened it ? "

" It was meant to be opened," said Sarah. " Letters generally are."

" Another relation of Mrs. 'Arris ? " gibed Henry softly.

" It was meant for a friend of mine—I suppose you saw the name on the envelope ? "

" I'm afraid I didn't pay much attention. I saw Miss Blake's name on the envelope, but that didn't help the postman very much."

" Did you say anything about that letter to Mr. Fair ? "

" Of course. I wondered if anything of the kind had ever happened before. By the way, he's out of town for a couple of days, his secretary tells me."

" I see." (She didn't for an instant believe he had rung up the office in Bishopsgate.) " You've been very clever, Henry. Blocked every bolt-hole. I know now what a rat feels like in a trap. It can't get out and presently it's compelled to realise it can't get out. There are only two alternatives. It'll die by inches or whoever set the trap will dispatch it in his own good time. I wonder which alternative you've fixed on for me."

Dr. Forbes had written a name on a card and this he now handed to Henry. " Many thanks," said the latter. " I'll get in touch at once and give your name as an authority. I may say it's extremely urgent ? "

Dr. Forbes bowed his head. " I propose to telephone myself this afternoon." The nurse fluttered in an angular manner in the background.

" Mrs. Prentice has been here for some time," she insinuated.

" We're on our way," Henry declared. " Come along, Sarah. We've taken up much more time than we've a right to as it is, doctor. I hope next time we come you'll be able to give us a more cheerful verdict."

Back in the car Sarah said hopelessly, " Aren't we going to have any lunch ? There's nothing at home."

" I thought perhaps you wouldn't feel like facing a restaurant. I bought some sandwiches while I was waiting. It's quite a pleasant day for the time of year. We might stop in the woods on the way back and eat them in the car."

She said in the same tone, " I want to powder my nose."

" Oh, dear, what a pity you didn't think of that when we were at the doctor's. Oh, well, we might go in here for a cup of coffee." He caught her elbow and guided her into a café. The proprietress came bustling forward to find them a table.

" My wife's feeling a little faint," Henry explained. " I wonder if you've anyone——"

" I'm really not helpless," said Sarah. She moved forward. Henry gave the proprietress a sweet, appealing smile. " If you could," he murmured. " We've just come from the doctor. A great shock."

" This way, dear," said the proprietress. Sarah whirled round, her eyes wild. " Is there a back way out ? "

" A back—— ? "

" Yes. Can I get out without my husband seeing me ? I'm in danger, in dreadful danger. You must help me. Have you a telephone ? "

" There's one in the office."

" Let me use it."

The proprietress looked dismayed. " I thought you wanted . . . Oh, well, this way, but . . ." They turned into another passage. Henry came forward.

" Now, Sarah," he reproved her. " At your old tricks again ? I've tried and Dr. Forbes has tried to prove to you that nobody's your enemy, nobody's hatching a plot against you, nobody wants to do anything but get you back to your normal self. All this crazy telephoning to strangers, bringing the police out at all hours, writing to people who don't exist. . . ." He turned apologetically to the proprietress. " I must apologise," he said. " But when my wife told me she wanted to powder her nose— I suppose I should have suspected it was a trick. It's a nervous breakdown, she'll be all right again after treatment."

" Poor thing ! " said the woman, a Mrs. Alice Rose.

" I'm sure you understand," continued Henry. " I can see you're married yourself."

" I haven't had a baby," exclaimed Sarah violently.

" No, no, dear. Of course not."

" I don't see why you say of course not. There's no reason why I shouldn't, only I'm thankful I haven't. And the trick's on his side, not mine. It's all part of a plot."

" I'll tell that girl to put on a kettle and make you a nice cup of tea," said Mrs. Rose soothingly.

" You're very kind," said Henry. " I'm afraid we're creating a great disturbance."

" That's all right. We're not so busy now. It's past the lunch-hour."

" It can't be," ejaculated Sarah. " It was only twelve o'clock——"

" You were a long time with Dr. Forbes, and then he kept us a little late for our appointment." He drew a bottle from his pocket. " I think you should take one of these, my dear. They're sedative tablets. . . ." As he had anticipated, Sarah flung out her hands in a gesture of repudiation.

" No. I won't. I don't want them."

" It's always the same," Henry confided to Mrs. Rose. " She thinks we want to poison her, though why we should nobody could explain. If only you could get things straightened out in your mind. . . ."

The girl brought the tea. Sarah regarded it with

mistrust. " I don't think I want any, thank you." And yet, how she longed for a cup of tea.

" My dear, I assure you I've had nothing to do with the making of it. You can't suspect everybody you meet."

" You take and drink a cup," urged Mrs. Rose. She poured out three cups. " Now we're all going to have one. You choose first."

Reluctantly Sarah took one, sipped the hot liquid. " It's very good," she said. " You're being very kind. It's not your fault if you're deceived. I was deceived, right from the start, and I had far more reason to know him than you. But will you do one thing for me ? Will you call a policeman and let me make a statement ? "

Henry made a gesture of despair. " Sarah, what use would that be ? The constable has only to apply to Dr. Forbes, and he'll confirm what I've just told this lady. You're not yourself, you've had a shock. . . ."

" Who gave it me ? " she asked slyly. " And what was it ? You tell me."

" I was unfortunately compelled to leave my wife alone in our cottage one night recently, and she thought a burglar was breaking in. It's a very lonely spot, Goblin Cottage at Spartan End. You may have heard of it. It's very old and all sorts of legends cling to it."

" They do say that part's haunted," agreed Mrs. Rose ; " but of course, sensible people don't believe it. Take my word for it, dear, all you heard was an owl."

" I saw——" began Sarah, and stopped.

" Poor young lady," said the woman, with genuine compassion. " Come to think of it I wouldn't like to be alone in the wood of a night. But now your husband's back. He'll look after you. You leave everything to him."

To her horror, Sarah felt that wild ungovernable laughter rise in her throat once more ; she flung her hands over her mouth, her body was contorted, her face convulsed with the effort she made to retain control. Mrs. Rose said in a low alarmed voice, " She's not going to have a fit, is she, Mr.——"

" Gould. No. It's a sort of convulsion. It's all part of the illness." He put a possessive hand on the girl's shoulder. " Finish your tea, Sarah, and then I think we'd better go straight back. You've had an exhausting time with the doctor, but this lady's right, don't give up hope. Put yourself in the hands of those who care for you and you'll be all right again. We're going to take her to a nursing home in London in a day or two, as soon as there's a vacancy," he added in explanatory tones.

" I'm sure I hope they'll put her right," said the motherly woman. " Oh, no, sir, there's nothing to pay. I'm sure I'm only too glad to do what I can."

" Then you must let me make a small contribution to your favourite charity," said Henry firmly, putting five shillings on the table.

" Well, I'm sure that's very kind. I was always a great one for dogs, and I do think our dumb friends ... Perhaps you don't care about dogs, Mr. Gould."

" Of course he cares about them," Sarah burst forth uncontrollably. " He's got one buried in the garden— buried in the garden. At least he says it's a dog, but perhaps it isn't, perhaps it isn't. Perhaps it's somebody who once wore that dress—that dress that belonged to your dear mother who died when you were a boy and then died all over again in a raid. Wasn't that strange ? " She turned excitedly to Mrs. Rose. " The house had a direct hit on it and his mother was killed outright—though he'd been an orphan for years—but none of her things was hurt, not her trunks or her dresses. . . ." She began to pound a soft silk cushion with her clenched fist. " You thought I was such a fool, you thought I was taken in. . . ."

Henry's voice changed, it became sharp and authoritative. The grip on her shoulder bit deep into her flesh.

" You're doing yourself no good, Sarah." And how right that was. He would never forgive her for this, for discovering his senseless blunder. He had known she was a source of danger to him the instant he rounded the bend of the stairs and saw her on her knees at the attic door ; now he knew the danger was more acute than he had supposed. He must act quickly. He drew her to her feet. " I must apologise again. I had no idea what I was letting you in for. Now, Sarah, come along."

" There's a private way out, sir, if you'd rather," suggested Mrs. Rose. " I mean, you don't want everyone in the café to see——"

" Let them all see," shouted Sarah. " Why not ? "

Henry put his hand over her mouth. Mrs. Rose grasped her arm. The waitress who had brought the tea stood goggled-eyed in the corridor. She vaguely hoped the young lady would snatch up a knife and plunge it into someone—but not Henry, of course. He was a lovely gentleman, you only had to cast an eye on him to see that. And awful to be burdened with a mad wife, like that Mr. Rochester in the film at the Troxy last month. She saw herself, the not-quite young, never very pretty waitress in the role of Jane Eyre. As the trio came past she tried to convey a sense of her deep sympathy to the man.

He smiled at her. " I'm afraid we've interrupted you. It's too bad," he said. Sarah was suddenly quiet, as if all virtue, all strength had suddenly drained out of her. She made no sound as Henry put her into the car, slammed and locked the door, and got into the driver's seat. The car moved off at a brisk pace.

" Poor young thing," said Mrs. Rose, turning back and almost cannoning with her helper. " Violet "—they went in for floral titles at the café, even its name was the Honeysuckle Luncheonette—" there's no reason for you to neglect your duties. I don't want the customers complaining."

" Poor man," said Violet romantically. " I was thinking, Mrs. Rose, it was like that film they had at the Troxy last month. . . ." She went back to her duties, and for the remainder of the day she was wrapped in a daydream that transfigured the monotony of her duties.

XVII

DAYBREAK DEPARTURE

HENRY DROVE back to Goblin Cottage by a roundabout route, travelling slowly, as if he wanted to give Sarah time to compose herself. At the post-office-cum-grocer they stopped and Henry asked if there were any letters. He seemed a little agitated, but was relieved when one was handed to him. Henry asked for a bottle of aspirin tablets and chatted about this and that, and Sarah suddenly emerged from the car, looking sheet-white, and bought a bottle of Chinese ginger. Then they went back to the cottage through a golden sunset. As Henry got out to unlock the gates she shot a sharp glance back and forth as if measuring her chances of escape, but she must have known they were nil. The lane ended in a thorny cul-de-sac, and even if she could have smashed her way through the brambles she would have found herself in a no-man's land of shoulder-high bracken, roots, shrubs, going on for ever. As for leaping out of the car and dashing back down the lane in the direction in which they had come, that, she was convinced, would be playing straight into Henry's hands. In the car he could overtake her in a moment, indeed it would be simple, if her disappearance was part of his plan, to engineer an accident —fleeing girl, half-crazy anyway, staggering madly this way and that and suddenly flinging herself under the wheels of the pursuing car. She remained where she was clutching her bottle of ginger. She had always had a predilection for the sweetmeat, and being convinced that at the nursing home she could be compelled to swallow one nauseous draught after another, it would be a comfort to have something to take the taste away, as Aunt Jessie used to observe in her childhood days. Henry re-entered

the car, drove it through the gates, and got out again to
lock them behind him.

" Why so much care ? " wondered Sarah aloud. " Who
was so much afraid of the world that he had to put up
those monstrous gates to protect himself ? "

" Any man with common sense," was her husband's
cool reply. " I wouldn't care to spend a winter at the
cottage without some sort of barrier between me and the
outside world. Tramps, thugs, maniacs, anybody could
break through a simple hedge, and then you would be
caught in your house like the proverbial rat in a trap.
Even if you were armed you could be caught by two
people, one behind and one in front. You wouldn't have
a chance. No, those gates are sensible. This place is so
isolated you'd never be heard, not if you shouted the
place down."

Her eyes, that had been averted, raised themselves
slowly to see his face. Was that intended for her ? Very
likely. She watched him lock the garage doors after the
car, then he was once more at her side and marching her
up to the cottage.

In view of the fact that he hoped to be able to take
her to London next day, he said, he thought it would
be a good idea if she went to bed immediately ; he
could bring her up a cup of tea.

" I don't want to go to bed yet," she said. " I'd rather
stay up and make the tea. If your plans come off I shall
be spending quite enough time lying down for the next
few weeks."

He smiled. " You must please yourself, my dear. I'm
not your gaoler."

She put on the kettle, found the loaf and made toast.
She didn't trust him an inch. She would not, she resolved,
go to bed until she had had all the food she intended to
take to-day ; if he brought her up anything to drink she
wouldn't touch it. She sat there, warming her hands at
the fire, feeling like something in a cage, going round
and round, looking for a way of escape.

And I like one lost in a thorny wood
That rents the thorns and is rent with the thorns
Seeking a way and straying from the way ;
Not knowing how to find the open air
But toiling desperately to find it out.

Presently she heard the faint tinkle which meant that the telephone receiver had been lifted ; she stole to the door, opening it an inch or two. Then she heard her husband's voice give a London number ; her heart beat fit to suffocation.

" Is that Milton 1704 ? . . . My name is Gould—Henry Gould of Goblin Cottage, Spartan End, Mereshire. I believe Dr. Forbes rang you earlier to-day about my wife. He hopes you'll be able to treat her as an urgent case for admission to your nursing home." (Pause.) " Yes. Yes." (Pause.) " I see. Thank you very much. Oh, I'll give you my number in case of emergencies."

She stole back to her place just before he hung the receiver up again.

A moment later he appeared. " As no doubt you heard just now," said he pleasantly, " I've been ringing Dr. Mortimer's home. You're very fortunate. There'll be a room for you in the morning. Dr. Forbes seems to have pulled some strings. I've said we'll be up about midday, which means an early start. Don't worry about the house here. I've looked after it single-handed before and I can do it again. And don't worry about packing. You won't need very much, as you'll be in bed. Anything that is wanted I can bring up when I come to see you."

Sarah stood in an agony of irresolution. Might it not be wiser to agree with Henry's suggestion, to go to this Dr. Mortimer's home ? The whole medical profession couldn't be in league with Henry Gould. From the home she could write to Mr. Fair and explain the situation. She was his client and probably he would agree to come and see her. Also, from London she could get in touch with Jonathan.

" Very well," she said submissively. " Mind you, I'm not really ill, but if it will satisfy you . . ."

He smiled, showing his excellent teeth. " I was sure you'd be sensible. How good that toast looks." He came and sat on the arm-chair by the fire. She curled herself on the fender-stool. They were a perfect picture of domestic happiness.

" It only needs a cat," she said suddenly.

" A cat."

" Then we should be a perfect design for a Christmas card," she explained.

He smiled in a benevolent way. " What an imagination you have, Sarah."

Imagination ? Ah, but she had never imagined anything like this. As the evening progressed the rain began to fall. Rain in the country falling among trees has a quality of mystery ; it sounded like footsteps coming through the garden, hands tapping on the window. " No, no," she told herself. " I must keep my head clear." Later the wind began to rise ; it was obvious that a storm was brewing. Sarah collected the teacups, washed them, put them away. Henry was busy with his own affairs. Suddenly there was a crash of glass.

" What's that ? " Henry had appeared on the staircase. " Had an accident ? "

" No. I thought it was you, perhaps."

" Must be the storm." They went round the house. Up in the bedroom glass lay scattered on the floor.

" Hallo, wind must be pretty powerful to have done that. Now what ? We shall have pneumonia unless we block the window. I like fresh air as much as any man, but we shall be floated out of bed if this goes on much longer." And indeed the rain was already splashing heavily through the hole in the glass. " Of course," went on Henry, " it had to be this room, but that's how things are." He went downstairs and into the outhouse where the chopped wood and a number of sacks and half-used tins of weedkiller, etc., were kept, but he could find nothing there suitable to stop the hole. " What we want is a piece of plywood," he said ; " something we could fit into the framework. Carboard's no good, it would be soaked through at once. No, it seems to me that only thing we can do is to close the shutters and leave the door open. Do you have a phobia about sleeping with an open door ? "

" I could sleep in the spare room," she offered quickly.

" As a matter of fact, I thought you might like me to sleep there. I'll leave my door open too, and then I shall hear you if you call out."

" Why should I ? "

" Well, you do sometimes, in your sleep. To-morrow on my way back I'll call in at the village and try and get a chap to come up—have to bring him up, I should imagine—to replace the pane. Even if the house is going to be shut up for a bit, as soon as you're fit enough to travel, we don't want to leave that window broken."

He closed the shutters and put the heavy bar in place. Sarah was right ; whoever planned this house had made it as safe against invasion as a medieval castle. It only wanted a moat to be utterly shut off from the world, and the lane that was a cul-de-sac, the stiff hedge and the locked gates were even more efficacious, she thought. Closing the shutters made the room very dark, but it would be dark in any case at this time of year. Sarah made herself a bowl of bread and milk ; she suddenly found she was dog-tired, and there was one thing about going to Dr. Mortimer's home ; it did mean that Henry wouldn't play any tricks with her food. They would be expecting her to-morrow, and he would see to it that she was delivered safe and sound.

" Forbes gave me some stuff for you to take, a sedative really," said Henry, in what was almost an apologetic voice. " I haven't unwrapped the bottle. You'd better take it along with you to-morrow, in case they want you to go on having it, though my experience of these places is that no two doctors ever agree on the same medicine. Like to back their own fancy."

" I don't know that I shall want it," said Sarah obstinately, taking the bottle nevertheless. Henry's shrug said that clearly she must please herself. She went up to her room where a lighted lamp threw patches of gold on the pale walls, and great shadows across the ceiling. She packed a few things ready for the morning. " We shall have to start pretty early," Henry had warned her. Then she got into bed with the feeling that she never wanted to leave it again. She was quite extraordinarily tired, and yet she couldn't sleep. She heard her husband moving about softly downstairs, closing windows, fastening shutters. Outside the wind howled and battered at the panes. " Go to sleep, go to sleep," that was what it seemed to say, but its very fury drove sleep from the room. At last in despair she sat up, broke the seal of the wrapping on Dr. Forbes' bottle of sedative, took a generous dose, and almost at once floated away into a shadowy world where nothing was real any more. Her last waking thought as she drifted into unconsciousness was that this was the last night she would ever spend at Goblin Cottage.

Henry was up early the next morning, got the car out of the garage, came softly into the room where Sarah was still sleeping to fetch her case and her little jewel-box— " Better take them with you," he had said ; " you may not want to come back here before we go abroad "—and stowed them neatly in the car. He seemed the ideal husband as he put on the kettle, made the coffee he liked for breakfast and took a tray up to her room. It was a grim morning, the rain still falling though nothing like so heavily as it had done during the night ; the garden had a forlorn look with its decayed vegetation and the scanty leaves beaten off the black branches. He washed the crockery and cleared the larder, he tapped the barometer, which fell down as it always did, went round making final preparations, then called out, " All set, Sarah," and went out to the garage.

Old Mrs. Potts heard a car going past the post office and twitched aside her bedroom curtain to see who it was. For all her years her sight was still keen and she could identify it as the big blue car from Goblins. In the country people are more often referred to by their address than by their names. " Poor young thing," she reflected, letting the curtain fall back into place, and curling up in her warm bed, " glad it's not me being taken for a drive this hour on a wet morning. She'll need that jar of ginger if she wants to keep warm." And, chuckling a little, she once more fell asleep.

And the dark-blue car, unaware of her scrutiny, went over the brow of the hill and up the road and took the turning for London. In the cottage in Goblin Wood everything was as still as death.

XVIII

CROOK TAKES A HAND

UP IN LONDON there had been developments. Crook had his own way of getting information and the crowning virtue of not looking back once he had put his hand to a plough, no matter how futile the furrow he seemed to be ploughing. He believed that Sarah was in real danger, assuming that her Henry Gould was also Greta Mannheim's Henry, and Beryl Benyon's Henry and hapless Flora Ransome's Henry. Which was assuming a good deal. Still, he thought in his optimistic way, it should be possible to get some sort of proof. The first thing to do was to find out where he was living now. As a matter of form he made inquiries—or rather caused them to be made—at the address given at the registrars, but, as he anticipated, this led them nowhere. Henry had occupied the rooms for the minimum period necessary to put up the banns, and had left, leaving no address.

" Letters ? " murmured Crook, but it appeared there
had been no letters. The landlady, however, remembered
him at once. "Such a delightful gentleman, such charming
manners. . . ."

" Probably married him herself if she'd had half a
chance," reflected Crook. " Well, if she can't help us, we
must try Fishers. The chap must have written from
somewhere. You can't just walk into Fishers on the spur
of the minute and say you want a room for the night."

" What beats me," said Jonathan, " is how he got into
Fishers at all. It's more like a club than an hotel. New
members have to be proposed and seconded."

" You don't know yet what we're up against," Crook
told him benevolently. " A chap who can get away with
murder, which I'm fairly sure he'd done, and I dare say
more than once—murder becomes a habit like any other
vice—wouldn't find it hard to get round that one. He'll
probably claim acquaintance with half the peerage, and
you admit yourself he's got something, must have or all
these women wouldn't fall for him the way they do. Mind
you, I know dames are daft, but all the same, they
wouldn't fall for me like that." The grin with which he
said the words was tantamount to a challenge. " Of
course," he said, doing a bit of underlining. " It may be
different for you. I always heard Adonis had his jam
served up on a gilt-edged plate."

Fishers, as Jonathan had remarked, is very exclusive
indeed. Probably they had never seen anyone remotely
resembling Crook come over the threshold before, and
when he casually asked for the manager he was told as a
matter of course that that gentleman was engaged. Also,
that the hotel was booked fully for the next few weeks.

" Me," said Crook, with the alarming simplicity he
affected on such occasions, " I prefer my own bed. Like
to know who's above and below me, too. No, I simply
want to make inquiries about a chap who was staying here
on . . ." He supplied the date. " Gave the name of
Gould," he said. " Came up from the country."

" I am afraid it would be quite impossible for us to supply the address of a client," said the receptionist in freezing tones.

" Play it your own way," said Crook. " But it's me or the police."

" The police ! "

" That's what I said. You know who I mean. The human bluebottles who direct the traffic and do a little investigation into crime in their spare time. The fact is " —he waxed confidential—" we've every reason to believe that the lady staying as Mrs. Gould had no right to the title. Me," he continued expansively, " I represent the real Mrs. Gould."

He produced his card. " Lawyer," he said. " You may have heard of me. I get around a bit."

" Are you suggesting—you are seeking evidence for divorce ? "

" Not me," said Crook. " Never touch it. If A and B don't hit it off and want to break it up, that's their affair. No, what I had in mind was murder."

" Murder ? "

" That's what I said. Police don't come into divorce, you know," he added kindly, " not without you get a spot of murder thrown in. Of course, if you'd prefer to have them haunting the place and taking statements— you won't like it, you know. I can see you don't know as much about them as I do. A nosey lot, the police." He spread himself over the desk. " And if it turns out it isn't murder you'll have had all that trouble for nothing. Mr. Gould won't be pleased, either, and nor will those friends of his who recommended him to come here." The receptionist looked somewhat at a loss. He felt that by rights he should indicate he had nothing further to say and let the stranger depart, but for form's sake he went to have a word with the manager.

The manager of Fishers knew nearly everyone, by reputation that is, and if the receptionist hadn't heard of Crook the manager had. " Crook here ? That's rather off his beat," he said. " Who is this fellow, Gould ? Has he ever been here before ? "

They turned up the correspondence. It seemed that Henry's publisher who was well known to the hotel had brought Henry there to lunch one day, and afterwards Henry had said he would be bringing his wife to London for a night or two in the near future, and had made the arrangement on the spot. Later he had confirmed it from Goblin Cottage. (Nobody at that stage, not even Crook, though he could make a pretty accurate guess, had known that the wife Henry had in mind hadn't been Sarah. He had met the Bird of Paradise on one of his visits to London and their acquaintance had ripened with a rapidity to which he was perfectly accustomed. Mrs. Lily Abbott was a woman of the world ; she had had one husband and a number of lovers ; she was not in the least averse to adding Henry to her list. She was a well-to-do woman who believed in living for the day. When Henry suggested a second meeting she agreed without demur, and when at the end of the evening he proposed remaining in London overnight, adding carelessly that he had booked a room at Fishers in the sure and certain belief that her reactions would match his, he hadn't had to break down much resistance.) There hadn't been the smallest reason for the manager to suspect that they weren't a suitably married couple. Fishers never figured in police court news, and certainly they had never anticipated being connected with anyone as sensational as Arthur Crook. He thought on the whole he had better see the fellow. Crook went bouncing in like a sorbo ball. He had already taken from Jonathan a snapshot that he carried about with him, though he hated to admit it, and this he laid on the manager's desk.

" If this is the lady who was with Gould then Bob's your uncle," said he. " And I don't mind telling you it'll be a weight off my mind if I can be assured it is."

" I told you," began Jonathan in a tense voice, but Crook stamped smartly on his foot.

" What the soldier said ain't evidence," he reminded him. " Likewise, two witnesses are better than one if you're sure they're going to agree."

The manager, loathing the situation and Crook even more, made some inquiries and presently a middle-aged chambermaid with virtue stamped all over her like a utility label was brought in. She said unhesitatingly that it wasn't the same lady. She had noticed particularly—she would, thought the graceless Crook, even the best of them weren't proof against Henry's unscrupulous charm —because the lady had seemed rather old to be married to such a striking man.

" Still, gold gilds even the fading lily," said Crook in his outspoken fashion. A dull colour stained the woman's cheeks. " Another of 'em," he thought. " What's this chap got that I haven't ? Ah, well, whever it is he can keep it. It's goin' to bring him to the little covered shed before he's through or I'm a Dutchman, and nobody who's ever heard my accent would believe that." As soon as Crook had got what he wanted, which included Gould's address, he marched out of Fishers.

" Now you've only got to write to your girl," he said. " If she answers, well and good, if she don't, we'll go down and take a looksee ourselves. We can't go down right away, we haven't a grain of evidence that anything is wrong, beyond the fact that Henry G. has a catholic taste in dames, and I at least knew that at the start."

So Jonathan, whose time was not his own and who had to be very cunning to get any time off at all, went back to his office and this night he wrote to Sarah. He waited a few days, but there was no reply—which was not Sarah's fault, because she never got the letter. Henry saw to that. By the time Jonathan had come to the conclusion it was time he appeared personally in the affair, it had made enormous strides, and the curtain on the third act of this fantastic melodrama had just gone up.

Jonathan waited four days for a reply to his letter ; waited with eagerness that changed to apprehension and apprehension that moved into a furious determination to discover the truth. It was on a wet and gloomy Friday night that he once again sought Crook's company.

" I'm going down to this place to-morrow," he announced abruptly. " It may be all right, but I don't think it is. I've been scouting round and I can't find a single person who's heard from Sarah since she was married. No letters have gone to her landlady's address. Of course, she may have filled in a P.O. form—I've no way of finding out—but if she was all right she'd have answered my letter."

" And you're off to Philadelphia in the morning ? Better take your man of affairs with you." His eyes were as bright as a robin's.

" It's very good of you," murmured Jonathan a little uncertainly.

" You're like the lady who married into the peerage and then had to pretend her mother was her old nurse," Crook accused him. " As a matter of fact, it's good old Henry Conscience behind the suggestion. Y'see, what you haven't grasped is that you're dealing with a killer. I'm pretty sure of that. Now, say it don't suit his book to have inquiries started as to his latest wife's present whereabouts, what's to stop him sending you to join her under the gooseberry bush—assuming she's there, that is ? No, I'm not talking through my titfer. I know these chaps. There comes a point when they think they're perfectly justified in gettin' rid of any obstacle that presents itself. You go down to this fairy cottage, ring the bell, announce you're a buddy of Mrs. G., and what happens ? ' Come in, my dear fellow, come in.' " Crook's voice changed with a suddenness that startled his companion. " In you go, and nobody sees you again until the woods and quarries give up the dead that are in them. You think I'm screwy, don't you ? All right, go down on your own, and presently, to-morrow or Monday, seeing Sunday's a general holiday, get through from the Other Side and tell me I was right. You see, livin' in a place like that the odds are he can do what he pleases, and who's to tell ? Now, you and me, if we was to try and put a body in the garden or drop it down a rubbish tip, we'd be seen sure as fate. There's always a Nosey Parker in a town with nothing better to do than inform on his neighbours and tell himself what a good citizen he is. But, as I read it, there's miles and miles of empty country down there—I was lookin' it up on the map and Rip Van Winkle could wake up in that cottage and not know what century he was in. Well, in you go in your feet and out you come in a sack, say. How many people had you thought of tellin' you were goin' down there ? "

" I've told you," Jonathan pointed out.

" And I've told you—and other chaps till my tongue's stiff—that what the soldier said ain't evidence. Mr. Murdering Gould's only got to say you never arrived, and it might take a couple of years digging up the woods proving he's a liar, and with the export programme and the rearmament programme and the forty-hour week, there ain't the labour to spare."

" What about my car ? " Jonathan reminded him.

" Chap's only got to drive it away and leave it in a wood or something. I wouldn't put it past him to put on your hat and coat and let everyone see you speedin' in the opposite direction. No, no, you're dealing with a very clever chap—within his limits. Luckily for us, those limits are very narrow. Now, if I come with you—it's what these writing chaps call a paradox. Twice one is two and twice two is four, but twice two is ninety-six if you know the way to score. I may only appear to be one person to you, but actually I represent the whole British public. Y'see, no chap wants to commit a murder in front of witnesses—too incriminatin'. Besides, he's goin' to be very nippy to put both of us out at the same time, and while he's coming bald-headed for you I can kick him on the shins or bang him on the head or something. So, you see, you'd get a witness to the crime if nothing more."

" That would be a great comfort," agreed Jonathan concisely.

" Cause of abstract justice," gabbled Crook. " Anyway, haven't you got any sense of duty to the community ? You oughtn't to release a killer."

" Have it your own way," said Jonathan. " Actually, I'd be very glad for you to come. Then if a rough house does develop and Sarah's still on the premises one of us might get her out of it, which is the main thing."

" Your mother ought to have christened you Lochinvar," said Crook approvingly.

The next morning dawned bright and clear, though the roads were still slippery after thirty-six hours of almost continuous rain. But the sun had come out and the first buds of spring were pushing through the black boughs, and Jonathan felt his heart lift as he climbed into Crook's ridiculous car, and they set forth.

" It's inaction one can't stand," he confided to his companion.

" I wouldn't know," said Crook simply. His enemies said he worked even during his sleep. If there was a hell anywhere he knew his share would be to sit with folded hands all through eternity. In fact, he couldn't do it.

They took a little longer to reach Spartan End than they had anticipated, thanks to taking a wrong turn. Once they were through Kings Benton the world seemed deserted.

" P'r'aps everybody goes to sleep on Saturday round here," hazarded Crook. " Or it could be we haven't noticed and we've driven right through into Sunday morning." Finally, however, they came to a narrow half-made road—a track, Crook called it, with a little notice saying, To Goblin Cottage Only. The notice was half-obscured by roots and long grass, and probably Gould was perfectly satisfied that this should be so. A traveller with less sharp eyes than the Criminals' Hope would probably have missed it altogether.

" Lucky we didn't bring your little biscuit-box," said he cheerfully, bumping up the lane. " The Gates of Hell couldn't stand against the Scourge."

But when they reached the gates of Goblin Cottage they found they had had their trouble for nothing, since these were not only locked but padlocked, and there was a label tied to one of the links inscribed in printed capitals : GONE AWAY.

" You wouldn't have said he was a chap who took risks, would you ? " mused Crook. " Pity he didn't leave a date for us. Then we might know where we were."

He dismounted from the car and walked a few steps farther up the lane. The quickset hedge made the cottage almost invisible, but he persevered until by making himself into a human croquet hoop, he could peer through and see the little building, desolate and dark, all the shutters closed, and an air of the end of the world hanging over everything.

> " I shall come back at last
> To this dark house to die,"

murmured Jonathan in his ear. " What next ? I'd like to get my hands on the fellow," he added with sudden ferocity.

" Take it easy," said Crook. " Leave these things to the chaps whose business it is, which don't mean us. If Henry Gould ain't the professional husband we think he may be he hasn't earned a rope round his neck ; and if he is, let the right people put it there."

" We've got to get Sarah away by hook or crook," Jonathan insisted, but his heart was sick within him.

" Queer things, dames," mused Crook. " If anyone was to invite me to make a place like that my home I'd be suspicious right away. Talk about a moated grange. Only a guilty conscience needs all that screening." He straightened himself and came back to the Scourge. " ' We traced her footprints to the bridge and farther there were none.' Well, he's beaten us to it. Now we better go back and try and pick up his trail. Getting dark, ain't it, for the time of day ? " And indeed the clear morning sky had given place to a brooding purple that betokened storm. " No sense getting drowned, always heard it was a damned uncomfortable death," Crook went on. " No, our best line is to get back to that green-grocer-cum-post-office we passed on the way in and find out if he left an address and when they beetled off. Y'know," he added, as the Scourge turned with a dexterity that would have done credit to a London taxicab, " this may be the answer—as to why you haven't had a letter, I mean. Say, they're moving about, she may only just have got yours. Or it may still be waitin' till they come back." His big capable hands grasped the wheel and they went bumping back along the road they had so laboriously climbed, leaving behind them the little dead house in the gathering storm.

At the post office an old lady who looked like Jack-in-the-Box's twin sister popped up from behind a counter.

" Mr. Gould ? You've missed him. Went up to London early yesterday morning with that poor young wife of his. She's going into a home or something. Don't know what's come over the young women nowadays. When I was a gel you weren't always running to doctors every time you had a stomach-ache, but when I was a gel you paid your own way and that made you think twice."

" What's wrong ? " asked Crook cheerfully.

" If you're asking me," said Mrs. Potts mysteriously, " I should say she wasn't but ninepence in the shilling."

" What rubbish," Jonathan began, but Crook shut him up with, " When you see what marriage does to people you can't blame a chap for stopping a bachelor. Give us the gen, Grannie," he went on.

" All I know," said the old woman, " is that they stopped here and collected a letter, and Mr. Gould told me they were going to London and he didn't know how

178

long it 'ud be before they got back. As soon as the young lady was able to travel they'd be going abroad."

" Didn't happen to mention where ? " drawled Crook.

" He did say Paris for a few days and then something about flying south. All this dashing about ! " The old mouth drew itself into a thin line. " Your own home town was good enough when I was a gel. My son—he wanted me once to go to London with him. Not me, I said. Better the devil you know than the devil you don't." Crook looked at her with a kind of reverent horror. Never to have seen London ! As well might some saint say he wasn't particular about visiting Paradise. " But this I do know," she went on, " he's been getting letters from that travel place—Bensons—with a London post-mark."

Crook silently applauded the interest taken by the countryman in his neighbours' affairs. " That the letter he came in for that last time ? "

" That's it."

" H'm. They might know. Now, tell me something else. Did Mr. Gould leave a forwarding address ? "

" He said he was going away to get quit of his troubles, and any letters there were could wait till he came back. *Poste restante* they call that," she added nonchalantly.

" Good for you," applauded Crook. " And Mrs. G. the same ? Or did they leave the name of the nursing home ? "

" She never had but one or two letters all the time she was here ; only wrote the same. So you couldn't expect more, could you ? Well, women with houses to look after don't have the time to waste on this everlasting scribbling."

" You don't happen to know the name of her doctor, do you ? "

Mrs. Potts bristled. " Who are you to ask me that ? "

" Matter of fact, I represent her. Lawyer, see."

" Lawyer ? " The old lady's little black eyes popped like corn. " Money troubles, p'r'aps ? "

" Money is the root of all evil, or so they say," Crook reminded her. " Now it's absolutely of the first importance that I get in touch with Mrs. Gould at once. Matter of life and death, really."

" Whose death ? " inquired Mrs. Potts.

" Wish I knew."

" Well, I don't know her doctor, and that's a fact," acknowledged the old woman regretfully. " All I know is they came here, and it was easy to see she was queer— white as a sheet she was. Funny how fine weather seems to make it worse to be ill ; ungrateful, I call it. Well, he picked up a letter like I said, and . . ." She stopped. " There's one thing now I come to think of it. He rung up somebody in London on the Thursday."

" That 'ud be a trunk call, which means you'll have a record."

" I don't know as I ought to give it you," demurred Mrs. Potts.

" You'll know all right if the police get dragged into this," prophesied Crook darkly.

" Well, I suppose there's no harm, seeing how it is. Hope not, I'm sure. Wait a minute and I'll get it for you." She stumped off, and Crook said :

" Rang up Thursday, went off Friday, left no address ; girl looked damned ill, house locked. Letter from Bensons. I don't like the look of it."

Mrs. Potts came back with a number written laboriously on a slip of paper. Milton 1704.

" Milton—that's the doctor's quarter," said Crook. " Well, you may have saved everybody's bacon this time, ma. If you say your prayers, put in one for us."

He got back into the Scourge and they shot London-wards. Jonathan glanced at his watch. " How late can we ring this number on a Saturday ? "

" If it's a nursing home, any hour."

" What do we do next ? "

" If she's there you go round to-morrow with a nice bunch of flowers."

" To be greeted with the news that she's allowed no visitors."

" When I was a young chap there was a saying about faint hearts and fair ladies," said Crook rather disgustedly. " All right, if you don't make it, round I go, representing Mrs. G. If they say I can't come in I'll offer 'em the police. Funny when you come to think of it how all foreigners are supposed to say ' Your police are wonderful,' but the British themselves would sooner have a gorilla to tea than a bobby. I shall say I've got to be sure that this really is Mrs. Henry Gould ; you'd better come along and do the identification."

" And then ? "

" Don't cross your bridges before you come to them. What worries me is that the bridges may have been blown up before H. G. beat his retreat to the Continent or wherever he is at this moment. In words of one syllable, that she may not be in the home at all."

" And all this elaborate telephoning is a blind ? "

" Could be," said Crook. " Could be." And thereafter maintained silence until they reached London. He stopped the car opposite 123 Bloomsbury Street and went hurrying up the endless stairs at a pace the younger man could envy. Bill was waiting, apparently quite unperturbed. " Get this number, there's a good chap," said Crook. " You've got the sort of voice a matron likes to hear. I just want to inquire for Mrs. Henry Gould."

Bill got through without difficulty. It was only after that the trouble started, for the porter who answered the telephone said there was no Mrs. Gould on the list of patients.

" I thought as much," said Crook, snatching the receiver away. " Hallo, who's that ? . . . I want to speak to the Matron. . . . Who ? Mrs. Henry Gould's legal representative. . . . Yes, I know Mrs. Gould isn't there. If she were I could talk to her herself. All right, tell the Matron the police are on their way."

This brought the Matron at a run. " Who is that ? " she demanded.

Crook began explaining all over again. " I understand you were expecting a Mrs. Sarah Gould on Friday."

" That is so," said the Matron. " Have you news ? "

" We're asking you," Crook pointed out. " Last we know of Mrs. Gould is she was coming Londonwards with her husband on Friday—yesterday, that is. You were expecting her ? "

" Certainly we were expecting her. Mr. Mortimer had gone to a great deal of trouble to make a room available, we refused another pressing case, but Dr. Forbes had made such a point of her coming in at once that Mr. Mortimer said——"

" We've got that part," Crook interrupted. " Any excuse why she didn't turn up ? "

" Mr. Gould rang up about half-past nine—his voice was rather faint—but he said Mrs. Gould had given him the slip and he wondered if she'd come on her own."

" Why should she do that, when she could be brought cosily to the door in her hubby's car ? " asked Crook sensibly.

" With these mental cases you can never tell."

" Mental ? "

" Well, it's what we call a nervous breakdown. Persecution mania. Think everyone's your enemy." Matron was being charmingly forthcoming. " I can only imagine there's been some accident."

" That's the way it looks to me, too," said Crook grimly. " Though I don't know that I'd call it an accident."

When he had hung up he sank back into his big shabby chair, looking both tired and deflated, an unusual circumstance with him. " Question : Where do we go from here ? That's a lonely road we came up, lots of quarries and measureless woods. . . ."

" But what's the sense of all this elaborate pretence ? " burst forth Jonathan. " Why drag all these extra people into the case ? "

" Oh, I don't think there can be any doubt that he

meant Mrs. Gould to believe it was all shipshape and above board. ' It's all right, my dear, kind Dr. Forbes has fixed up for you to go into a nursing home, we're going up in the morning.' Off they go—and somewhere he sheds the real Mrs. G. and carries on with the Bird of Paradise. Come to think of it, it's all Lombard Street to a china orange against his taking the chance of putting her in a home. Whatever yarn he tells the Matron won't cut much ice in the face of an expert's opinion, and if your young woman was in possession of her senses sooner or later she'd convince the doctor of the fact. Besides, we don't know what she may not have to tell."

" He seems to have hazed this Dr. Whatsisname all right."

" Because he was on the spot. But he can't be on the spot in a nursing home. No, it's as clear as the nose on my face that he never meant her to get there."

Jonathan looked quite frantic. "What can we do now?"

" Nothing more to-night. Now, my dear chap, do be reasonable. If anything's happened, as I rather fear it may —if he's the chap I think he is he's an expert at losing wives—it's too late to do anything about it. If he hasn't put out her light already the odds are he's got some reason for keeping it burning, and it'll be burning to-morrow as much as it is now. In the morning we'll go along to Bensons—no, I was forgetting, it's Sunday, they won't be working."

" The police ? " suggested Jonathan.

" Can you see them looking down their long noses when we say we're gunning for a husband whose wife's run away from him ? ' What the hell's it to do with you ? ' they'll ask. Tell you what we might do, though. Go along to London Airport. I'll spin a yarn."

" We don't know that he went by air."

" Forgetting what he said to that Jill-in-a-box at Kings Benton, ain't you ? Flying south with the swallows."

" I didn't realise that was meant literally. Will they tell you ? "

" You wait," said Crook.

Jonathan went home, sick with fear. " Oh, Sarah, Sarah," he whispered. She wouldn't have recognised this pale distraught young man for the composed young architect who had hitched his wagon to a star and was so lordly about not getting married until he could pay for everything cash down. But she couldn't hear him ; she wouldn't have heard him if he had been standing at her side and shouted in her ear.

XIX

THE SECRET OF GOBLIN COTTAGE

" THE SECRET of success," remarked Crook, " don't lie in a chap being brighter than the average or havin' second sight or anything of that kind, or even in knowing more than the next man. It's mainly knowin' the right people." Crook exemplified his creed ; he had buddies everywhere so it wasn't really surprising that he should prove to have a friend at court at London Airport. This man, whose name was Hitchcock, had been in a bit of a jam about a year previously and he still had reason to be grateful to Crook for his present life and liberty. Crook turned up as fresh as the morning, a haggard Jonathan beside him, and sought (and obtained) audience with this friend.

" Keep it under your hat till I give the word," he said ; " but I believe I'm on to the biggest thing since George Joseph Smith. Nice sensible name, Smith. Well, Gould's not so bad either. At a pinch I'd say there are probably a couple of thousand of them roaming round the country-side and quite a number of them might be called Henry."

" Who's your Henry Gould ? " asked Hitchcock patiently.

" I was tellin' you—reincarnation of G. J. Smith. Now, I've reason to believe he took off with a dame some time Friday. Paris flight. Can do ? "

He found, with satisfaction, that the bar was open and settled down to enjoy a pint, in the temperate manner in which pints can be enjoyed in 1950. People popped in and out, with or without luggage, the great planes stood about on the tarmac or roared away into the sky, and he watched them all with pleased satisfaction. Not that any of them impressed him to the point of wishing that he was aboard. " If man was meant to walk he'd have had four legs," he used to say, " and if he was meant to fly he'd have had wings." Anyhow, London was good enough for him. Say England to Crook and he saw London instantly, Piccadilly Circus and the milling crowds, Hyde Park with its nursemaids and dogs and lovers, Bloomsbury with its cosmopolitan population, the great red buses like reincarnated dragons, the long cars like hammer-headed sharks, and driven by chaps not altogether unlike 'em in many cases, the shop windows, the waterfront, the narrow alleys, the secret houses—he revelled in them all. You would have to gouge him out with a sardine server to get him away. Presently he got the V-sign from Hitchcock, who was looking puzzled.

" This chap of yours," he said ; " got his address ? " Crook supplied it. " Booked through Bensons. That's right. Only—you said Mr. and Mrs. Gould. But this chap only booked one passage."

Crook whistled softly. " Return ? "

" Yes. Went on Friday morning on the ten o'clock plane. Hope he found the weather better in Paris."

" Got the list of passengers ? "

" I could."

" Find out if there was a dame, London address, I fancy, also booking a single ticket."

And that was how Crook discovered the name of the Bird of Paradise.

" All the same," he confided to Jonathan, " it don't add up. The time factor don't work. He leaves the cottage early on Friday, but not so early the old lady don't have a word with him. I don't reckon she'd be down before, say, eight o'clock—besides, there was that letter he collected—and it's the best part of three hours to the airport. Well, no, not if he came direct with no stops and had a good road and no punctures. Say two hours forty minutes. But he couldn't do it under two hours. Well, then—he takes the next plane. But he didn't. Joe said he was on the ten o'clock. Then he has to leave about seven, passes the post office, say, seven-fifteen. Well, the letters might be in, though it ain't likely in a place that size, and even less likely the old girl would be feeling chirpy enough for conversation."

" Do we know for certain he saw the old girl ? "

" They both saw her. Don't you remember her sayin' how poorly Mrs. G. looked, and how it seemed more ungrateful to look ill on a fine day ? " He stopped abruptly, then pounded to his feet. " Suffering cats ! " he exclaimed. " I'm slipping, I'm slipping right down into the ditch. Almost time I signed up for the sunny side of the work'us wall. Come on. There's not a second to lose."

" Where do we go from here ? " asked the bewildered Jonathan, following him into the Scourge.

" Remember what yesterday was like ? Stinking black rain, all the morning. Joe just said, ' Hope he found the weather better in Paris.' Then how come Mrs. Thing——"

" Potts."

" Potts or Panns, it's all one. How come she said that bit about fine weather? Of course, it's as clear as mud now. Gould didn't call at the post office and get his letter and have his chat with the old dame on Friday morning, but *on Thursday afternoon*, when the sun was shinin'. I know the rain came on later, but the odds are they got back in the fine. He got his letter and knew everything was set for the morrow, he rang up Mortimer or the nursing home, and got everything fixed. All that was Thursday. He could have started at crack of dawn on Friday, most likely did."

" And Sarah ? "

" Don't you see ? " Crook sounded the klaxon and a Rolls-Bentley just ahead nearly jumped out of its shining armour. " Who's to say she ever left the cottage ? She didn't go to the nursing home, she didn't go to the airport. He didn't mean her to go to the nursing home, would be my guess. Why, he couldn't have done it in the time, and you don't dump patients at homes at that hour in the morning. He hadn't bought her a ticket—no, my guess is she stayed at home."

" But—the cottage is locked."

" Maybe that wouldn't worry her," said Crook, more grimly than ever. " Remember nobody saw her leave the cottage and my guess 'ud be she never did."

" Then—what now ? Where are you making for ? "

" Telephone. We've got to get Bill on to this. He's the neatest hand with a padlock outside a gaol, and he'd have most of 'em inside beat to a frazzle if it came to an open competition. We can't start going places till we've got through that gate." He found the public telephone and dived for it. " Until we're angels," he went on, waiting for his connection, " we can't fly over that hedge, and that's too long to wait."

Bill received the news that he was wanted at Heath Row with his usual composure.

" Has he got a car ? " asked Jonathan.

" He'll get one. Now, there's nothing you can do till he comes. No sense us going on in advance. Besides, he don't know the road, and this is on the direct route. You've just got to possess your soul in patience till he arrives."

It seemed to Jonathan a lifetime before a thin dark man with a ruined face that must once have been handsome came towards them, limping a little. He asked no questions, just got into the Scourge, and never turned a hair during the heart-shaking ride that followed. It was a tight squeeze for the three of them, particularly when one of the three was Crook, but the Scourge that looked as though it would fall to pieces if anything heavier than a kitten got into it took the load with equanimity. It was another of those deceptive clear mornings only too apt to turn to storm later in the day. They made a good pace, though it seemed to Jonathan that every vehicle on the road was in a conspiracy to bar their way. Nobody spoke, Crook and the young man were entirely concerned with thoughts of Sarah and her probable whereabouts ; as for Bill, no one ever knew what was passing in his mind.

They reached the cottage without mishap. Despite the sunlight it still had a desolate air. Now they could see more clearly that all the shutters were closed, and even the birds seemed to foreswear that deserted garden. Bill got out of the car and set to work with what seemed to Jonathan an intolerably leisurely air. He ranged up and down the lane, saying, " There must be some other way over." But the hedges grew high and thorny, and there was a drop of twelve feet on the other side ; as for plunging through them, that was an impossibility.

" Unless you want to be St. Sebastian the Second," said Crook. " Make a nice paragraph for the *Record,* but it wouldn't do your young woman much good." The padlock was an intricate one, and even when Bill had got that unfastened there was still the lock on the gate. This, however, presented few difficulties to one of Bill's attainments, and at last they were all hurrying up to the house. To Jonathan's surprise Crook paid no attention to that but went plunging round to the long ill-kept garden at the back.

" Do you think he's likely to have left a window open ? " gasped Jonathan, who for all his advantages in years and girth had his work cut out keeping up with the Criminals' Hope.

" Window hell," said Crook. " I don't expect to find her in the house at all. Well, be your age. He comes back with the fixed intention of going to Paris to-morrow with another lady. He's got to dump this one somewhere. And it had better be somewhere where she can't attract any attention. If she's in the house what's to hinder her opening one of the shutters and climbing out ? Oh, I know not many come up the lane, but you can't afford to take even hundred-to-one chances if your name's Henry Gould."

" Always supposing," said Jonathan, " that she's still alive."

" I'm not supposing that," said Crook grimly. " Only a fool leaves a dead body above ground." He was rampaging down the weed-grown path as he spoke, his sharp little brown eyes glancing ardently this way and that. " Drat the rain ! " he remarked. " Wipes out every trace of footprints. Who was the chap who flourished like a green bay tree ? "

" The ungodly," said Jonathan in a choked voice.

" Fits like a glove," acknowledged Crook.

Bill appeared round the corner of the cottage. " Hey, Crook. Something here that might interest you."

Crook spun round on his axis. " Where ? "

" In the garage."

Crook moved faster than you'd have thought a fat man could, Jonathan following on his heels. " You better wait a bit," Crook counselled him. " What is it, Bill ? "

" A sack," said Bill, and even the hardened Crook sickened a bit. He plunged into the building, but the sack Bill indicated contained nothing suitable for an inquest. It was half-full of a white substance.

" Lime," said Crook, and presumably it was the half-light of the garage that gave his plump face a yellowish tinge.

" Lime ? How does that help us ? "

" If ever you're dated for the little covered shed," Crook told him, " on the morning you go for your last walk they give a receipt for your body and for two sacks of lime. Now get me ? "

" Yes," said Jonathan. " To destroy the corpse, and prevent identification."

" Well, it ain't so easy to do that. There's teeth and bones and—oh, you'd be surprised what the nobs can discover these days. All the same, what does an honest man want lime for ? Not for the garden, not in this instance. The earth must have looked a bit like this before the Spirit breathed on the waters and brought the first signs of order out of chaos. What's that in the corner ? A spade ? Bring it along, Bill. It might be useful." The three of them left the shed and marched down the garden. At the pseudo rockery they paused. " Someone's been mucking about here fairly recently," said Crook. " Those branches and those swathes of grass pulled off. Can't say how recently because the rain's evened everything off, but it's worth digging, I'd say."

Jonathan stood with his hands in his pockets. "Oughtn't we to get in touch with the police ? " he asked in a choked voice.

" And find there's nothing here but a once-cherished pussy-cat ? Not much. I don't want to give the slops a chance to laugh their fat heads off at me. . . . Of course, if we find anything else . . ." Bill took up the spade and started to dig. He hadn't been at it very long when he struck something hard and white, something that had once been part of a living creature. " Go steady," Crook warned him. " It could still be a big dog."

But what they turned up during the next few minutes had never belonged to a dog.

" All the same," said Crook, " that's not your girl. I'm not a graveyard expert, but I know enough to tell you that's been underground quite a while before last Friday. I'd say it was a matter of years rather than months. Well, no need for us to trouble ourselves over that. This is where the police come in."

" In the meantime," said Jonathan in choked tones, " there's Sarah."

Bill was bending imperturbably over their discovery. " Lost a top finger-joint," he said.

" Sarah hadn't." You could have a sackful of corpses for the delectation of the police for all he cared, so long as Sarah's wasn't among them.

Crook walked back up the garden and stood staring at the back of the house. A jagged hole in one of the windows caught his eye. " Wonder how that happened ? Looks as if someone threw a stone. Now, why, if you want to attract attention, chuck a stone from the back garden ? And who would be in the back garden ? Only H. G. and spouse, one would imagine. Had she locked him out, and he threw a stone ? But why that window ? Well, then, suppose the stone was thrown from inside ? " He moved nearer. " If the stone came from outside you'd expect to find glass under the window. But there ain't none. Then it came from inside ? And why ? I'll tell you. If it's raining cats and dogs and there's a hole in the window it's obvious you'll have to close the shutters. Here, Bill, you can leave that for the minute—I never was one to do the police's job for them—and get us into the house." He stepped up and rattled the back door. " This is bolted as well as locked," he said confidently ; " chap must have left by the front." Bill came round and tackled the lock. There was a mortice as well as an ordinary lock, but even that didn't defeat him. All the same, it took time. The hall into which they eventually stepped was pitch-dark, because all the doors opening on to it were closed. When Jonathan turned the handle of the nearest, the door didn't open, because that was locked too.

" Locked from the outside," Crook confirmed. " Key taken away. I like this less and less. Don't waste time down here, Bill, go for that room with the smashed window." All the rooms upstairs were locked, too, but they weren't proof against Bill's cunning. Breaking and entering was child's play to him, and the police could say what they liked when they appeared on the scenes. While this was going on Crook who had taken a torch from his pocket, flashed it on to look for the telephone. But when he lifted the receiver he realised they weren't going to get the police so easy. Henry Gould was a man who believed that what is worth doing is worth doing—if not well, certainly thoroughly, and before leaving the cottage he had cut the wires. In a corner of the staircase something white glimmered faintly ; he stooped and picked it up. It was a linen handkerchief, with no name on it but a laundry mark, and it was sticky with some sweetish substance, like syrup or jam. Only jam would surely have left a coloured mark, however faint. On the whole he didn't think it was jam, and most probably it didn't matter anyhow. He felt a little aggrieved that it wasn't embroidered H. G., but the laundry mark would prove identification enough.

A shout from Bill brought him upstairs at the double. He had got the door open, but when he tried to push it back it jammed against something lying along the floor. Push though he might he couldn't force it back more than an inch or two. A sound broke from Jonathan that startled both men.

" Hold your horses," said Crook. " This is the best bit of news we've had since we started. Don't you see, if that's Mrs. G. blocking the road, as it must be, then she was alive when he locked the door. Well, obviously. You try lying a body across a threshold and then shutting and locking the door. It can't be done. Mind you, I don't say . . ." He flashed on his torch. The room was in darkness, because of the shutters, but the nature of the obstacle was now clear. The body was, however, lying close up to the door and the crack was too narrow to admit the passage of even a woman's hand. None of the men could hope to make it.

" The hinges ! " exclaimed Jonathan, but Crook shook his head.

" Not from this side." He stooped down. " The face is the other end," he said. " There's only one thing for it—shove. Luckily the door's flush in the middle of the wall. There's no question of crushing the skull. All the same, it's taking a chance, but at times like these there's nothing else to take."

It seemed to Jonathan an interminable time before the door had been forced open a few inches. Then Crook crouched down and balling his fists, pushed at the soft thing lying there in the dark. And so after much terror and suspense Bill, the thinnest of the three, was able to wriggle through and pull the body clear.

X X

ENCOUNTER IN A LANE

HE LAID HER on the bed and Jonathan went across to open the shutters, but these were padlocked on the inside shutting out not only light but air. He turned abruptly. " What did he do to her ? "

" Nothing positive," said Bill, who had an amazing repertoire of abilities. " Heart's still going," he announced briefly, after a minute or so. " Weak, but—well, she's starved, and nearly suffocated." He reached a hand into his hip pocket and brought out a flask of brandy.

" I'll get a doctor," said Jonathan in an agony of dread. " The telephone——"

" Cut," said Crook. " You stay and give Bill a hand. Get some water boiling. Blankets." He looked round and tore open a wardrobe, pulling out the clothes hugger-mugger in a way that would have made a woman weep.

Bill was still stooping over the unconscious girl, forcing the brandy between her set teeth. Crook's torch supplied the only light, for when they examined the lamp they found the oil had burned dry.

" There must be candles somewhere or more oil," said Crook impatiently. The light of the torch fell on the girl's hands ; they were raw where they had battered in vain against the panels of the door, scratched and bleeding to show how she had torn, equally vainly, at the window fastenings.

" She's drugged on top of everything else," said Bill in a puzzled voice. " That's queer."

" Not really," contradicted Jonathan in a rather unpleasant tone. " If he was going to oil out he'd clearly drug her first so that she wouldn't hear."

" The effects of a drug don't usually last so long." Bill's voice was still quite impersonal. " After all, Gould cleared out on Friday morning early, this is Sunday afternoon. If he gave her the drug before he left the effect would have worn off by now. No, she must have taken something herself. Because, you see, she's hammered her fists raw trying to get out. Then I suppose she realised just what her loving spouse had in mind. She was to stay here a week, a fortnight—who knows ? Anyway, by the time he came back she wouldn't be in any fit state to argue with him."

" This is ridiculous," said Crook crossly, and Bill reflected with some surprise that in all their years together he had seldom seen Crook out of temper. " We've got to have some light on the scene. This fiddling little torch. . . . You "—he turned to Jonathan—" go down and bust open the kitchen door, get some oil, find a kettle, get a fire going. Go on, what are you waiting for ? It's your girl, isn't it ? "

While Jonathan methodically kicked down the kitchen door—Bill couldn't be spared from his duties as sick nurse —Crook went down on all fours and crawled round the room flashing the fiddling little torch into every corner. He found two objects of interest. On the floor under the bed was a bottle containing sleeping mixture ; a good part of the contents was spilled on the floor. He sat back on his haunches considering.

" Not difficult," he said. " Girl must have decided it was easier to peg out from an overdraught than slow starvation, and however dotty she may have been—to marry him in the first place, I mean—she wasn't dotty enough to suppose he'd come back while she was still in the land of the living. There wasn't a hope she could unfasten the shutters or attract attention in any conceivable way. But—by this time, I dare say, the lamp had gone out, and no matter how brightly the sun was shining outside you wouldn't see anything in this room—so she grabbed for the bottle and what with the cold and being a bit light-headed, I shouldn't wonder—she dropped it. Mind you, she must have taken some of the tablets, but not a fatal dose." He stopped. Both men had an uncomfortable vision of the distraught girl groping about in the dark, talking to herself, perhaps, laughing even—delirium did funny things to you—saw the wavering, uncertain hands feeling in the blackness for the tablets that would bring release but (mercifully as it turned out) never quite locating them.

The other thing he found was a bottle of ginger in syrup which stood on the bedside table. None had been taken out of the jar, but it had been opened, as a faint sticky rim betrayed.

" Funny that," said Crook. " You'd think a girl who was starving would have wolfed even preserved ginger. There's a long fork and everything left ready on a pretty plate with roses round the rim. No knife though. That significant ? "

Bill looked at him questioningly. " Significant ? "

" Well, look at the size of the pieces of ginger. You or me might push a great slab like that into our mouths, but a girl with a dainty trap 'ud just naturally look round for a knife and a plate. Whoever left that bottle there wanted to make sure the ginger 'ud be swallowed whole. Me, Bill, I'm a simple chap. Cause and effect are good enough for me, and if I see a set-up like that it's just second nature to me to be suspicious. Specially when I see it's been opened. Now supposing you open a bottle of anything, what's the idea ? " He lifted his arm and went through the motions of drinking. " You don't open it just because you've nothing else to do for the time bein', now do you ? If the little lady had opened the bottle it 'ud be because she meant to sample what was inside it. But it ain't been sampled, Bill. That's the important point. It ain't been sampled. Ergo—she didn't open it. Ergo, Mr. Murdering

Gould did, there bein' no one else on the premises. Opened it and put it nice and handy by the bed, with a nice long fork alongside. I'd stake my davy, Bill, when they come to examine that jar they'll find the top two or three pieces have been cut open and a little something's been put in. Or maybe not the first two or three pieces."

" Poisoned ? He's not a chemist, is he ? "

" Flora Ransome that was died of an overdose of hyoscin, and I don't think it was accident and I don't think it was suicide. If our Mr. G. could do that, doctoring a bit of ginger would be child's play."

" How's he going to explain it away to the authorities? "

" Easy as winking to a chap of his experience. He's already prepared the ground with Matron. I think when he comes back in a day or two he'll unpadlock everything and find his dear darling wife has had a fit of melancholia and taken her own life. Sleeping tablets, see ? He had to be away on business ; she was supposed to be going into a nursing home, but wouldn't go. Insisted on being left, wouldn't have a friend to stay, and then as soon as she was alone—hey presto, for the high jump."

" It doesn't sound too good," said Bill doubtfully.

" If it's good enough to get him off the gallows it'll be good enough for Mr. G. Wonder if she had any money ? Must have had something or he wouldn't have married her. How's she doing now ? "

" That chap below must be cutting down trees to make a fire," said Bill sourly, but at that moment Jonathan came in carrying a tray of tea—kitchen pot, odd cup and saucer, lashings of sugar, condensed milk, and a stone hot-water bottle, which, he said, was all he could find.

" Is she going to be all right ? " he asked feverishly. " They cook on oil here, which is very nice, I dare say, but it takes a whale of a time getting going. I've brought some up, and a couple of candles. I'll fill the lamp and then we can see a bit better."

" She'll do with Bill for head nurse," Crook told him " Me, I'm going to look for a doctor. And the police

But they can wait. We don't want our patient harried by a Sense of Duty in a blue uniform."

"Turn 'em loose on the bones on the lawn," said Bill. Jonathan filled up the lamp and adjusted the wick. When the flame had steadied to a garden glow all three men had a horrible shock. Scrawled in crazy uneven capitals on the surface of the looking-glass and on two of the walls themselves was the word MURDER.

The fact that the letters were a flaming scarlet made it the more shocking.

"Lipstick," said the knowledgeable Crook. "Don't touch those. They're going to be a big help in getting our Henry underground. And don't tell me," he added to Jonathan, "that your girl's the kind that won't testify against a husband, because it don't matter if she is. He'll be like the psalmist's buddy who was hanged out of his own mouth."

He left them to it and went down the stairs like a ton of bricks and out to the waiting Scourge.

There would be a telephone at the post office, and old Ma Potts could tell him the name of the nearest doctor. He had noted the name Forbes on the bottle of sleeping mixture, and an address at Redmondstone. "Went pretty far afield to get advice, and who could blame him ? " he reflected characteristically, getting the little car going. He had rounded a couple of bends when his quick ear caught the sound of another engine, and he slowed almost to a walk. A few seconds later a handsome dark-blue car came round the corner and stopped abruptly with a squeal of brakes. The tall dark man at the driving-wheel was as handsome as the car.

Crook leaned out. "This is a cul-de-sac," he yelled, "and why the blanketty blanketty so-and-so who owns the house can't put a notice at the mouth of the lane to say so, beats me."

"How inconvenient for you," said the stranger, with a smile that had knocked dozens of women off their demure perches. "Were you paying a call ? "

197

"Do I look dressed for poodle-faking?" Crook demanded. "Anyway, there only seems to be one house up there and that's locked up, so if you were planning a surprise visit——"

"I'm so sorry," murmured the stranger. "It happens to be my house. I've been away. And you know there is a notice at the foot of the lane saying, To Goblin House Only."

"Must have missed it," lied Crook glibly. "Well, what happens now? Can you pull over a bit?"

"Will that car of yours climb the bank?" The stranger's voice was very dubious.

"If there's no other way," Crook promised him, "she'll run up your bonnet and over your lid."

This was a situation he hadn't foreseen, and he wasn't yet sure how best to tackle it. On the one hand it was important to get doctors and police on the scenes as early as possible, and it would be a scoop to find the murderer-elect there, too. On the other, it was going to take all of fifteen minutes to get to the post office, make his connection and persuade a doctor that he wasn't playing a practical joke. The nearest doctor was probably at Kings Benton, and he had got to come out—that would mean holding the fort for approximately half an hour. Meanwhile, there were the two men and the unconscious girl in the cottage. Both kitchen and bedroom were at the back of the house, both men were absorbed in their life-saving task, Gould could steal up and surprise them before they were aware of his arrival. The big iron gates were unfastened, and his first glimpse of them would warn Gould that he was in a very nasty spot indeed. Crook didn't doubt for a moment that he was armed, nor did he imagine that he would scruple to use his weapon. And to Crook, at all events, it was no consolation to realise that Mr. Henry Gould's race was, in any case, pretty nearly run. If he didn't keep the last bullet for himself—well, the police would provide a very nice rope. But what of Jonathan and the girl? None of that would be much use to them if they had taken the first instalment of bullets. As for Bill, Crook would sooner have lost an arm or leg than his partner of twenty years standing. And not simply because Bill was so useful. He would have told you he hadn't much use for hearts, unless they belonged to sheep and were served up piping hot, stuffed, with greens as an accompaniment, but in their unsentimental way Bill had been playing Jonathan to Crook's David for a long time now. " And that's the way I like it," said Crook. " And I don't see why H. G. should be allowed to muck things up for us." It was different for the women, of course. They were natural suckers. . . . So, " If you can pull back a bit, round the next corner, say, I'll see what I can do," he suggested politely.

The driver of the blue car looked doubtful. But since they clearly could not spend the rest of their lives bonnet to bonnet, he drew back. " Come on," he called a minute later, " go slow for Pete's sake. A crash here would be no joke."

" No more it would," Crook called back. " But," he added, standing on the accelerator and going hell for leather round the bend, " it's just what you're going to have."

It was madman's tactics and he knew it, but then he also knew it was their one chance. He couldn't allow Gould to go up to the house and chance him picking off those three, or any one of them, and there was no other way in which he could stop him. As he rounded the bend he twisted his steering-wheel furiously to the right so as to avoid a direct impact. But the shock was quite severe enough. Gould, taken completely by surprise, was knocked half-silly by the collision.

" What the hell do you think you're doing ? " he stammered. " Might have . . ." Crook, his cap almost covering his eyes, reached out, hooked a brawny arm round his assailant's neck and banged his head hard on his own steering-wheel. For good luck he banged it again. Of course, by the law of averages the Scourge should have taken the major part of the punishment, but the Scourge was like her owner, always doing the unexpected. Gould groaned and Crook did a little choking on his own account, not enough to be fatal, but enough to ensure that there couldn't be any chance of the lady-killer continuing his journey for a while. Then he methodically frisked him for his gun, and noted with satisfaction that the car was in no better shape than her driver. The Scourge wasn't exactly a picture, either, but Crook had no fears for her. Any car that had triumphed over so many vicissitudes would (he was convinced) live to fight again. Anyway, there was no time to spare for her at the moment. Henry would recover soon enough, but he owed it to Bill to get a doctor to Sarah as soon as possible. Disentangling himself from the wreckage, limping a bit because, however well you plan these encounters, it's almost impossible to get off scot-free yourself, quite unaware of a bleeding cut over one thick red eyebrow and a long angry scratch on his cheek, he set off down the lane, Henry's revolver swinging in his hand in the most melodramatic manner conceivable. It had seemed quite a short journey in the Scourge, but it seemed as long as the path to Paradise now. He had a growing suspicion that his ankle wasn't quite as weather-tight as it had been before the smash, but he limped savagely on till he reached the mouth of the lane. All things considered, it really wasn't surprising that a small boy riding a bicycle that was too big for him without holding on to the handlebars let out a roar of terror and promptly fell off.

"Serve you right for showing off," said Crook unsympathetically, stooping to rescue, not the child, but the bicycle. "Here, I'm going to hire this for half an hour. I'll leave it at the post office." He thrust a ten-shilling note into the boy's hands, and shakily mounted the machine. It was as well that he wasn't a self-conscious man or he might have followed the little lad's example, and fallen off with humiliation into the dust. He had tossed the revolver into the basket in front, and once he was well away he realised that it wasn't even a boy's bicycle he was riding, but the boy's sister's. He hadn't been astride a cycle since the year he stayed in Norfolk and found the forgotten village and the corpse in the vestry, and at least that had been built for an adult. He wasn't a tall man, but he was broad and heavy, and the handle-bars were lost in his huge palms, while his ginger-bright posterior bulged over the diminutive saddle. He panted as though he were climbing a mountain and he pedalled away like one of those society women who ride a stationary cycle to reduce weight. Luckily the road seemed quite empty until round a corner he happened on an A.A. man in his striking yellow uniform. Crook stretched out a hand. " For the Lord's sake help me to get off this thing," he bawled. The fellow was so surprised that he caught the arm, and the next instant found himself supporting both Crook and the bicycle.

" What's the idea ? " he demanded. " Doing it for a bet ? Fallen off once already, haven't you ? " Then he saw the revolver in the basket, and he turned pale. " Is that thing loaded ? "

" You bet it is," said Crook. " Don't go pointing it at people. And for the Lord's sake get the police—and a doctor—and don't ask any questions. We've got two probable corpses on our hands, and I want to save 'em both."

Overwhelmed by Crook's exuberance the A.A. man unlocked the yellow box and lifted the receiver. Crook shoved his head inside. " And get a mechanic. There's two smashed cars as well as two near-corpses," he shouted.

" Don't believe in doing things by halves, do you ? " said the A.A. man in injured tones. " And you'll have another claim for a deaf aid if you go shouting in my ear like that."

He put out a hand to shove Crook back into the road, and Crook went. His ear had caught the sound of a car coming in the opposite direction and he hailed it madly, for it had a label DOCTOR on the windscreen. He wondered why. Of course during the war doctors had labelled their cars, when petrol was short, and a man with a car had to explain what right he had to be on the roads at all. Crook wondered now as he had often wondered then how many unofficial doctors had been driving round England during those five years. Not many, he decided, anyway, not for long. Even he, who didn't approve of handing bouquets to the police, had to admit that quite often they did know their onions.

" Hey ! " yelled Crook, and the car stopped abruptly. He still had no notion how ferocious he looked. The cold wind had dried up the blood over his eyes and the wide scratch on his cheek, but he still didn't look the sort of person you would expect to meet on a harmless English road.

" You making a film ? " asked the doctor brusquely, " or been in an accident ? "

" See any film-van ? " inquired Crook equally brusquely. " As for an accident, murder's nearer the point."

The doctor looked round and saw the little boy's bicycle that had belonged to a girl. " If you've been riding that you've been asking for whatever was coming to you," said he.

Crook wrenched open the door of the car. " Right along and up the lane," he said. " Murder was the intention, but you may just be in time. Come to that," he added violently, " you have to be. Can't start changing my motto at my time of life. Crook always gets his man, that's what they say. Well, I've got him all right, and living or dead who cares ? But it's the little lady. . . ."

" Shock," thought the doctor charitably. " Chap's had a shock. What little lady ? " he asked aloud.

" At Goblin Cottage. Tell me, Doc, how long can a girl live in a locked room ? How many days, I mean ? "

" Depends on how much air can seep in. Depends on the condition of the heart. Depends if she loses her nerve and tries to put an end to her own life."

"I wouldn't know about that," said Crook, but his mind was full of a picture of a bottle of sleeping stuff that had rolled under the bed. "Never say again, I don't believe in Providence," he reflected. "She's breathing," he said aloud, "or she was when I left. Turn here," he added ; "but go slow after the first five minutes. There's been a jam."

When the doctor saw the two cars interlocked he said in angry tones, "Chaps who try to pass in a lane this width deserve anything that's coming to them."

"Oh, he didn't know it was me coming," explained Crook, as if that explained everything. "He's not your patient anyway. The police are coming for him. That chap in the A.A. box was calling them—and a doctor. Your girl's up at the cottage itself."

"The police are going to be nearly as pleased as I am when they see the set-up here," the doctor told him. "Hope to heaven they have the sense not to ram my car." He got out and walked up to the wreckage.

"Not dead, is he ? " asked Crook anxiously. "I don't want him dead."

The doctor didn't answer for a moment. Then he said, "Concussion. That's all. Should be all right with proper attention. They'll want an ambulance, though, and they'd better get a breakdown gang to clear all this muck away."

"What are you calling muck ? " asked Crook, looking with yearning eyes at the little red car crushed up against the handsome blue one like a kitten against its mother. And not the sort of kitten a pedigree mamma would be keen to own at that. But Crook saw her as the heroine of Charles Kingsley's poem saw the doll lost in the hayfield.

> One arm trodden off by the cows, dears,
> And her hair not the least bit curled.
> Still for old sake's sake she is still, dears,
> The prettiest doll in the world.

He felt like a deserter when he scrambled round the edge of the wreckage and led the way up to the cottage.

XXI

THE NET CLOSES

WHEN THE A.A. man came out of the yellow box and found the road empty his face was good enough for ITMA. The child's bicycle lay in the road, and the incredible man who had been riding it—and he was good enough for Variety Bandbox—had disappeared. Not even a note. The A.A. man looked up and down the road and then lifted his eyes on high, as though he expected to find Crook up a tree like Zaccheus or even hovering in the air like some Picasso type of angel. But he had simply disappeared. "Gone back round the corner?" he reflected, for the road ahead stretched straight for a mile or more and there was no traffic on it at all. He hurried round the bend leading the bicycle and saw a figure in the distance approaching him at a good pace. But it wasn't the stout man in the brown suit, but a little boy clutching something in his hand. When he saw the A.A. man he began to run.

"Golly, another of 'em," groaned the A.A. man, but it became clear after a minute or two that it was the bicycle and not its leader who was his objective. "Where did you come from, sonny?" he asked. "Hey, what are you doing with that bike?"

"It's my sister's; she loaned it me. Leastways——"

The A.A. man grinned a little. "You mean, you borrowed it."

"She wasn't using it," said the little boy defensively.

"And what's that in your hand?"

"That's a note." He sounded more defensive than ever. "*He* gave it me. The man with the gun."

"So he tumbled you off your bicycle and gave you ten bob and went off on it, the machine, I mean. H'm. Who did you think it was? Dick Barton?" The little boy directed upon him a look of such scorn that he almost shrivelled up. He felt himself turning red.

" Reckon you don't know much about Dick Barton," said the little boy. " And this money's mine. He give it me. For the bike." He looked round. " Where is he ? "

" Just what I was wondering. Here, take your machine."

The little boy paused in the act of mounting. " Where's the gun, mister ? "

" The gun ? Oh, yes. I've got it here."

The little boy got off the bicycle again. " Let's have a hold of it."

" Not likely," said the A.A. man. " It's probably loaded."

The little boy's face became positively ecstatic. " I wouldn't press the trigger. Anyway, there'll be a safety-catch."

" You can't teach kids anything," thought the A.A. man. He retrieved the gun. Gingerly. The little boy was right. There was a safety-catch. And it was up.

" Now, look," he said in serious tones. " I can't let you touch this, because of fingerprints."

The little boy's eyes resembled those of the dog in the fairy tale that were as large as saucers.

" Coo, mister. You don't mean—murder ? " It was clear that this was the most wonderful moment of his life.

" Don't ask me. I wasn't there. I only know . . . Ah ! " Round the farther corner came the familiar sight of a police car. " Now, you get along," he said. But the little boy wasn't having any. The police—and a chap with a gun—and ten bob—all at the same time. He shoved his free hand into his pocket and waited.

The police took charge of the revolver, looked askance at the little boy, asked where Ginger had got to, listened with disfavour to the A.A. man's admission that he'd just disappeared, and then turned their attention to the youngster. " Come down that lane," said the little boy. " Goes to Goblin Cottage, that does. Nowhere else.

Waving the gun, he was. Knocked me off my bike and went off on it. Cor, didn't half look funny."

The police still looking distrustful, went on up the lane ; they hadn't gone far when they found their way blocked by a dark-green car. Beyond that was a blue car, and beyond that something that looked as if it had been made out of a couple of red biscuit tins. Inside the blue car was a body. Some chap driving up, tenant or owner of the cottage, most likely, crashed into by the red monstrosity. (They weren't London police and they didn't recognise the Scourge.) As for the third car, it was clear that had belonged to a doctor, though why he hadn't stopped to do something about the injured man was anybody's guess. They were still wondering about this when they were joined by the little boy on the bicycle.

" Is it a murder, mister ? "

" You go on home," said one of the policemen.

" You can't do that to me," said the little boy, who seemed clearly aware of his rights under a democracy. " Why, I'm a witness. I see the fellow come down the lane waving a gun. Blood all over his face, he had, shouting something terrible."

The doctor who had accompanied the police and one of the policemen stayed with the wreckage, and the little boy stayed too ; the other policeman pushed past up the lane. They would want an ambulance for the man in the car and there would be a telephone at the cottage. He couldn't be expected to know the wires had been cut.

The cottage hummed like a hive. At first glance it seemed full of people. The man who had been waving the revolver, with a face still patched with blood, came down to the door to greet him.

" Nice work," he said. " I could have stowed a couple of corpses away in the time. Still, she ain't going to peg out this time, no thanks to you. One day the force 'ull realise it's there to prevent crime. You'd better come in," he added, standing aside.

" What's all this about ? " asked the policeman.

" Attempted murder, that's all."

The first doctor, whose name was Peterson, appeared on the stairs.

" Who's that ? "

" Police."

" I can't have my patient disturbed at the moment. She'll be able to make a statement later, but not now. She's suffering from shock and exhaustion, but there's no actual injury. When they've cleared the lane you'd better get her away from here."

" Who is she ? " asked the police.

" Mrs. Sarah Gould—so far as she knows." (That was Crook, of course.) " My guess 'ud be she's still Miss Sarah Templeton. You'll have to wait till the chap in the car comes round to get all the facts."

" Who's he ? " asked the policeman, standing squarely at the foot of the stairs so that no one could get by.

" Bluebeard 1950, would be my guess," said Crook. " There's one corpse in the garden, by the way. Been there some time by the look of it, and for all I know, the place is strewn with 'em."

" And how much do you know ? " The policeman's voice was curt. He didn't take to Crook. For some reason the authorities hardly ever did.

" Ever hear of a chap called Kiss ? " inquired Crook. " A Bulgarian, he was. Had a way with him with servant-girls. Used to lure 'em to his villa and, when he was through with 'em, they were all found in the garden laid out in neat rows. All except six. They were in jars in the cellar. Cemetery full, see. I haven't got down to H. G.'s cellar yet."

Jonathan came out of the room upstairs to say, " Is that the ambulance ? Well, we'd better get one right away."

But a faint voice from the bedroom whispered his name and he went back as though someone had jerked him on a string.

" Can't you open some windows ? " asked the police. " The place is dark as pitch."

" The chap in the car has all the keys on his ring," Crook assured them. " We had to break the door down to get in. Not that Bill couldn't oblige if you insist." He came down till he was standing level with the police officer. " I'll put you in the picture," he offered generously. " This is a case of attempted murder. I told you that before."

He had to admit that the story he proceeded to unfold sounded unlikely enough, except that the police know that no story, however fantastic, is too strange to be true. This one took down Crook's tale, had a word with Dr. Peterson, and came up to look at Henry's last victim. Sarah was conscious now, but in no position to talk. " That can wait," the doctor urged. " She'll be all right. She was suffering from starvation, locked in here with not even a biscuit so far as we can tell."

Jonathan had found candles and lighted them all over the room ; they hadn't tampered with the padlocks on the shutters, because Crook said it would be better to touch as little as possible until the police arrived. The officer looked round.

" There's a bottle of Chinese ginger there," he said. " Funny she didn't touch that."

" P'r'aps she didn't like ginger," said the doctor.

" If she didn't like it what was it doing here ? "

" One to you, brother," said Crook generously. " I'll tell you what I think. See this handkerchief ? Gent's. Sticky, but not stained as it would be if it had been wrapped round a jar of jam, say. But suppose you open a jar of ginger and then wipe your hands on your hanky— well, I leave it to you. You better take that ginger in charge," he went on. " Exhibit No. 1. Lucky for the girl she didn't take it. Maybe she thought it a bit queer it should be opened so carefully for her. One thing, she wasn't out when Gould left the cottage, because she must have got off the bed and rolled herself to the door to get some air into her lungs. That's where we found her," he added politely to the police. " Rolled up against the door. Had a job to get it open. Lucky for her, anyway, these old cottages let in a lot of draughts. Next time our Mr. G. wants to put a wife out he better have a draught excluder nailed on the door first."

Most of this was Greek to the police, but Crook kindly explained his meaning.

The policeman didn't precisely thank him, but took charge of the jar of ginger, which was much more to the point, and went off to call an ambulance.

" Two ambulances," suggested Crook. " Or don't married folk rate an ambulance apiece ? Next thing," he added nonchalantly, " is to find out about the Bird of Paradise—our chap's next intended. If she's still above ground I'd guess she's making the sort of noises that 'ud startle the rest of the B. of P. race into fits."

Henry was certainly giving the police a good run for their money. He had them working for him all over the place, like any bloated capitalist. One lot took charge of the bones in the rockery, another had Sarah on their hands, a third were keeping watch over Henry himself and, unbeknownst to them at the time, a fourth was having a pretty warm quarter of an hour with Mrs. Lily Abbott, Crook's and Jonathan's Bird of Paradise.

That very Sunday morning she had been as contented as any woman living, sitting in a café in Paris with the most delightful man in the world, drinking chocolate and listening to his plans for an excursion for that afternoon.

" Don't want to spend the whole day here," said Henry, with more truth than she could conceivably realise at that stage. " You wait here for a few minutes and I'll find out about getting a car. By the way, I left most of my notes at the hotel. If you've got any by you it would save me going back." Trustfully she handed him her wallet ; he abstracted the large notes and handed it

back ; then off he went as debonair as a spring morning,
and that was the last she saw of him that side of the
Channel. She waited quite a long time, watching people,
enjoying the stir and bustle and colour all about her. She
ordered more chocolate and drank that, and then it
occurred to her that Henry was being an unusually
long time. And she began to wonder if something had
gone wrong. It shouldn't take all this time to arrange to
hire a car, and if he couldn't get one why hadn't he come
back to tell her ? She was instantly sure that there had
been an accident, and remembered the ferocious driving
of Parisian motorists. Quite likely Henry, whose middle
names were surely Bayard Galahad, was lying in a French
mortuary. She started up, paid for the chocolate, and
hurried away. If there had been an accident she supposed
the information would be sent to the hotel, but half-way
there it occurred to her that Henry might have stopped
to buy her a *cadeau*. She had taken the precaution of
smuggling £100 of English money over with her, as well
as some valuable jewellery ; she told Henry it was quite
safe. You bought some Paris gowns and said they had
been given you by a friend resident there. She had a
woman who would alibi her. In short, she was the
greatest possible contrast to Flora Ransome, and yet she
was as easily trapped as that unsuspecting spinster had
been. As she neared the hotel she saw someone looking
remarkably like Henry going by in a taxi, and she thought,
" He'll look for me at the café and perhaps he'll be
annoyed to find I've left." She knew men hated impatient
and exacting women, so she turned and hurried back to
the café, pausing on the way to buy a *cadeau* herself, to
soften Henry's possible annoyance. She was confident
that she would find him waiting and when she got back
and found he wasn't there she was sure the worst had
happened—he had arrived, found her gone, and departed
in a huff. But that would only have been a trifle. The
worst was something she hadn't even considered. She
spoke excellent French and she approached a waiter and

asked if he had noticed Henry come back, but the waiter hadn't and nobody else could give her any information, for the excellent reason that Henry hadn't come back to the café at all. Thoroughly disturbed now, she hailed a cab and was driven back to the hotel. Here she learned that Henry had packed his luggage and departed at very short notice. He explained that he had a message recalling him to England.

But he left some note ? For the sake of appearances the Bird of Paradise put up a pretty good bluff, but her heart was sinking like a stone. Henry *couldn't* have had a message. The hotel would know if a telegram had been received and it seemed that it hadn't. Nor had anyone telephoned him.

She said in as casual a voice as she could manage, " No doubt he will ring me up this evening and return to-morrow." But up in the room they had shared she looked round in despair that presently accentuated into rage. A quick search revealed the fact that not only was all his baggage missing but also her jewel-case. Her wallet, containing her return ticket and passport, was still in her own possession, but she had recklessly passed Henry all her large French money. What she had left would barely get her home. Now she was in a pretty pass. To go to the British Consul meant uncovering the truth of the episode, which was—*tout court*—that she had agreed to come to Paris with a man she scarcely knew, whom she had met in an hotel bar some weeks ago in London, with whom she had spent a night soon after that solitary meeting, and who had bamboozled, robbed and ditched her in a Paris hotel. Nevertheless, unlike Flora Ransome, she was a woman of spirit. She was also a woman of the world and cared little for anyone's opinion. Sitting in a low chair staring out of the window, seeing nothing of the scene beyond, she prepared her story. Henry was a married man—so much he had told her. His wife was a nervous invalid from whom he could not, on account of her poor health and spirits, obtain a divorce. He had proposed that they should start an *affaire*, give each other a good time, he said. She began to wonder if the wife was part of the myth. It wouldn't be the least surprising if she were. As for tracking Henry down, the only address he had given her was a London club, and there was no reason to suppose that he was even a member of that. Nevertheless, recalling the value of the jewels, she didn't intend to let him get away with it. The British police were not concerned with morals unless they constituted an offence against the law. The money, the one hundred pounds she had illicitly sneaked out of the country, she could not claim, but the jewels were worth much more than that. It was fortunate that it was a Sunday. Henry couldn't dispose of them before morning, and before morning she intended to be on his trail.

Hurrying out of the hotel again, she drove to the airport, where she explained that she was to meet her brother, Mr. Henry Gould. The airport officials couldn't have been nicer. They said Mr. Gould had departed on the last flight. He had left no message for Madame, presumably anticipating that she would follow by the next plane. Thanking heaven she still had her return ticket and passport, she went back to the hotel, explaining that there had been a message at the airport for her to join her husband in England. It was something that Henry should have paid the hotel bill—probably they had refused to let him go until he did—and she had some English pounds that she encashed at the hotel. It was late when she got back, for she had had to wait till the afternoon was well advanced to get a place on a returning plane. As soon as she had dumped her luggage she went round to the police station where she preferred a charge against Henry for theft. As she had anticipated, the club whose name he had given had never heard of him.

" Bensons would know," she said, and the police observed dryly that Bensons were not open on a Sunday evening.

Reluctantly she agreed to wait till the morning, but she

gave a description of the jewellery to be circulated to all business houses.

" These women ! " said the police officer who took her statement. " You'd think by that age they'd have more sense. Of course, if he's an old hand it's san fairy ann, so far as her stuff's concerned."

His companion was looking thoughtful. " This reminds me of something," he said.

" She does ? I could tell you——"

" No. The set-up, I mean. There was a case like this some time back, suicide, it was. Lady came home to find her stuff had disappeared and not being like this one, she went off and took an overdose. Husband didn't turn up at the inquest. Now, Sarge, that chap was tall and dark and had a way with him, according to the landlady, and his name was Henry something-or-other. Could be coincidence, of course, but——"

" All marked for promotion, aren't you ? " suggested the sergeant sarcastically. But all the same, he felt there might be something in it. Chaps of this colour were apt to repeat themselves.

" It wasn't a London case," added the young officer. " Matter of fact, it was my sister that got so interested. She had the house at Frampton where they were staying. Mind you, the lady didn't take the stuff on her premises, but she'd remember the chap's name, and I dare say she could identify him if it comes to that."

" The chap who brings the criminal low is the Invisible Witness," was one of Crook's cliches. " It don't matter how careful you are or how clever, you can never bet on a dead certainty. Some woman walking her dog, some chap selling flowers or playing a mouth-organ in the gutter, they're the people who upset your case, the people you can't guard against, because you don't know they're going to be there." And he used to quote Rouse, who set fire to a car at 2 a.m. and, hurrying from the scene, found himself face to face with two strangers returning from a local dance. " No man deserved his success better than

Rouse," Crook would say handsomely. "To this day nobody knows who the chap was whose body was found in the burning car—but he got his ticket all the same from those two young fellows he'd never heard of and whose names nobody remembers. It's the long arm of coincidence, and you take my word for it, its longer than the arm of the law. Henry—saves time to call him that, and it's a nice short name anyway—couldn't dream that the Frampton landlady was going to have a brother in the police force, and that brother, out of all the police officers there are, was goin' to be concerned in his next deal but one."

So here were all these inquiries, like spokes in the same wheel, all pointing to the hub of the case, said hub, of course, being Henry G. As for him, for the first time in his infamous career, he knew cold feet. When he awoke to find himself in a hospital bed it took him a little while to get his bearings. A nurse told him, after the fashion of her kind, to lie down and stop worrying, he was perfectly safe, everybody was looking after him, he had nothing to be troubled about.

"That's all you know," thought Henry. Memory came back slowly. He had left Paris and that stupid woman in the café, got back with the jewels and the money that he had successfully smuggled through the Customs, contriving to dispose of his jewel-case en route, and reclaimed his car. He had been almost home when disaster overtook him in the shape of a maniac driving something that should by rights be in a museum, if any museum would give such an object house-room. It was what had happened subsequently that was worrying him. The vital question was : Had they gone on up to the cottage and found the gate padlocked ? On that point everything depended. He had had his story neatly mapped out. His wife, Sarah, had been in a very nervy state, a fact that could be confirmed by Dr. Forbes. He had arranged for her to go into a nursing home, while he himself made a brief business journey to the continent. When the morning came she had refused to stir ; her attitude towards him was such that he judged it best to leave her alone, just for the short period he would be away. She seemed to have taken a sudden dislike to him, though until just recently they had been as happy as two love-birds. He had concluded his business (no need to mention the Bird of Paradise), and he had come speeding home to find that during his absence she had taken an overdose—by accident or design he couldn't swear—and there he was, faced with her dead body. There would be no evidence against him. She would have eaten the doctored ginger, and since there was hyoscin in the sleeping mixture Forbes had given her— he had asked Forbes particularly about its composition— it would be assumed that she had taken her life during a period of melancholia. Of course, there were holes in the story. Some humanitarian busybody might object to his leaving her in such a state, but he would explain that she had refused to accompany him, to enter a home or to remain under the same roof. Henry had laid the foundations of that story when he saw Fair in town a little earlier. " Any history of melancholia or hysteria in the family ? " he had asked. Fair would remember that now. Well, then, there the distracted husband was. If he stayed at the cottage Sarah would depart, and where was there for her to go ? She had no relatives and apparently no friends, for if she had would she have been driven to writing to an imaginary Miss Blake ? She was quite capable, Henry would explain, of dashing into the woods, giving him the slip while he was at work, and if she was lost there she would die of starvation and madness. So on the whole, it had seemed to him best to stick to his original plan. Of course, there would be the cut telephone to explain, but he had thought up an answer to that one. Sarah had heard him making the arrangement with the nursing home, and had been quite demented. As soon as his back was turned she had deliberately cut the wires, shouting that the next people he would ring up would be the authorities to take her to an asylum. He had supposed the best thing to do was leave her alone. In the event, it hadn't proved a fortunate decision, but he had been at his wits' end. On the whole, he thought it would be yet another case of the coroner offering the bereaved husband the sympathy of the court. It wasn't only what you said on these occasions, it was the way you said it, and you could trust Henry to get ninepence for fourpence every time.

And now all that was ruined if the police had discovered the padlock on the gate. Even if they hadn't the red-haired maniac had, for he had said as much. Of course, he had no witness, which was something to be grateful for and if he, Henry, could get up to the cottage before any nosey parker started messing about with things, he believed he could still carry it off.

When they told him a policeman wanted to see him and the doctor considered he was fit, he stiffened and mentally rehearsed his answers. If they had found the padlock he had another story to tell, but it wasn't a very convincing one, and it certainly wasn't one that would win him any sympathy. Still, so long as it kept him from the gallows, it would do. Henry Gould's career was practically over in any case—and there was one point on which Crook would have agreed with him. The policeman gave him a fresh shock. He didn't mention Sarah. He said that a Mrs. Lily Abbott had preferred a charge against him of stealing certain items of jewellery of which accurate descriptions had been given and that had been found among his baggage. This was a pretty kettle of fish, and one Henry hadn't anticipated. For one thing, he had not thought the Bird of Paradise would track him down so soon, and for another, he had rather thought she would prefer to lose the jewellery to taking her story to the police. This august body has little sympathy for a woman of mature years who lets herself be fooled by an adventurer. Lily, however, would have retorted with spirit that she didn't want sympathy, only her jewels returned to her.

" There's some misunderstanding," said Henry, knitting his brows. " Mrs. Abbott herself put the stones into my hand. We met by chance," he improvised glibly, " crossing to Paris, and—you know how it is on these flights, you get friendly with your neighbour—and she happened to mention that she wanted to sell some of her jewellery, and she showed it to me. I brought it back with me because I know a man who would be likely to give a good price."

" That's not the lady's story," the policeman assured him.

" I've a witness," said Henry. " At the hotel she put the case into my hand. ' I want you to have these,' she said. ' Are you sure ? ' I asked her, and she said—and the proprietress of the hotel can confirm this—she said, ' Yes, I'm quite sure. You take them.' "

All the same, the policeman told him he was under arrest on a charge of theft, and that nearly drove Henry silly. Because it meant the police would never take their eyes off him till he had been brought up before a magistrate and officially charged. Still, he reminded himself, calming down, he needn't return to the cottage till after that had happened. There was still, he thought, a chance of saving his bacon.

XXII

ACCOUNT RENDERED

WITHIN TWENTY-FOUR HOURS, however, he knew he could say good-bye to that piece of bacon for ever. Mrs. Lily Abbott and her jewels faded into insignificance when another policeman came to see him, a vastly superior person, the kind that handles murder trials and gave it all to Henry on a plate. He said the police had been called in in connection with Mrs. Sarah Gould, and he asked Henry if he agreed that Sarah was his wife and that his permanent address was Goblin Cottage. Henry said, Yes, and what was all this leading up to ? The policeman said that two members of the public, acting on their own initiative, had broken into the cottage on the previous Sunday and had found the place locked at every turn, the telephone wires cut, and Mrs. Gould in a condition of collapse in a locked and darkened room.

Henry said quickly, " Is she dead ? " And the policeman said she was on the danger list, and hadn't been able to make a statement. All the same, he would like to ask Henry some questions, though he wasn't compelled to answer them until he had seen his solicitor, but if he cared to make a statement it might ultimately be used in evidence.

" What is this ? " asked Henry, with an air of very creditable bewilderment. " If my wife is alive—I mean, you sound as if you were going to charge me with something."

" All we want at the moment is information," said the policeman stolidly.

" I'm so much in the dark," said Henry, " I think I'll wait and see my solicitor." The policeman intimated that that was O.K. by him, and as he turned to go, set Henry's heart fluttering again by asking if he knew anything about a skeleton, part of which had been found in the rockery of the cottage.

" A skeleton ? " exclaimed Henry. " You mean, a dog ? "

" No," said the policeman. " The bones were those of a human being."

" How horrible ! " Henry shuddered. " Have they been there long ? "

The policeman said he understood a considerable time.

" Well," said Henry, " I never set eyes on the cottage till 1941. I was working at a first-aid post in London, and I got thoroughly run down after all the 1940 raids, and my doctor advised me to go away for a bit of a change. Of course, it wasn't very easy to find any place, with the mass evacuations that were the order of the day, but the authorities didn't want Goblin Cottage, because it was so isolated and had no amenities as town dwellers understand the word. It suited me down to a T. The owner was called Smith and offered it to me for as long as I wanted."

" And you've been there ever since ? "

" On and off. Oh, there have been long periods when I haven't set eyes on the place, but it's nice to have it as a hideaway. I suppose that's why this fellow, Smith, bought it in the thirties. Thought he might want a roof over his head during slump periods, I dare say."

" Do I understand that you bought the cottage ? "

" Oh, no. Strictly speaking, it's not mine. No, as I told you, I was at this first-aid post and when I crocked, Smithy offered me a rest here. Afterwards I could stay as long as I liked so long as the rates were paid."

" And you paid them ? "

" Yes. Each quarter."

" Who were the demands made out to ? "

" Smith, of course."

" And you pay them in the name of Smith ? By cheque ? "

" In cash. Things hadn't been going too well for me—that's why I was so grateful for the offer of the place—and I sometimes had to sell some of my possessions. There were some cuff-links, I remember—I lived quite a while on those—and I used to send the money in a registered envelope, and having got into the habit of doing that over a period of years, I do it still."

" It does save a lot of trouble," agreed the policeman smoothly. " Do you mean to say you've been paying them ever since ? "

Henry said, Yes, he had.

" What about the owner all this time ? "

" That's the mystery," said Henry frankly. " I stayed at the cottage for some time and then I went back to London. I returned to the first-aid post, to find it had been blitzed, there had been several casualties, everyone had been dispersed. I could get no news of my pal or anyone else."

" You mean the owner had been killed ? "

" I've always wondered," said Henry. " I never had another letter or any visit. No lawyer ever wrote, nobody came to see the cottage. It might only have existed in my imagination, except for the rate demands that came at regular intervals. But legally, it's still only on loan to me, by a person who may be dead. It's an odd situation."

" If this chap, Smith's, death had been officially reported, the cottage must have been included for death duties."

Henry looked vague. " Suppose death duties didn't apply ? If it was a small estate——"

" It would have to appear in the valuation. Even if it was only a case of presumed death——"

" But—if there was no one to report the death, or presumed death, no one who took any interest. Of course, I do see that if I hadn't been there to pay the rates, questions might have been asked, but I was, and I shall go on paying them, unless, of course, I decide to let the house go. I'm sure it has very unfortunate associations with me now."

All through this gruelling period Henry was remaining remarkably calm. " I can't make that chap out," the Inspector confided, " he's as cool as a cucumber." Questioned about the clothes in Bluebeard's cupboard, he said he had bought them second-hand from time to time, as he travelled in second-hand clothes, though he could not produce anyone who had ever employed him. He insisted, however, that he had sold many articles through the medium of advertisements, and there was, in fact, a notebook found in the cottage recording a few sales. Sold M.'s fur tie £6, a wretched price. Asked to identify M., he said at once, " Mamma." It was a very old-fashioned piece of fur but good of its kind. There was no record of the person to whom he had sold it. Then a Mrs. Young enters the story. She said she had answered an advertisement in a local paper for a coat, reputed to come from one of the best makers, being offered at a bargain price. It was a black coat with a cape and a quilted lining. The gentleman had brought it to her house and she had pointed out that it was shorter than the prevailing fashion. The gentleman had said that had it been the right length his wife would not be parting with it, but with women's fashions changing so arbitrarily, it was probable that by the following winter it would be the modish length again. Eventually she had bought the coat after a good deal of haggling for seven pounds. The coupon system was then in existence, and so second-hand clothes still retained a considerable value.

" Did you give any coupons ? "

" No. The gentleman did not ask for any."

" Did he give you a name ? "

" No. There was just the advertisement in the paper, a box-office number."

" How did he get in touch with you ? "

" I answered the advertisement, giving a telephone number and he rang up and said he would be in the neighbourhood the next day, and would bring the coat."

" Did he give you a receipt ? "

" No. I never thought to ask for one. After all, I had the coat."

Faced with Henry, she said he looked like the man, but after so long she couldn't be certain. Tall dark men were not uncommon, but she seemed to remember that the gentleman had been clean-shaven, whereas the man who now confronted her had a small moustache.

The extraordinary thing about Henry was that he always spoke as if what hung over him was just a passing trouble, a misunderstanding that would soon be cleared up, and then he could resume his usual way of life. His solicitor, Davidson, asked him once, " Can you really be as calm as you sound ? Don't you realise the hideous position you're in ? "

" I think I realise it, but there's nothing to be alarmed

about. They've found a body in the garden of the house I'm temporarily occupying. Well, it's very melodramatic and all that, but it doesn't actually affect me. I don't know who the woman was——"

" Who told you it was a woman ? " asked Davidson sharply.

" Oh, the police gave me to understand it was a woman though they didn't go into any details. Who was she ? "

" No one knows."

" But——"

" She's been there a good many years, remember."

" What about clothes ? "

" There weren't any. She was buried nude. There were no rings on her fingers."

" Or bells on her toes ? " suggested Henry.

Davidson looked shocked. " Do you realise this may be a murder action ? "

" Murder ? Sarah's not dead, I understand. As for this corpse in the garden even the optimistic police can't hope to tie that round my neck. It's ten years since I started staying at the house, or very nearly. During that time I've been away for long periods, anybody could get in. . . ."

" Don't you usually keep the gate padlocked ? "

" You saw how easily that London chap broke it open. Besides, I wouldn't like to swear I never left the gate open. The body may have been there when I first saw the house."

" If so the reasonable assumption is that Smith put it there ? "

Henry's eyes positively sparkled. " Are you suggesting it's the remains of Mrs. Smith ? "

" That's for the police to discover. And they will. You may not believe it, but there are certain signs, idiosyncrasies, there are the teeth—sooner or later they'll identify the poor thing."

" And then they'll discover who popped her into the rockery. I must say I'm glad I didn't know. I should

222

never have slept quietly at night. It's no wonder Mrs. Truelove and the others saw ghosts in the woods."

" There's one thing you seem to have forgotten," said Davidson, honestly amazed. " What about telling your wife that you'd buried a favourite dog in the rockery ? "

" Dog ? I never had a dog. Too much of a tie. And if Sarah says so—by the way, it's news to me she's able to make a statement—then I fear it must be recognised that no unsupported evidence she may offer is worth the paper it's written on. She's been suffering from illusions—or do I mean delusions ? Yes, I think delusions is the word. Let them put Forbes in the witness-box. He saw her only a day or two earlier, he'll testify——"

" Like hell he will," remarked Davidson grimly. " Nothing puts a doctor out more than getting mixed up in a murder."

" I've just pointed out to you, there is no murder charge in the offing. These fools don't even know who the woman was, nobody missed her till they started rooting about on my property."

" I wasn't thinking of the bones, I meant your wife."

" I understand you to say she's just made a statement."

" That will only strengthen the police's hand when they come to take you on a further charge of attempted murder."

" Nothing of the kind," said Henry robustly.

Davidson looked at him curiously. " What explanations were you thinking of offering ? "

" Ever heard of shock treatment, Davidson ? It horrifies the lay mind as a rule, and yet doctors will point to cases of complete cure as a result. Sarah, as I've told you, was becoming increasingly hysterical and unbalanced every day. I could see nothing ahead for her but an asylum. I had hoped Mortimer would work miracles, but at the eleventh hour she refused to go near Mortimer, cut the telephone wires, said she wouldn't stay in the same house as myself, had nowhere else to go—I tell you, I was at my wits' ends. I argued, I cajoled. No use. Then I thought I'd fire the only other shot in my locker. I'd see what shock treatment would do. If Sarah were to wake up and find herself alone in a dark cottage, all the doors locked, absolutely isolated, it might be like a douche of cold water, bring her back to her senses. She'd be overwhelmingly grateful to anyone who rescued her—and naturally I intended that person to be me."

" Are you," inquired Davidson in an awed voice, " going to tell that story in court ? "

" It's the only one I have," said Henry simply.

" And—the poisoned ginger ? They found hyoscin in the three first pieces they examined."

" I know nothing of that. I've never possessed hyoscin."

" You'll have to prove that."

" On the contrary, the police will have to prove that I did."

" You know all the answers, don't you ? " retorted Davidson sourly. " It doesn't always pay to be too clever with the police."

But Henry still believed in his luck. Other men might hang but not he. He had been fooling the police and the public, to say nothing of his various wives, for so many years he simply couldn't believe in his own defeat. He was front-page news by this time, and he had all the papers sent in. There was a photograph of him that was reproduced simply everywhere, and he complained that it didn't do him justice.

" I don't look like that," he asserted. " It's a libel. Look at that profile. . . ."

But if Henry didn't think it a good likeness there were plenty who did. Mrs. Derry saw it, and exclaimed, " Why, Tom, I swear that's the man we saw with Greta that evening after the cinema. Do you remember ? "

" I didn't notice," said Tom. " You'd better be careful how you say these things. You may find yourself in court. On a slander charge."

" Giving evidence, more likely."

Tom Derry looked rather disturbed. "Look here, are you certain ? Because if so——"

"I shall go to the police," asserted Mrs. Derry. "I've always thought it queer that Greta should disappear as she did. I mean, it wasn't like her. She never even sent me a card."

"Well," said Tom dubiously, "of course, if you're certain." He looked at the photograph again. "It's not such a very unusual type."

"My dear Tom, if there were many men as handsome and enchanting as that going about——" She stopped because she didn't quite know how to finish her sentence. But she went to the police and made a statement, and was asked to attend an identity parade. Here she hesitated. After all, she had only seen the chap once. The authorities asked her if she would recognise any of Greta's possessions, assuming any of them were among the treasures found in Bluebeard's cupboard, and here she was on much surer ground. For she recognised at once the dress she herself had given to Greta. "She altered it and added a very striking belt," she told them eagerly. "I remember wishing I'd thought of it myself. It was rather a nice dress, a model. I've probably still got the receipt somewhere." But though that went to show that Greta had been one of Henry's monstrous regiment of women it didn't get them very much further, because a verdict of death by misadventure had already been passed on the dead girl, and however many suspicions the police and the public might cherish there was no possibility at this stage of proving that it hadn't been an accident. At Marchester a great many people saw the photograph and thought it had a familiar air, but it was Mrs. Carstairs who said, "That's the man who married Beryl. I swear it. Oh, it's no wonder she was never heard of again. Why, that skeleton they found in the garden may be *hers*. It doesn't bear thinking of."

The skeleton had been there for a period of years, her husband pointed out. "Besides, wasn't there something about a finger-joint missing from one hand ? Beryl was particularly proud of her hands. We used to chaff her, I remember, wonder how she could risk spoiling them doing all that cookery."

" Yes, that's true. All the same, it was queer she never wrote or anything. John, I'm going to have a word with Sergeant Place, if only for my own peace of mind."

The evidence piled up. There was a fur cape in Bluebeard's cupboard that was identified as the property of Miss Beryl Benyon by the Marchester furrier, who had had the care of it every summer for ten years. He knew its weak spots and pointed them out to the authorities. The investigation went deeper, coming to a full stop at the inquest on Mrs. Beryl Gardiner. . . . " That's the man. She was marrying a Dr. Henry Gardiner. He said he was going back to South Africa." A jeweller came forward with a flat gold watch inscribed To Henry from Beryl, that had been left with him by a gentleman greatly resembling the picture in the paper, though he hadn't given the name of Gould. True, his man had been clean-shaved, but these little moustaches took no time to grow. Then came a cloud of witnesses from the Parade Hotel, Sunhaven, whence the jeweller also emanated, all convinced that Henry Gould was identical with the Mr. Grainger Flora Ransome had married. And she had come to a sticky end, too. The police went on patiently, one foot in front of the other, one foot in front of the other, and so to the top of the mountain. Henry Grant, Henry Gardiner, Henry Grainger, Henry Gould. Mrs. Robins, the Frampton landlady, had particularly noticed the ring Flora habitually wore, a square emerald, not big but of a charming colour, set in a rose of diamonds. Her engagement ring she had said it was. And a precisely similar ring was found on the finger of the unconscious Sarah.

In the meantime Sarah had made her statement. She said :

" When I awoke on that Friday morning, the room was

very dark, and I couldn't hear the sound of anyone moving in the house. I got up and went over to the window to draw back the shutters—my husband had fastened them the night before because one of the panes broke in the storm." (" Not it," intervened Crook. " Someone bashed that with a boot from inside.") " To my surprise, I found they were padlocked. That made me angry. I thought my husband was trying to make me believe I was really going out of my mind. I ran over to the door and to my amazement I found that was locked, too. I tried to remember turning the key, and then I realised it was fastened from the outside, making me a prisoner. I rattled furiously and shouted and banged on the panel, but he didn't come. I thought perhaps he was still asleep. I had no idea of the time because it was perfectly dark in the room. I found the matches and lighted the lamp, but when I looked at my watch I realised I had forgotten to wind it the night before. There are no striking clocks in the cottage, and no church clock within hearing distance. I banged on the door again and listened. I thought my husband must hear. It was quite a long time before I understood that he had gone away and I was alone in a locked room. I wasn't frightened at first, I thought he was doing it as a sort of revenge or perhaps to make me so furious I should sound unbalanced. I swore I wouldn't play his game, so I went back and lay down on the bed. I don't know how long I stayed there, it seemed hours, but then time always does when you're alone and waiting feverishly for something to happen. As the time went on it seemed to me the only thing that mattered was that he should come back and let me out. I felt I'd agree to any suggestion he might make if only he'd come back. I've never suffered from claustrophobia but as the time went on and there wasn't a sound so that I might have been the last living thing in a dead world, I began to understand what such people might suffer. Those words, the last living thing in the world, began to ring in my head like a bell, until I began to think. Living, but for how long ? I thought he had gone off for the day, perhaps, leaving me alone—he'd know it wouldn't kill me to spend a day without food, alone. I was determined to keep my head—but I'd forgotten about the lamp, that the oil wouldn't last indefinitely, I mean. I had to have it on, there wasn't a gleam of light from anywhere. When I lay down by the door and tried to peer under the crack I saw nothing but darkness. Then the lamp began to flicker, the flame leapt up, sank, leapt more wildly, it threw crazy shadows on the ceiling—shadows of my fears, I thought. I shook the door and battered on the panels, though by this time I knew he wasn't there to hear. There's a sense of emptiness about a house that's been deserted, an atmosphere, a chill, and it was creeping over me. I let go the door and came back to the bed. Then the light went out and I was absolutely in the dark. I hadn't any way of telling the time. Perhaps, I thought, it was only four o'clock when I woke, perhaps it's only five or six now, perhaps I'm getting myself into a state for nothing. I was furious with Henry for locking the door, but I believed it was part of his diabolical plan, though I didn't realise then how diabolical it was. He'd been trying to persuade a doctor that I was peculiar. Well, the time dragged on, I was desperately hungry. I remembered I'd seen a jar of ginger on the table, and I put out my hand to feel for it. I touched the rim and it was sticky and that seemed wrong. Then I realised it was sticky because it had been opened. And that meant Henry must have opened it. I remembered, too, I hadn't brought it upstairs, I was sure it hadn't been there when I put out the light. That meant Henry must have come in while I was asleep, and of course he had—to put the padlocks on the shutters.

I don't recall exactly when it was that I realised he wasn't coming back at all, not till it would be too late for me, I mean. Then I went nearly frantic. I ran round and round the room, falling over the furniture, banging on the walls and the windows and the door. I screamed, I rattled the shutters, but of course nothing happened, no one came. I could scream myself mad and no one would hear." Her voice shook, her face was icy-pale. " I couldn't see a ray of hope. I kept thinking, A miracle must happen, a miracle, but I couldn't see any reason why it should. Trifles that I'd hardly worried about before came back to torment me. I remembered the room he called Bluebeard's Cupboard, all the women's clothes there. I'd wondered why he kept them—he said they belonged to his mother, but I knew that wasn't true. And suddenly it came over me that before very long my clothes would be hanging there, too, and I'd be—I'd be . . ." She paused to regain control. " Then I was convinced this wasn't the first time," she went on after a minute. " I mean that there had been other women who had conveniently disappeared. Nobody knew where I was, except Mr. Fair. Henry could tell any story he liked. He could even say I'd run off, and the doctor would back him up. Everyone would believe his story, people always did. I thought about the ginger again, and I felt that had some part in the picture. I couldn't argue it all out, but I was resolved not to touch it. I don't know how long I stayed there before I felt I should really go mad soon, and I felt for the sleeping stuff and tried to take a lethal dose. But I was shaking so, and it was so cold, the bottle fell out of my hand, and I had to crawl about in the dark feeling for the tablets. I swallowed all I could find, and lay down thinking that must be enough. I can't tell you what it was like. I remembered a man who was condemned for a murder some years ago swearing on the threshold of death that he was innocent— innocent, but couldn't prove it. I knew the awful helpless- ness he must have known. Then suddenly I didn't want to die, I rolled off the bed and went to the door and lay down and gulped in the air. I thought perhaps someone will telephone, and when there's no reply will come up to the house, and then I thought of course Henry would have locked the gates. I wondered how long you could live, if you'd slowly become unconscious. Then I thought somebody should know the truth and I felt about for my bag and got out my lipstick, and scribbled MURDER on the looking-glass, and I felt for blank places on the wall, and wrote it again. But I didn't succeed very well even at that, because the lipstick broke off in my hand. It was rather low, and I'd meant to put a new one in the next morning. . . . You won't let him come near me again, will you ? He meant to kill me, he did, really."

" Tell me something," said Crook. " Had you signed your will ? "

" Yes. But it wasn't witnessed. Henry said we'd get two people to witness it the next time we were in a town."

" That wouldn't make it legal," said Crook grimly. " The witnesses have got to sign at the same time as the testator."

" That wouldn't matter," returned Sarah in the careless way of women. " I mean, nobody would know."

" Well," said Crook, " here's an interesting thing. That will's been found, and two witnesses' signatures are appended. It seems your Henry ransacked your drawers for it and persuaded two village chaps to sign just to oblige him when he was out one day—they wouldn't know what they were signing, but it would make everything hunkydory for him."

" Do you mean you think he'll escape after all ? " Sarah's voice was incredulous.

But Crook shook his big red head. " Not he, sugar.

" Stormed at by shot and shell,
Right to the gates of hell
Crook on the trail as well

and Crook, you know, always gets his man."

XXIII

CROOK GETS HIS MAN

ARTHUR CROOK was a queer creature. No Trade Union would have had him in its ranks. He simply didn't understand the essential justice and sweet reasonableness of the forty-hour week. He might say, " The labourer is worthy of his hire," but he didn't always assess that worth in cold cash. " Me," he used to boast, " I'm one of the enemies of the Welfare State. I like to stand on my own flat feet. And I never was good at taking orders. Knock off now, Crook. You've done your share. Down with competition. Flat rates for all. Be sure you get your Union rate of pay. Besides, I'm a capitalist. I can afford my bit of pleasure." At the moment his pleasure seemed to consist of doing a good deal of work that wasn't his concern, without pay. " My bit of social service," he explained to a plain-clothes man who found him nosing round the site of what had once been the Bampton Road first-aid post. Whatever he learned there, if anything, he wasn't prepared at that stage to confide his discoveries to the police.

" Well, would you ? " he inquired frankly. " Just think what a fathead I shall look if it comes out I've been enjoyin' pipe dreams." Not that he ever smoked a pipe —cigars were good enough for him.

" What are you after ? " demanded Jonathan who, said Crook candidly, had more time off from his job than was the rule when he, Crook, had been a young man. " Nose to grindstone, that was our motto. You young chaps ! "

" Just thought I might be able to pick up something from someone who remembered our Mr. G. in the piping days of sirens," he replied.

" Do you suppose he ever really worked here ? " Jonathan sounded scornful.

" I'm wasting my time if he didn't."

" What do you expect to learn ? "

" I have a hunch that he could tell us more about this Smith who owned the cottage than he cares to tell."

" You mean, you think Smith worked here too ? "

" That was the idea."

Jonathan frowned. " How does that help ? Or do you think he's gone on using the cottage because he put Smith underground ? "

" You read me like a book," said Crook admiringly. " But—the skeleton in the rockery's a woman."

" Oh, yes. So the police say, and of course the police can't be wrong."

" I don't get it," said Jonathan.

" You will," said Crook encouragingly ; " you will."

So it happened that before the police had traced the elusive Smith, Crook sent a casual invitation to a certain retired Detective-Inspector Cobbey to meet him at the Running Dog near the Elephant one Wednesday evening. Cobbey was the exception that proved the rule that the police didn't like Crook. Cobbey had found himself confronted by him on various occasions and had always had a good word for him.

" Of course he breaks the rules," he would agree. " No, I don't know why the Law Society hasn't moved against him, but I suspect they have the good sense to know he's a lot safer in the fold than out of it. It isn't as a lawyer that he's made his name. The fact that he is one is a help, of course, particularly to the chaps who consult him, gives him an excuse, see ? But he can do a lot of things we can't, because we're public servants who come under the law. If Crook comes under any law it's one that hasn't yet been framed. Besides, he does get his man, and you can't help liking a chap who does that."

Most of the police didn't agree with him, but that didn't deter Cobbey at all. Mind you, he had no illusions about Crook, didn't think he was a noble-hearted Sir Galahad, or out to establish justice on the face of the earth, but he had a vivid recollection of a tame-looking old lady who had once put a hand on his arm, and said, " You can't help liking him, can you ? When you're in trouble he's so kind."

Crook would have had an apoplectic fit to hear that, but more people would have agreed with her than he would have thought possible.

When Cobbey arrived at the Running Dog he saw his man leaning against the counter, deep in conversation with someone who (Cobbey was convinced) he had never set eyes on before. " Chap would have made an ambassador," Cobbey reflected. " Now we're all democrats and know that beauty's only skin-deep. Come to that, he's not any odder to look at than some of the chaps we do send abroad to represent the country."

Crook hadn't turned his head, hadn't stopped talking, but he knew Cobbey had come in, and by the time the ex-policeman had reached the bar a pint of the best (" Not so hot," said Crook apologetically, " but you know how it is these days—equal sacrifices for all—though how a teetotaller can talk that way beats me ") was waiting for him. After a minute or so the two men picked up their tankards and found a small table against the wall.

" What is it you want from me to-day ? " Cobbey asked. " Don't pretend it's the pleasure of my company because I know better."

" What moralists don't seem to understand," mused Crook, " is that it takes two chaps to tell the truth, one to give and one to take. No, I want you to do a bit of dirty work for me, Cobbey."

" You're not forgetting I live on a pension," Cobbey murmured.

" When did I ever ask a chap to do what I wouldn't do myself ? Matter of fact, it's only my consideration for the force that gets me to put up a proxy."

Cobbey jeered gently. " Go on, share the fun. What a greedy blighter you are, Crook. Which case is it anyway? "

" The Lady-Killer, our Henry, the most-married man in England."

" You're not representing him ? " Cobbey really did look shocked.

" Don't you read anything but the betting news ? No, I've been dragged into this by Jonathan Trent who's already planning to marry the widow."

" Assuming she's going to be a widow."

" Oh, Henry'll swing all right. Y'know, when these humanitarians scream for abolition of capital punishment they don't give much thought to the scoundrel's family. Yes, I know if he gets a life-sentence she can ask for a divorce after three years, and trail all her dirty linen in public, but what sort of a start does that give her if she wants to marry again ? What I had in mind was the probability that she never was Mrs. Henry Gould. I dare say there are half a dozen women tucked away in quiet corners who went through a marriage ceremony with him. Anyhow, he's not goin' to stand his trial for attempted murder, not if I can help it, and I expect I can."

Cobbey expected so, too.

" No, he went the whole hog and now he can pay his shot. It's about this Smith the police can't trace."

" Are you offering to lead them to him ? "

" They wouldn't come if I did. You know the police, conservatives to a man, I don't care what way they vote at the elections. They love me about as much as Attlee loves a communist. But if a well-behaved ex-dick like you was to go to them and say, ' What's holding you up ? Can't you use your eyes ? And if they're a bit weak, what about the free glasses you get under the Health Service ? ' Well, then, they might begin to take a bit of notice. Mind you," he went on earnestly, " I'm not asking you to take my word for all this. I've got all the evidence in the bag, only—I don't want to make their faces red."

Cobbey went into a roar of laughter. " Nothing would please you better. Come off it, *where is Smith* ? "

" Mr. Smith, Christian names George William, bought Goblin Cottage as a hideaway in 1936, and died in 1938. He's buried in the municipal cemetery at Bustard Common and any chap with five bob to spare can get a copy of his death certificate."

" And this chap, Gould, says he met him for the first time in 1941. What a liar he is ! "

" Oh, no," said Crook gently, " on this occasion he told the truth."

Cobbey frowned. " Meaning he met him before 1941 ? But he said——"

" What he said was the true gospel. Hallo, there's Bill —and the lady."

He half-rose as Bill Parsons came towards the table, accompanied by a battleaxe of a female who looked as though she could take on any two gentlemen present and make mincemeat of them. Crook put out a huge hand.

" Miss Willsher ? Pleased to have you meet Detective-Inspector Cobbey, late of the Yard. Yes, we're moving in high society to-night, Bill and me. Cobbey, this is Miss Willsher who's going to dot the i's and cross the t's for us. Bill you've met."

Cobbey had—in the days when Bill was on the wrong side of the law. But that was a long time ago. Cobbey said once that Providence must have a poker mind to have thought of a chap like Bill at all. No one, sometimes not even Crook, knew what he was thinking.

" What's the lady going to take ? " Crook went on.

" Whatever you're having will be good enough for me," said Miss Willsher in a voice that would have made a sergeant-major quail.

Crook beamed at her. " Do the honours, Bill," he suggested, " and you might say ' Same again ' for Cobbey and me while you're about it. Miss Willsher knew our Henry in the war," Crook explained. " Lent a hand at the A.R.P. post."

" First-aid," corrected Miss Willsher. " He was on the gas side, and about the right place for him. I never knew

a man with such an oiled tongue and he would do it on
the sort of coffee you got from the amateur in charge of
the kitchen there. I tell you, Inspector "—she swivelled
her great green eyes at him and he felt as if, swimming
under water, he had suddenly found himself confronted
by some immense marine monster—" I sometimes felt as
if I was running a matrimonial bureau. In the spring a
young man's fancy—you know—though he wasn't as
young as all that. Still, he was younger than a lot of the
women I had. It was a funny thing," she added, taking her
tankard from Bill and saying briefly, " Here's to Crime."
I noticed he never paid much attention to the girls,
and that gave me a funny feeling. Because when a chap
of, say, five-and-thirty, only makes the running with the
widows and the elderly gals we had there, you can start
smelling rats till you're ready to faint with the stink.
Mind you, the women encouraged him all round the clock.
He was only on for eight hours, but that was seven and a
half hours too long, and if he'd only been there half an
hour in the twenty-four he'd have made trouble. Put the
come-hither on them by a look or a word. Mind you, his
beard may have had something to do with it—I never saw
anything like it. Ever seen a good marksman bowling
over rabbits ? That's what Henry Grey did. That's what
he was calling himself then, and if he did change his name
afterwards—well, I don't doubt he had at least one woman
to match every name. And some of 'em were tough old
birds, mark you, as tough as I am." She drained her
tankard and handed it back to Bill with a meaning glance
that said, " Same again." Bill obediently took the hint.

" There was one widow there, ten years older than Don
Juan if she was a day, made herself so conspicuous I called
her in and told her not to be more of a fool than Nature
made her. ' That chap's about as much use to you as a
bomb,' I said. ' What's more, he's making you look pretty
silly.' I tell you, if a genie had appeared out of a bottle
and given her one wish she'd have turned me into a toad
for the pleasure of putting her foot on me. ' You couldn't

be expected to understand," she said. No wedding ring, see ? What married women never appreciate is what a lot of confidences we spinsters amass. Common sense, if you ask me. You start telling another married woman what a raw deal you've got with your husband and how much sympathy do you get ? I'll tell you." She held up a massive thumb and forefinger shaped to a great O. " The married woman's thinking, ' Why, she doesn't know anything. She should be married to my Bill or Tom or Augustus.' But spinsters—they ooze sympathy. ' My dear, how *awful* ! ' In a way," added Miss Willsher candidly, " they rather enjoy it all. Shows 'em that if they've missed the roses they've missed getting scratched to bits on the thorns, too. ' Well, are you proposing to marry him ? ' I said. She had a lot of the root of all evil from her late husband, according to her own account, and of course H. G. had his pop-eyes on that from the word Go. Not that he did have pop-eyes, but a telescope wouldn't find a missing comet for you quicker than Henry could spy a bank balance. Of course, My Lady flung up her head and rolled her eyes and pursed her mouth, and said how disgusting, and that was spinsters all over— didn't believe in a true friendship between a man and a woman, and they don't," added Miss Willsher ; " not when the man's Henry Grey, Gould, whatever he calls himself now. She was what our doorkeeper called a meaty armful, but that wasn't her charm for him. When he told me his doctor was sending him to the country because of a strained heart I was relieved. A couple of days later My Lady sent in her resignation. I don't mind telling you I didn't think either of them was any loss, though I did wonder if she mightn't find her useful war-work in the same part of the country as Don Juan was doing his recuperating."

" And that's the last you heard of her ? " asked Cobbey, playing the obvious lead.

" Till she turned up in the garden at Goblin Cottage," amplified Crook. " Now d'you see why I said Henry G.

was telling the truth for once in his chequered career ? He said, ' I met the owner of the cottage, name of Smith, for the first time in 1941.' Well, actually I suppose it was probably '40, but that's no odds. And your great goggle-headed Police Force jumped to the conclusion that Smith had to be a man."

" You can't blame them," said Cobbey instinctively defending his own. " Like some maternal hen gathering her chickens under her wing," murmured the shameless Crook to Bill Parsons. " If a man refers to a body by a surname it's usually another man. You must admit that."

" Ah, but remember where Henry met his friend, Smithy. At a first-aid post. Now, you ask Miss Willsher if all the C.D. establishments didn't go in for calling each other by their surnames, irrespective of sex."

" Surnames or diminutives," boomed Miss Willsher. " Mrs. Smith was known as Smithy. I," she added, with a grin, " was known as the Willing Horse for obvious reasons."

And now that she mentioned it she did look remarkably like a horse if you can conceive of a horse with green eyes. And very nice, too, decided Crook. A lot nicer to look at than plenty of so-called human beings.

" If you go through H. G.'s statement with a pair of opera-glasses," Crook went on in a voice juicy with relish, " you won't find a single reference to Smith as ' he.' It was always ' my pal ' or the ' owner ' or just plain Smith or Smithy. He said, if you recall, ' Smithy said I could stay on at the cottage if I'd pay the rates." Mind you I don't believe that bit. If she was dotty about him she wouldn't bother about who paid the rates, but he had to find some explanation of why he was paying them. If they weren't paid someone was going to start asking questions, and if Smith (male or female) had died openly as it were, there'd have been the question of death duties, and rolling up the estate in general. Matter of fact, Smithy led him up the garden path, giving him (and everyone else, for that matter) the idea that she had a nice little fortune.

Smith left him the cottage and damn all besides, and what there was Henry soon ran through, after which she was simply a burden hanging round his neck. Mind you, I don't know precisely why he decided to put her underground. If you ask me, I'd say it was a spur-of-the moment job. He didn't go in for these secret burials as a rule, not so far as anybody knows, which may not be saying a lot. It could be she rumbled him, or he'd been playing some hanky-panky with her money, such as it was, or maybe he'd already started on the next female. Patience wasn't his strong suit, if he'd been a bit more patient he mightn't be where he is now. Or, maybe patience ain't the word. The fact is, he was greedy, couldn't bear to let any chance go. If he'd stopped to tidy up things at the cottage before gettin' involved with the Bird of Paradise, he might be proposin' to another idiot female at this very minute instead of languishin' in durance vile. But no, there was a bit of gold and he was after it like a leprechaun legging it for the foot of the rainbow. Or p'r'aps she did a bit of spying on her own. That's what sealed his last wife's fate, or precious near it. Y'see, once she began to suspect he wasn't all he represented himself to be but a whole lot more, she became a danger to him. And any female would start thinking twice when she found out about Bluebeard's chamber. All that female gear under lock and key—even a nit-wit might put her thinking cap on then. Anyhow, whatever it was, she'd served her turn and was next in line for the Cemetery Stakes."

Cobbey turned to Miss Willsher. " You knew Mrs. Smith. Was there anything special that would enable you to identify what's left of her ? "

" The missing finger-joint," agreed the Willing Horse promptly. " She used to make great play with that. She'd made munitions in 1918—well, there was no sense pretending she was just a little lass in rompers during the First World War, because I had all their dossiers in my office, all with ages attached. There had been some accident and she had lost this joint. You might have thought she was the original two-toed sloth deprived of half its toes to hear her talk. ' If you didn't draw people's attention to it,' I said, ' no one would notice.' I've lost one myself, come to that," added this astounding woman. " But had you noticed ? "

" I hadn't," confessed Cobbey. He glanced at Crook, but naturally Crook had. Crook noticed everything. He noticed everybody's tankard was empty and arranged for them to be refilled.

" There was a ring she used to wear, an emerald affair set in a rose of diamonds. ' You're not supposed to wear jewellery here,' I told her. ' Take it off and lock it up in my cupboard, and don't wear it to-morrow.' But the next day she'd have it on. ' I don't trust that woman in my flat,' she'd say. ' Give it to your bank,' I said. ' Better still, give it to the Red Cross.' But not she."

" Might have been better for her if she had," agreed Crook soberly. " It was probably the ring that drew H. G.'s attention to her."

" She had a string of pearls, too, that was worth—oh, a couple of hundred, probably more—Smith, I gathered, had been a successful speculator at one time."

Crook nodded. " I wonder what he got for *them*. There weren't any pearls at the cottage. It could be he wouldn't like to risk selling the ring. It was—kind of distinctive. Pearls now, they're more anonymous. Now, you see, Cobbey, what we want you to do. You happened to rub up against Miss Willsher and you got talking, and something she said gave you the idea that her Henry Grey might be our Henry Gould, and her Smithy might be his Smith which equals the body in the rockery which equals, skipping one or two stages, a nice piece of hemp, two sacks of lime and a nameless grave under the prison flags. Y'see, if I was to approach them they'd only give me some forms to fill in, and H. G. could live to be an old man before they'd gone the rounds of the departments, but you—you're a Name, you're a Reputation, you're

One of Us, not a sneaking yellow dog of a lawyer going round nosing out the policeman's bone."

Miss Willsher said, " Neither cash nor credit ? " And Crook burst into a great guffaw and explained he had all the cash he could do with, and if he had any more it would only be taken by the Exchequer. And as for credit, when the day came that he had to hang around a police station with his hat out, waiting for a good word, he would be ripe for his numbered seat in the Eventide Home kind Mr. B. was going to provide for everybody, when he had finished providing houses.

Then the barman called, " Time, gentlemen, time. Glasses, please," and the party broke up.

XXIV

THE ROGUE AND THE RING

HENRY GOULD went to the gallows furiously protesting his innocence. Almost up to the instant that he saw the judge reach out for the black square before proclaiming sentence he had believed in his immunity. Other men might hang, other men made mistakes, other men paid penalties, but not Henry Gould. (It was ascertained that his real name was Miller, and that he was, in fact, the convict from B—— Prison whom Mr. Carstairs had recognised at Marchester. He had exchanged identities and documents with the dead man who had been buried in the name of Miller, but these facts were not made · public until after the rejection of his appeal.) When he heard the dreadful words—" taken hence to a place of lawful execution and you be there hanged by the neck until you be dead "—there ensued a wild scene during which he effectually drowned the judge's concluding words and had to be forcibly silenced by warders.

And yet, as Crook remarked later, it was a very little

thing that hanged him. The connecting link between a number of the women he had married and (said Crook) for whose deaths he was subsequently responsible, though he was tried only for the murder of Elsie Gertrude Smith, was the emerald ring set in a rose of diamonds. This ring was sufficiently striking to attract the attention of various women who had seen it on the fingers of Henry's successive wives. It was found with Sarah in the blacked-out room at Goblin Cottage. Mrs. Robins remembered commenting on it to the lodger she knew as Mrs. Flora Grainger, and she recalled also that Mrs. Grainger was not wearing it on the day she returned from London, nor was it found among her possessions after her death. Records of the inquest on Beryl Gardiner (née Benyon) had no mention of any such ring, and it was supposed that Henry had found some excuse for taking it into his own custody on that day, saying possibly that the stone was loose or even that it was unwise for her to wear so valuable an ornament when driving alone in a comparatively untenanted district. But there were witnesses who remembered seeing it on Beryl's finger. The final touch was given by a jeweller, a Mr. Hartley Rampole, who had made it to order for a Mr. George William Smith in 1928. It was a wedding gift to his second wife, a woman some twenty years his junior. Mr. Smith, an elderly man, was a speculator who had done well during the twenties, and had afterwards, as the police learned, fallen on leaner times. When he bought Goblin Cottage in 1936, it was to be a refuge, a roof over his head when other roofs became untenable, and he did in fact live there for a couple of years. The manner of his death was debatable, though no suspicion attached to his widow; the coroner had returned a verdict of death by misadventure, but there was reason to believe that he had taken his own life. His affairs after his death were in wild disorder, and his solicitors had only been able to save a small portion for the widow. Mrs. Smith, however, a buxom lady of forty who had earned her living before her marriage, turned to and found herself employment, keeping the cottage, which at that time nobody wanted, in any case, for an emergency. She used it occasionally, and sometimes was seen with a friend or friends in the neighbourhood. With the outbreak of war a flood of evacuees filled Kings Benton, and there were so many strange faces that her coming or going would pass unnoticed, but no one remembered seeing her for a great many years. The cottage was so remote that comings and goings thither would scarcely be noticed ; at no time had anyone stayed there for any length of time until the man calling himself Henry Gould had arrived with a young wife.

Henry's counsel insisted that the evidence of the ring was insufficient proof of guilt, but Miss Willsher proved an unshakeable witness, and Mr. Rampole showed the police a minute intertwined monogram—G. & E.—on the inner side of the ring which was good enough evidence for the police and the jury. In addition, the black coat sold to Mrs. Young was conclusively shown to have been made to Mrs. Smith's order by a tailor in Old Brompton Road.

" I suppose H. G. didn't like to try and sell the ring in case it was recognised," said Crook. " And he was too greedy to chuck it in the sea. It's queer the blunders these fellows make. If Samuel Dougal hadn't passed on Miss Holland's jewellery to his light-o'-loves at a time when he was insisting she was still alive he might have died in his bed a nonegenarian. It's what the old song says :

" It's the little things that matter, don't you see ? "

During the trial it was shown that a number of ladies had gone through a form of marriage with the prisoner, always in a different name, and many of them had been lucky to get away with their lives. Their property practically always passed to the spurious husband. H. G. saw to that. In the main they were dressmakers or elderly spinsters with small incomes they could be persuaded to commute, and as soon as the proceeds of these negotiations were forthcoming their dear Henry disappeared, and so did the cash.

The police believed he had been associated in one way or another with more than fifty women in about twelve years ; he hadn't, of course, married them all ; some had scarcely known him a month. All had been losers in one way or another through the connection.

The last word is Arthur Crook's.

" Dames ! " said he. " They've got me beat. You no sooner save one from a scheming husband than she's rip-roaring mad to take another chance. Mind you, I don't say Jonathan Trent's in the same class as Henry G.—but how does she know ? Henry seemed all to the harps and haloes when they first met. It's their form of gambling, I suppose, and you can't cure 'em, because they're like all gamblers. They may have lost all along the line to date, but they know this time they've picked a winner."

And so far as Sarah was concerned, this time she had.

THE END

>>> If you've enjoyed this book and would like to discover more great vintage crime and thriller titles, as well as the most exciting crime and thriller authors writing today, visit: >>>

The Murder Room
Where Criminal Minds Meet

themurderroom.com